SCRAPS OF LOVE

Recycled Fabric Binds a Family Together in Four Romantic Novellas

TRACEY V. BATEMAN
LENA NELSON DOOLEY
RHONDA GIBSON
JANET SPAETH

BARBOUR PUBLISHING

ISBN 1-59310-254-2

Scripture quotations are taken from the King James Version of the Bible.

Published by Barbour Publishing, Inc., P.O. Box 719, Uhrichsville, Ohio 44683, www.barbourbooks.com

Our mission is to publish and distribute inspirational products offering exceptional value and biblical encouragement to the masses.

Printed in the United States of America.
5 4 3 2 1

Introduction

Marry for Love by Janet Spaeth
Wild prairie-born Brigit Streeter is a totally inappropriate match for the cultured new minister, Peter Collins, who has come to the Dakota Territory from St. Paul. She lacks the domestic and social skills she needs to be part of his life. When Peter's supervising elder brings Brigit a gift of fabric to make her wedding dress, Brigit is lost. She can't sew. Can Brigit become a Proverbs 31 wife?

Mother's Old Quilt by Lena Nelson Dooley
Maggie Swenson's life has taken a tragic turn, and she is alone on the family farm without even a dog to keep her company. John Collins tries to help by chopping firewood and doing chores, and he even brings Maggie a puppy wrapped in his mother's old quilt. As John starts to fall in love with Maggie, he wishes he could restore her trust in God.

The Coat by Tracey V. Bateman with Frances Devine
When Leah loses not only her husband to the war, but her job to returning soldiers, she does what she must to take care of her son, Collin. The boy's coat, lined with an heirloom quilt, causes him to be the target of teasing at school. As headmaster of Collin's school, Max's heart goes out to the boy—and to his mother—but he has to remind himself that his scandalous past could ruin them all.

Love of a Lifetime by Rhonda Gibson
Though her culinary skills are lacking, Colleen Halliday vows to keep open the bakery her grandmother left her. Postman Adam Walker is raising his younger sister after their parents are killed. When his sister must complete a scrapbook for a school project and Colleen receives a box filled with memorabilia, Colleen and Adam discover piecing together the scraps of the past to be a link to their future—together.

SCRAPS OF LOVE

Marry for Love

by Janet Spaeth

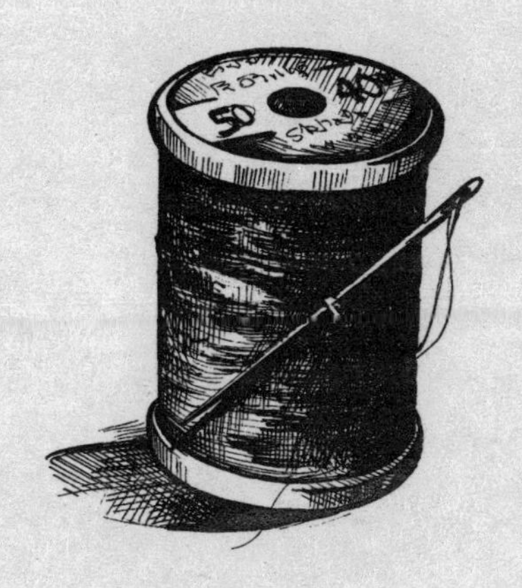

Dedication

To my parents, Margaret and Bill,
who gave me the patchwork of my own history.
Daily the hand of God draws thread through
that cloth and binds us all closer.

A woman that feareth the LORD, she shall be praised.
PROVERBS 31:30

Chapter 1

Dakota Territory—1879

Brigit Streeter ran into the small house, hooting with laughter. "Fulton and I just raced a rabbit," she said to her father, "and we won."

Mr. Streeter sighed, and Brigit knew she was in for the usual litany of *Why can't you act like a girl instead of a wild animal? Do you think this is a barn instead of a house? When will you grow up?*

"It's good exercise," she protested as he opened his mouth. "It keeps Fulton healthy so he can pull the plow. Horses need to stretch out their muscles, you know. Plus, running and riding keep my arms and back strong. What would you do with a weak daughter?"

Her father seemed to shrink, and Brigit wished she could bite back the words she'd just spoken. She didn't have the life he'd wanted for her, presiding over a grand house with lace curtains and plush carpets. Instead, she was a farmer, working just as hard as any son would. She knew it pained him.

She stepped behind his chair and threw her arms around his shoulders.

"Oh, Papa, you know I didn't mean anything by that except that I love being here with you and I will never, ever leave you."

He smiled, and she relaxed. The crisis had been averted—for the moment.

They'd been on this farm, just the two of them, since she was born. She'd never known her mother, who had died giving birth to her. All of Brigit's life, there had been her and Papa, and it was enough.

It always would be.

But now Papa had a crazy thought rolling around in his head—that she should be thinking about getting married.

What a foolish idea that was. First of all, she had no interest in getting married. Second of all, there was no one in the entire Dakota Territory who was even faintly husband material.

That pretty well summed up her situation. It didn't bother her one whit that her prospects were at best slim. She didn't care. She was perfectly happy staying on the small farm with Papa, watching the sun set on the Dakota fields.

Days like these were precious, the first true moments of spring with their fragile beauty, so full of promise. She could feel life bursting from the land right into her veins.

"What did you do this afternoon, Papa?" she asked, flopping into the only other chair in the tiny room. This one was hers, and the thin cushion on it now fit her body perfectly.

"I went into town to see about some new boots. These are getting to the point where they're like vanity: from the eyes they look good, but from the *sole* they're sorely lacking."

Brigit laughed at father's pun. He was a God-fearing man, always had been, always would be. Even her mother's death hadn't swayed him from his abiding belief in the Lord.

"Papa, why didn't you become a minister? You would have been a wonderful preacher." It was a question she'd pondered for many years, and although she'd asked it before, she'd never gotten an answer that totally satisfied her.

"I'm a farmer. It's in my bones and in my blood. A minister is a farmer, too, I suppose. He plants the seeds of hope and love and awe in the hearts of his congregation. And that's lofty work. But me, I need to feel the dirt in my fingers, and in my hair, and yes, in the cracks of my feet."

He lifted up his foot and smiled ruefully as the sole flapped away from the upper. "If I don't get these boots fixed soon, I might as well go barefoot."

"You said you went into town to get some boots. Why didn't you?"

"I guess I got waylaid by some news. And mighty big news, too."

Brigit wriggled to the edge of her chair. "Tell me! What happened?"

"A new minister is headed our way."

"Really?"

"Really. Our very own minister! Just for us."

Archer Falls was so small that it didn't have a minister. Marriages and baptisms had to take place in Fargo, a two-hour wagon ride away. For Sunday morning worship services, the townspeople relied on each other, with the sermon duty handed from man to man.

Brigit didn't mind it at all when her father brought the message, but she dreaded the days that Milo Farnsworth, the owner of the feed store, stood in front of the congregation. Mr. Farnsworth apparently felt that the significance of his sermon could be absorbed only if he hollered it so loud that Brigit's ears rang for the rest of the day.

Mr. Streeter smiled at his daughter. "And this new man, according to the rumor, has two very interesting attributes."

Brigit knew he was teasing her. "Attributes, huh? Let me guess what they are. He's breathing, and oh, let's see, what else would be important? Wait, don't tell me. Could it be—he has a heartbeat, too?"

"Very good. But I was thinking of two more. One is that he is young, fresh out of the seminary, and the other is that he's a bachelor."

The joy evaporated from the day. "Then let me guess two more things, Papa. He will be as horrid looking as a dusty toad, and he'll be equally as boring."

"Brigit, don't do this. All I mean is, he's going to be our new spiritual leader, and we're certainly in need of that."

Immediately she regretted her outburst. She knew that her father had longed for the presence of a permanent minister, not just for Sunday services, but to expand his own understanding of the Lord and the world. She'd seen his subtle grimace—although he must have thought it hidden—when Milo Farnsworth bellowed forth dire predictions of a fiery afterlife for those who didn't follow in his oversized bootsteps.

She kissed her father's sun-dried cheek and smiled. "We are indeed. And he can start working on my heart right away after words like that! I'm sorry, Papa."

"Not to worry." He smiled at her reassuringly. "Reverend Collins will be conducting services next Sunday morning. They're expecting an overflow crowd."

He touched her tangled strawberry blond hair, and she laughed. "Yes, my dear father. I will clean myself up and wrap this messy mop into a respectable bun. I'll look so splendid, even you won't recognize me."

"You're a beautiful young woman." His voice was so quiet that she knew he was talking more to himself than to her. "When did that happen? When did you stop being that little girl who ran beside me, catching grasshoppers as I put in the wheat?"

She dropped a kiss onto his head and noticed how his hair was starting to thin. As she was getting older, so was he.

She ignored the catch in her heart and answered lightly, "It just wasn't fun anymore when you made me stop putting them down the back of your shirt. But if you're getting nostalgic about that, well, dearest Papa, we still have a quarter to plant. Better guard your back!"

The train shuddered to a stop. The newly ordained Reverend Peter Collins leaned over to retrieve his hat, which had slid to the floor with the last jerk of the brakes.

He glanced out the window at the station. The presiding elder had told him that someone would be waiting for him, but which one was it? The man wearing overalls? The presiding elderly woman, balanced on her cane? The family of three, finely dressed in what must be their Sunday best?

Excitement fluttered in his stomach. This was his first real assignment as a minister. He'd been given it so easily, he suspected no one else had wanted it.

How could they not, though? Who wouldn't want to live in a town like Archer Falls? It had the best of two worlds: it was small and rural enough to be a true community yet large enough to have the world of possibility open to it.

And the Dakota Territory! The very words evoked the images of a land rich in soil and belief. The closest he'd ever come to being one with the earth was putting a petunia on his windowsill at the seminary.

As he stepped out of the car, he blinked at the vast panorama that greeted his eyes. He'd underestimated the expanse of sky and the stretch of land sprinkled with the bright green of new grass that seemed to go all the way to the ends of the earth.

And it was now officially where he lived.

"Reverend Collins?" The fellow in the overalls spoke, and when Peter nodded, the entire group moved forward. He took a moment to realize that they'd come to greet him—and that they were all beaming as happily as he was.

Introductions were made—names Peter knew he would know better soon—and he was taken to a waiting wagon.

He had never been happier. Never.

God had truly brought him home.

Brigit struggled with the bag of rice, succeeding at last in spilling half of it across the table. *Waste not, want not,* she reminded herself, but her attempts to sweep the grains back into the bag only sent them skittering onto the floor.

A call at the front door diverted her attention. It was Mary Rose Groves, her best friend, motioning madly to her.

"Brigit, did you hear? Did you? A new minister, and he's single!" Mary Rose's slightly nearsighted brown eyes glowed with excitement, and she pushed up her wire-rimmed glasses with a finger.

The two of them plopped on the edge of the shallow porch boards.

"Papa told me. I just hope he isn't going to scream the Word at us the way Mr. Farnsworth does. My ears can't tolerate that anymore." Brigit shuddered at the thought.

"I think the damage has been done." Mary Rose frowned. "There's something already wrong with your ears."

"What?" Brigit watched an ant industriously carrying a minuscule bit of something under the boards.

"Didn't you hear a word I said?" Mary Rose demanded. "I said he's single. Not married. A bachelor."

"If there were any hope that he's handsome as well, I might let myself get excited, but the fact is, Mary Rose, there isn't a man in this territory that I would have for a husband. Not a one."

"You shouldn't be so negative, Brigit." Her friend stared at her earnestly. "This could be the fellow, the man you'll share your life with. You never know."

"Oh, I know perfectly well. I know all about the so-called eligible men in Archer Falls. I'd have to be a desperate woman to marry one of them. Look who I have to choose from: Lars Nilsen, who doesn't speak a word of English, at least as far as I can figure." Brigit rolled her eyes.

"Jerrod Stiles would make a terrific husband, wouldn't he, assuming I could wave my way through that constant plume of pipe smoke to see what he looks like," she continued. "Or maybe I'd be happiest with Arthur Smith, who's a hundred ten if he's a day but thinks he's fourteen."

Mary Rose kicked her friend's leg lightly. "You are exaggerating, but not by much. There aren't good pickings here; that's the truth."

Brigit grinned. "Between you and Papa, you'll have me married by the time I'm twenty-one or die in the trying."

Mary Rose's slightly myopic gaze got dreamy. "I only want you to be as happy as I am. Just think, by autumn I'll be Mrs. Gregory Lester."

"You had to go and get greedy and take the last good man in the territory," Brigit teased, "and look what you left me with. My choice of a fellow I can't understand, one I can't see, or one I can't abide."

"Maybe so," her friend argued back lightly, "but you've got to admit that this new minister might be just the one."

"If he is even palatable, Mary Rose Groves, I will eat my hat. I promise that to you. I will sit in front of the school and eat my hat, ribbon and all."

"I hope that hat is as tasty as it looks," Mary Rose whispered as she slid into the pew next to Brigit. "I've heard that straw is quite flavorful."

"Mmmm-hmmm."

"Don't you think Reverend Collins is handsome?" Mary Rose insisted.

"Mmmm-hmmm."

"Brigit, why don't you say—oh, I see." Mary Rose leaned back and smiled in satisfaction. "You agree with me. And for some reason, I think you're happy to lose this wager."

"Mmmm-hmmm."

The Reverend Peter Collins was the kind of man who had inhabited Brigit's dreams—when she'd dared to let her thoughts drift to that vague fancy that somehow, someday, she would find true love.

Standing to the side, silhouetted against the newly painted wall, was her hope personified. Tall, with dark hair that would silver elegantly when he aged, he stepped easily to the front of the small sanctuary. With every move, he stepped closer to her heart.

Then he turned and faced them. His gaze settled on each member of the congregation, as if recognizing every individual, and Brigit held her breath.

Finally, her turn came, and during that moment when their gazes met, she saw a true faith glowing in his deep brown eyes.

He began to speak, and his glance flitted away to the rest of the people packed together. But Brigit knew what she had seen, and she liked it.

Mary Rose jabbed an elbow into Brigit's side and motioned expressively toward the new minister. Brigit understood what the motion meant. Yes, he was handsome beyond belief. But more important, he radiated faith. That, as far as Brigit was concerned, was more important than his appearance.

She peeped at her father. His weathered face was not going to grace any advertisements for genteel menswear, that was certain, but she saw beneath the wrinkles and the leathered skin what was more valuable: a trustworthiness, a security, a steadfastness that far outweighed his physical appearance.

A pang stabbed her heart. She hadn't known her mother more than a few moments, just long enough, her father had told her, for the woman to hold her newborn daughter and whisper some words in her ears.

She'd often asked what those words were, but he'd turned away, sudden tears in his eyes even after all these years, and shaken his head. She no longer pursued the issue. She did not want to hurt him any more than he had already been hurt.

As if aware that she was thinking about him, he turned to her and smiled. From the relaxed expression on his face, she could tell that his heart was filled with gratitude as the new minister's words filled the room.

Piecing together their faith in this small town had been like making a quilt of scraps. Bit by bit, the ragged edges had become smooth, the small unmatched bits turned into a beautiful unity, with each color, each shape enhancing the others. *It has been,* she thought, her heart filling with gratefulness for her father, *an extraordinary work of love.*

Now Reverend Collins's strong, young voice filled the hall. ". . .Seminary in St. Paul, when the call came for this church. I was eager to come here. I have lived in the city my entire life. Admittedly, twenty-four years isn't an eternity, but I was ready to commit to another twenty-four years spent under God's sky, watching the country grow before my eyes."

His smile swept the crowd. "I was delighted to accept the assignment."

Then he paused. Only the sparrows chirping in the lilac bush outside the open window made any sound. The listeners stopped all motion and stared at their new pastor.

"I'm not being entirely honest with you," he said at last, his voice dropping to a near-whisper. "I have a confession to make."

The assemblage leaned in to hear his barely audible words.

"I begged to come here." He grinned at the surprised faces. "I wanted to come to the Dakota Territory—I have since I was just a lad and saw all those wonderful notices about life out here. More than anything, I wanted to see the sun overhead, the clouds floating like white puffs of God's breath against the blue vault of the firmament. I wanted to be able to look at the horizon and see the curve of the earth without any buildings crowding it from my sight. I wanted to be able to dig my hands into rich, black Dakota valley soil, to feel with my fingers where the seed finds its root and, I pray, where I might find mine."

If it were at all seemly, Brigit thought, the church would have stood and applauded. She realized she'd been holding her breath and exhaled.

Around her, the people of Archer Falls were smiling happily. This was the moment they had waited for, for a long time, ever since their community had been nothing more than a cluster of sod houses. It had grown board by board, building by building, until it lacked everything except a man of the cloth to lead them.

And now they had their minister.

Brigit looked at the new young minister, and he looked at her. . .and her heart stirred.

At that moment, Brigit Streeter fell in love.

Chapter 2

Reverend Collins, I'd like you to meet Alfred Streeter and his daughter, Brigit," Milo Farnsworth shouted at them.

Brigit's heart, which had been busily fluttering in her throat, seemed to rise even farther and take over her speech. She nodded mutely, unable to take her eyes off the minister's face, yet at the same time completely incapable of looking directly into his coffee-colored eyes for fear of what her own eyes would reveal.

This is ridiculous, she scolded herself. *You've just met the man.* She took a deep breath and tried to calm her shaking fingers as she reached to clasp his hand.

"I'm very delighted to meet you," he said, and she found herself returning his easy smile.

She'd always loved Archer Falls, always felt that she was so much a part of the prairie that its rich soil was part of her blood and bone. But she had never been as glad to be standing where she was as at that moment in the newly painted church with late spring sunlight streaming through the windows—and holding Peter Collins's hand.

She was suddenly aware of how she'd flown into her clothes this morning, having overslept by at least an hour, ripped a brush through her knotted locks, and quickly bound her hair into a braided bun.

Her shoes were probably irretrievably scuffed. Brigit looked down at the leather-shod toes that peeked from under her blue and white calico skirt and grimaced. Not only were her shoes dusty, one of them was untied and the lacing hopelessly frayed. She tucked the offending shoe behind the heel of her other foot and attempted a smile.

This man had the speaking skills that Lars Nilsen lacked. He wasn't wreathed in odorous pipe smoke like Jerrod Stiles. And he most certainly was nowhere near as old as Arthur Smith.

No, the Reverend Peter Collins was about as perfect a piece of work as God could have made. She could only pray that his heart was as good.

"I'm very delighted to meet you." She felt stupid and quite dense. He'd certainly think she was not very bright if all she could do was parrot back his line.

His smile was a candle in a dark room. "I'm looking forward to being here."

His fingers moved in her grip, and she realized that she was still holding his hand. She dropped it as if it were on fire. Quickly she mumbled a few incoherent words and turned, nearly tripping on her shoelace as it caught on her heel.

No wonder he was smiling. She was a foolish, foolish young woman. He was so elegant, so cultured, so perfect, and she was nothing more than a prairie chicken scratching in the dust.

Her father filled the uneasy silence on the ride home with a running commentary on the reactions to the new minister.

"That was quite the picture, let me tell you," he said to Brigit as Fulton pulled them along the lane. "Milo Farnsworth was puffed up, proud as a pigeon; and you know, I think I heard him claim responsibility for the Reverend Collins's presence here."

He slowed the wagon to look at a deer that wandered out of the shelterbelt. "Of course, Milo was part of the committee that requested a minister, so I do suppose he has some credit due him on that."

She didn't respond. She couldn't. Her mind was too occupied to manage speech at the moment.

He glanced at his daughter. "Remember, he's a bachelor."

"Mr. Farnsworth?" Brigit looked at him in confusion. "No, he's not."

"I didn't mean Milo," her father said. "The new minister isn't married."

Suddenly the day didn't seem as bright as it had. Couldn't she simply meet Reverend Collins without her father and who knew who else pushing them together? Didn't he think she was capable of finding her own sweetheart without his interference?

"He's not married," she snapped, "and interestingly enough, neither am I."

Her father didn't respond to her outburst. He merely reached across the wagon and patted her hand. "We farmers can only trust in our Lord for our daily bread, but He trusts us with the seed."

She loved her father dearly, but right now figuring out what he was talking about required more thinking than she was willing to do. Somehow, though, she knew this had to do with Reverend Collins.

She should guard her heart closely with the new minister, because there was no way he'd want a farming woman like her with calluses on her hands and no social graces at all. The gap between them was as wide as the Mississippi River.

Brigit sighed. At last someone who was handsome and charming and educated had come to Archer Falls, and she had no choice but to look the other way.

Her father had quit talking and was now singing softly. It was a hymn that she'd grown up with, "Rock of Ages." He'd hummed her to sleep with the melody many nights when she was a child, and it never failed to calm her.

Even now, she felt the tightness in her throat relax and her heart ease. God was good. He had given them a minister.

He would give her love, too—in time.

All He asked of her was patience.

Peter placed his new Bible on his bureau. It was the one that the presiding elder had given him as a first-assignment gift. The rich burgundy leather cover had his name stamped in gold letters on the front. He'd never had anything as fine, he had assured the Reverend Armstrong at the time, but that wasn't quite true.

His fingers ran across the words HOLY BIBLE on an older copy that was also on his bureau. The black leather was cracked, the pages were dog-eared and bent, but it meant more to him than the new volume.

This Bible had belonged to his father, and before that, his father's father. He opened the cover and let his fingertips trail across the notes that three generations had added.

The last page was the Our Family page. There were his grandparents' names, and his parents', and their children's. His brothers and sisters and their spouses were on the family tree, along with the "twigs," as he liked to call his six nephews and nieces.

But his branch was empty save for his name. No spouse. No twigs.

The only corner of his heart that wasn't filled with joy moved sadly—yet with hope.

Maybe here he'd find his love, and his tree would grow and bloom on this prairie.

God, he prayed silently, *dearest Lord, might I find love here? Is the woman Thou meanest for me—is she here?*

The image of a young woman, her hair the color of orange marmalade, floated into his mind.

Brigit Streeter. Brigit Collins?

The tiny empty corner of his heart seemed to sigh with a sense of hope.

If only Brigit hadn't decided to take a late afternoon run through the cottonwoods on Fulton's back. But the house had been too closed in for her. Spring was already nearly over. Summer was lurking behind every leafing tree, ready to leap out and embrace her.

The new minister had been there for five weeks already, and his sermon that morning had been about enjoying the beauty of God's creation. She had gone out of the house, not planning on doing anything beyond sitting on the log seats and doing exactly what Reverend Collins had suggested, when she discovered that one of the harbingers of summer had already arrived—the voracious mosquito.

She quickly slapped that insect into history and ran into the barn to saddle up Fulton. Mosquitoes were already in his stable area, and his tail switched furiously in a mostly futile attempt to keep the pests away.

Within minutes they were one being, woman and horse, and the memory of the nasty mosquitoes was left behind them.

These were the times she loved the most, when she could shake herself free of the responsibility of house and farm. Fulton seemed to enjoy it, too, and Brigit allowed herself the fancy that he was imagining himself running free across the prairie with no saddle on his back, no plow fastened to him, and only the wild grasses to feed upon.

At last they both tired, and at the end of the farthest tree line, they turned back, moving in a companionable canter as the ever-present wind cooled the sweat.

The mosquitoes found them immediately. Brigit brushed and swatted, swatted and brushed until they arrived home and she could lead Fulton into the barn and clean him up.

Voices were coming from the house, and Brigit glanced at the wagon that was parked in front of their house. It was probably one of her father's friends come to chew over the events of the day.

Fulton was, without a doubt, the best horse in the world, and Brigit told him so as she curried and fed him. "I wish I could do something about the mosquitoes, old friend. Someday someone will invent something that really works to make them go away."

She gave him one final pat and left the barn.

The voices still floated from inside the house in a quiet, murmuring stream. Automatically she began separating them. Her father. Mary Rose's father, Calvin Groves. But who did the third voice belong to?

She pulled the straggling bun out of her hair as she walked toward the house. There was no point in trying to keep it in place. The ride had effectively torn the hairpins from their moorings so that the chignon trailed down one side.

Men surely had it nice, she thought as she tried to untangle her hair from the pins. Just snip-snip and they were done. It certainly would be wonderful if she could have short hair, too. Her life would be much easier: no snarls to try to comb through, no trying to braid and wrap her hair behind her back.

"Hello, Papa," she sang as she stumbled into the house, her eyes not used to the darkness of the inside after the glare of the afternoon sunshine. A pin fell, and she dropped to her knees to find it. Her fingers searched blindly; against the floral background of the rug, it was nearly impossible to see the pin. "Fulton—"

Her words stopped mid-throat as she realized who the third voice belonged to.

The Reverend Peter Collins was in her house, and she was crawling on the floor, her hair a matted mess, her dress stained and wrinkled. Plus she smelled like a sweating horse.

Lovely, she thought. *Just lovely.*

There was no hope for her. None. At least, she consoled herself as she stood and worked up a smile for him, there was one good thing to be said for all this.

It couldn't get any worse.

Chapter 3

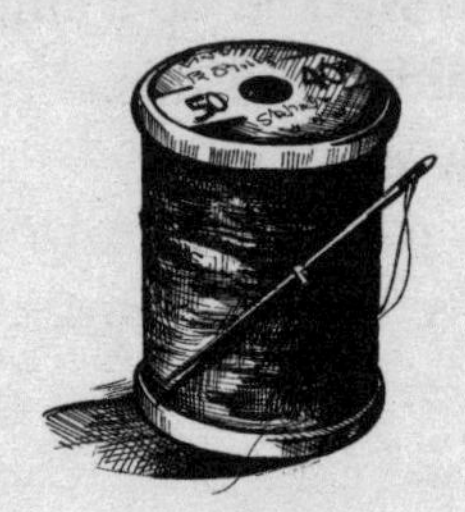

If Peter was horrified by Brigit's appearance—and her aroma—he didn't show it as he stood and bowed slightly to her. *He's probably too genteel,* Brigit thought. There was no way that he couldn't notice how disheveled she was.

She stole a look at her father. From the expression on his face, she knew that she looked as terrible as she feared. His left eyebrow was arched almost up to his hairline, a sure sign that he was dismayed at what he was seeing. She'd seen that often enough growing up to know it as a danger signal.

"Brigit," he began in his warning voice, but Peter interrupted him.

"You look as if you've been enjoying this wonderful spring afternoon that the Lord has provided us," the young minister said, his eyes alight with laughter. "We should take advantage of all of them without worrying about the winter that is always lurking around the corner."

Milo Farnsworth stepped from the shadowed corner of the room. "Brigit Streeter, sometimes I think you are more horse than woman." He smiled, a frosty action that touched only his lips, not his eyes. "How fortunate your father is that he has you as a daughter. Why, you are as strong and capable as any son. Didn't I see you last week plowing the field north of here?"

A quick retort sprang to her lips, but her father gripped her arm tightly. She didn't dare look at the minister for fear of what she might read in his expression.

These were not simple, innocent words. Mr. Farnsworth's sentences hurt. Like a vengeful hornet, he had found the most painful—the most effective—target for his sting.

Her father's fingers dug in a bit more, and this time she knew it wasn't done to keep her from lashing out at Mr. Farnsworth. No, the words had struck a spot in his heart that still ached with loss. Plus there was something else, something that even Mr. Farnsworth couldn't know.

Albert Streeter couldn't farm without his daughter.

They had never spoken about it, but she knew from the way he sank into his chair at the end of the day. He wasn't sick—she could tell that. He was simply tired. The farm he had was too big for him to run by himself.

So the two of them had done it together, father and daughter; and it had been a good partnership. Now it was, in her father's eyes, time for her to move into a marriage home.

He could sell off part of the farm, but she knew he'd never stop farming. He'd. . .

Her thoughts were abruptly ended when Reverend Collins turned to her and said, "She looks wonderfully capable to me. Any man would be fortunate indeed to have her grace his home."

The look on Mr. Farnsworth's face made up for any hurt that she was feeling. His cheeks were flushed, and for the first time in her life, Brigit saw him at a loss for words.

He started to speak, stopped, started again, stopped again.

Her father's fingers relaxed their hold, and he spoke behind her. "I am always proud of Brigit. Always."

Mr. Farnsworth harrumphed. "Of course, of course. She is an—"

Brigit had to suppress the smile that twitched around her lips as he struggled for the proper way to describe her. She could tell that he wanted to say more, but social correctness kept him from doing so.

She turned to look again at Reverend Collins and was surprised to see him watching her, almost as if he were studying her. He smiled. "No, there'd be no mistaking you for someone's son."

If she'd thought the day couldn't get worse, she hadn't figured on him saying *that.* The blood rose right from the tips of her dusty toes to her cheeks.

Oh, she hated blushing. Just hated it. She didn't turn pink or blush gently. No, her whole face flooded into a bright red. Why on earth had God ever thought it would be a good idea to make her face turn crimson whenever she was embarrassed? Couldn't He just have given her a brightly colored flag to wave or a sign to hold—"I am mortified"—or perhaps a trumpet to blare?

Reverend Collins smiled at her, and the world collapsed into a space that was just big enough for the two of them.

This was not real, a little portion of her brain told her. It wasn't possible to fall in love this quickly.

There were other people in the room. She could hear their voices indistinctly. Mr. Groves said something vague and left.

Mr. Farnsworth stood off to the side uneasily, as if not being at all accustomed to being in that position. He said a few words, something about a piano, and Reverend Collins turned to him and nodded.

"Friday evening? Why, thank you. I do enjoy good music, and from what you've told me, your wife is quite an accomplished pianist. I'm looking forward to getting to know you and your family better."

If he had thrown a knife right into her heart, it couldn't have caused more pain. The Farnsworth house was the grandest one in Archer Falls. The windows that overlooked the fertile valley were draped in snowy white organza. The dishes—she had seen the dishes—were blue and white patterned china. She'd never seen cups as delicate as these. Her father once described the Farnsworth china as "thin as a hurried promise."

She looked down at her stained dress and sighed, which reminded her that the Farnsworths undoubtedly smelled better.

But then, she thought, they'd never had the joy of riding Fulton full-bore along a young shelterbelt, nor known the satisfaction of seeing wheat that they'd planted themselves from tiny seeds sprout up in sun-warmed earth.

She summoned a smile from the depths of her soul and tried to stand tall and proud. What was done was done, and she couldn't do much to change that, now could she?

"It's been wonderful seeing you both," she said, imagining herself in front of a grandly sweeping staircase, "and I do hope you both drop in again to visit."

She put her hand on her father's shoulder, and as she did, she noticed a piece of straw dangling from her cuff. Of course it wasn't a small bit. It was at least four inches long and caught the late afternoon sunlight so that it glowed golden.

The men noticed at the same time. There was no way to ignore it, so she did the next best thing.

She held her arm up and admired the straw as it reflected the rays. "Look at this. God gives some of us gold in coins. For the rest of us, He grows it in our fields."

Her father's lips clamped shut, but she knew it wasn't because he was offended by her audacity. Quite the contrary, he was probably trying to control his amusement.

Mr. Farnsworth gaped at her, obviously astonished at her words.

Reverend Collins, however, smiled broadly and chortled. "Amen, Miss Streeter! Amen!"

Mr. Farnsworth glanced uncertainly at the minister and joined in the laughter. "Ha ha. Good one, Brigit. Gold in the fields. Ha ha." He harrumphed loudly. "On that cheerful note, I will take my leave. Reverend Collins, it is indeed a joy to have you with us in Archer Falls. Streeter, we'll talk more this week about putting some paint on the schoolroom walls."

Some people could simply leave a room, Brigit thought, but not Mr. Farnsworth. He took a good five minutes to finally get across the room and out the door.

"Farnsworth is a good man," her father told the minister. "A good man."

"I can tell he is," Reverend Collins agreed. "He certainly has the heart of a stalwart citizen. If I hadn't already been inclined to come to Archer Falls, he would have swayed me in this direction."

"We are glad you chose us." Her father winced a bit as he leaned back into his chair, and he rubbed his leg. "Brigit, would you walk the reverend to his wagon? I'd do it, but this charley horse has got the better of me."

"I'm sorry to hear about your leg, but I'd certainly enjoy Brigit's company," Reverend Collins said, touching her hand.

People had touched Brigit's hand before, many times. But the action had never had this effect. She had to remind herself to breathe as they walked out of the house and toward his wagon.

She was very aware of how the sun sat just so on the cottonwood trees. How Fulton whinnied softly to her from his stall. How the mourning doves cooed a forthcoming rain that the sky didn't yet show.

And how very tall and handsome Peter Collins was.

"It's quite lovely out here," he said. "This has a beauty of its own. The sky is incredibly blue. You know, in St. Paul I didn't get to see but patches of the sky. The buildings got in the way."

She looked at him, startled. Most of the city people who came to Archer Falls saw only empty prairie, barren and in need of more buildings, more trees, more things.

"In Dakota," he continued, apparently unaware of how much his words had surprised her, "the sky goes on forever. I am awed by what our God has done."

"He's done a good job." Her voice sounded small and tiny.

Reverend Collins glanced at her, and his lips curled into a grin. "Yes, He has. He has made many wondrous creations, I'm finding."

That furious blush started its crawl up her neck, and she

quickly changed the subject. "I hope life in Archer Falls is to your liking."

"Oh, it is. As I said in church on Sunday, Archer Falls is exactly what I've been looking for."

"It isn't too. . .backward?"

He reached down and picked a just-blossomed daisy. "Backward?" He studied the flower thoughtfully. "Not at all. Oh, the buildings aren't as grand as those in St. Paul, and the stores don't have the variety of wares, and there's no opera house, but none of those matter. What's important is the people. And the land."

"I'm glad to have you with us," Brigit said. Then she added hastily, "We've been in need of a minister for a long time. As it is, the men of the community have been trading off the sermon duties, and while my father's sermons are intelligent and thought-provoking, I can't say that's true of the other men's sermons."

"Does Mr. Farnsworth preach?" he asked.

"Oh, yes. He does." She thought she should stop with that short answer.

He continued, "And how are Mr. Farnsworth's sermons?"

"Loud."

The word popped out before she could stop it, and they both laughed.

"You know, Brigit," he said, "there's a lot of work ahead of us, building a church."

"Yes, there is."

"Can I ask you something? I don't want to rush you but. . ."

Oh, this is great, she thought wryly. *He's going to ask me to sew altar cloths or polish candlesticks or something, when my talent would be more in laying the floorboards.*

"I don't know if I can help you much," she admitted. It was better to get it out in the open, in case he hadn't figured out that she was sadly lacking in the finer feminine skills. "It's not my forte."

Reverend Collins seemed surprised. "Not your forte? What do you mean?"

"You want me to do something with the church, right? Embroidering pew cushions or hanging drapes?"

He didn't answer. Instead, he studied first her face and then the daisy. "Well, that would be helpful, but that's not what I had in mind."

She groaned silently. This wasn't sounding at all good. "Reverend Collins, I—"

He shook his head. "Let me finish. First of all, I like you—quite a bit. Would you be willing to let me visit you?"

"Of course," she said. "Our door is always open. Or almost always open. Except when it's closed."

Oh, stop babbling like that, she scolded herself. *Not only have you made a splendid impression on him with your first meeting, you've undoubtedly cemented his opinion of you with today.*

"I want to visit you," he began, and then he paused and took a deep breath. "I want to visit-you-because-I'd-like-to-get-to-know-you-better." The last words came out in one long whoosh of breath.

He handed her the flower, and to her amazement, he flushed a deep crimson.

If there had been any doubt at all, it vanished with that simple act.

"I'd be honored to have you visit," she said, aware that she'd never smiled as broadly and as joyfully before.

⁘

Peter got into his wagon, and as he drove away, he realized he was singing. This wasn't something he often did, for although God had given him many talents, singing wasn't one of them.

He warbled—shakily—the last line of the morning's hymn, and a flock of quail flew out of a cluster of brush by the road.

At least he thought they were quail.

She's the one, isn't she, God?

Life was good. God was good. The future stretched ahead like this road that seemed to head toward the horizon, a golden thread in the afternoon sunlight, a golden thread with no knots, no snarls, no—

Oh no!

He sat upright so suddenly that the horse whinnied a question.

He clicked in encouragement, and the horse continued down the road, but his afternoon had taken on a less glorious glow.

He'd forgotten about the evening of piano music at the Farnsworth house on the coming Friday. It wasn't that he didn't think he'd enjoy the recital—quite the opposite—but for some reason he didn't relish the evening.

Maybe it would be all right, he tried to console himself. Maybe it would be just a simple evening of good music in a lovely house.

In the interim, he had something wonderful to look forward to. Odd that Brigit hadn't mentioned it to him.

Brigit watched as Reverend Collins's wagon got smaller and smaller until it was part of the horizon. She hugged herself with delight, thinking of what he'd said.

She tried not to think about the upcoming evening at the Farnsworth house, though. The fact of the matter was that comparing Farnsworths to Streeters was like comparing silk to homespun.

"You must have found a lot to talk about," her father said when she came inside. He was grinning. "Even Milo Farnsworth doesn't take that long to leave."

The dear was trying so hard not to ask her what the minister had said to her.

"We visited about the community and the church."

"Yes?" His curiosity was ill reined, and Brigit didn't keep him in suspense.

"Yes. He also asked if he could come to visit."

Her father frowned. "Well, of course he can visit. Maybe he wants some information from me about the materials of worship that we have, or—"

She smiled broadly as the realization struck him.

"He isn't coming to see me, is he?"

"He could be."

"Or not."

Brigit stood in the fading summer light, watching hope play across her father's face.

She tried to refuse to let the nasty little voice in, the one that reminded her how unsuitable she was for the minister. *He really should be married to someone like Mary Rose,* the voice nagged, *someone who is well versed in the social graces.*

Someone not like you.

"I'm glad," he said at last. "Very glad."

He was smiling a bit more than she was comfortable with. She didn't try to figure it out. Her father was having some very strange moments lately.

She patted his hand. "He's a nice fellow, Papa."

He nodded and stood up. "I'd better check to make sure that chicken wire is still good. Groves brought over some of his newest hatchlings."

She grinned happily. Baby chicks! She loved them. Maybe Mary Rose could come over later and they could play with them. She loved the sensation of their little chick feet on her hands when she held them.

"You don't mind, do you?" he asked as he ambled toward the front door. "I meant to ask you, but just like old Groves's rooster, it flew out of my mind."

He stepped outside and almost immediately popped his head back in. "I did tell you that I invited Reverend Collins for supper, didn't I?"

Chapter 4

"You did *what?*"

Brigit's father turned and faced her, a faint frown creasing his forehead. "Didn't I tell you?"

She studied his face. Was that slightly confused expression also slightly faked? "No, you didn't tell me."

"I'm sorry. I certainly meant to." He sounded sincere, but a mischievous glint in his eyes gave him away.

She shook her head. What was she going to do with him? "When is he coming over?"

Mr. Streeter stepped out of the doorway before answering. "Tonight."

Tonight?

Brigit took a mental survey of what was on hand. It was a very quick survey: they didn't have much at all.

She slumped into the chair. There were some women in town who were quite adept at taking a chicken, a carrot, and a sprinkle of seasonings and coming up with something delicious. She wasn't one of those women. If she couldn't boil it, it didn't get cooked.

Why had her father done this? He knew how limited her culinary skills were. If he were really trying to marry her off, he had chosen an odd way of advertising her assets.

There was no ignoring her predicament, though. Her father had really done it this time. With a sigh, she pulled herself out of her chair and checked to see what was possible for a dinner.

She grumbled to herself as she gathered together a pile of vegetables. It certainly wasn't much, and it definitely wasn't going to be fancy.

The Farnsworths weren't going to be eating thick stew with carrots and potatoes cut into large chunks because Brigit didn't have the patience to dice them into tiny cubes. No, they'd be served food with French names that she couldn't pronounce on dishes that she didn't dare touch for fear she'd break them.

Here she'd be serving stew on heavy mismatched plates with chips in the sides. The delicate china that had been her mother's had long ago been discarded, the victim of her father's inept washings.

Why hadn't he asked her before he invited the minister to dinner?

She muttered as she chopped potatoes and sliced carrots. Griped as she cut up the chicken. Complained as she shoved wood into the cookstove and heated the small kitchen area to an unbearable temperature.

But even as she did so, part of her was rejoicing.

He was coming back!

She smiled at the unpeeled carrot she was holding. Had ever a vegetable looked so beautiful? How could its brilliant orange coloring develop like that underground? Had there ever been such a miracle as a carrot? She almost hated to scrape the skin off it, but into the pot it must go.

If only she had some of those seasonings she'd heard the women at church talk about. She'd never paid any attention to those discussions. Salt and pepper were all she and her father ever used.

The liquids began to burble in the pot. It would be awhile before it would be ready. She had time to turn Fulton out to graze one last time before evening. She didn't like to have him out after sunset. The mosquitoes were getting fierce at dark, even this early in the season.

Her horse whinnied softly as she went toward his stall in the barn. He'd been with her so long that she'd almost forgotten a time when he hadn't been there. Even so, his canter was still good and strong. She loved to watch him playfully fling his head or nibble the grass.

She couldn't resist. Within minutes, she was up on his back, racing down the road toward the river and then back again. There was nothing like the wind on her face to clear her mind of her foolishness, she told herself.

After they'd come back to the farm and she'd brushed him down, she turned Fulton into the fenced area of the yard.

Brigit watched Fulton soak up the afternoon sun for a while, and then she realized with a start that it was almost time for Reverend Collins to arrive, and she was still as smelly and messy as she had been—even more so since she'd added peeling an onion to her day's activities.

She tore inside and washed and combed and patted and

brushed until she looked as good as she could, given the circumstances. She had just finished when her father lumbered through the door, calling to her.

"Brigit, are you—Oh no! What is that smell?"

She poked her head around the corner, a ready retort on her lips. "I smell just fine, thank you very much, thanks to—oh, that's awful!"

She covered her nose and ran to the kitchen.

The pot with the stew in it had boiled dry, and the carrots and potatoes were now a hardened mass at the bottom. She gave them a tentative poke with the fork, but it was as bad as it appeared—and smelled.

"What are we going to do?" she wailed. "What are we going to do?"

Peter stood in front of the mirror and straightened his tie for the seventh time. It simply would not stay put. No, it insisted upon sliding over to the side, and that wouldn't do at all.

Not when he was going to visit Brigit Streeter. He was smitten. There was no other word for how he felt. She lived life with a vigor he envied. Customs and conventions didn't seem to hold her back.

He sighed. Customs and conventions were part of a minister's life. He had known that from the very beginning. And they fit him very well.

Brigit Streeter, though, touched that part of his soul that longed for a closer relationship with the Lord, one that saw His face in every flower, His hand in every bird.

She had also touched his heart.

"So what are we going to do?" Brigit asked her father again.

He shook his head in disbelief. "I don't know. I just don't know."

She opened the cupboard door and stared in at the nearly empty whitewashed shelves.

The stew was beyond salvaging, and there wasn't enough of anything left to make dinner from on such short notice.

She sank to the spindle-legged chair in the small kitchen and buried her face in her hands. This was not good. She wanted to make a good impression on Reverend Collins, not continue to reinforce what he must surely think of her—that she was a tomboyish mess.

There was something inordinately unfair here. Here she was, stuck on the prairie with the saddest assortment of "suitable" men imaginable, and what happened when the most eligible bachelor this side of the Mississippi showed up—and was interested in her, to boot?

The pain in her soul was almost palpable. *I want him to like me,* she cried silently, moving as naturally to prayer as if it were breath. *Dearest Lord, Thou art probably trying to teach me something here, but apparently I am a horribly slow student. What am I supposed to do? Please help me!*

A knock sounded at the door, and she raised her head, startled. She hadn't expected God to answer quite this quickly, and she dreaded His answer.

"Mary Rose, what a surprise!" Her father's voice rang through the small house. "I wasn't expecting to see you this evening."

Brigit stuck her head around the corner and stopped mid-step when she saw what her best friend was holding out toward her father.

It was round and wrapped in a blue and white checked cloth, and it smelled heavenly.

Could it be that God had answered her prayer in the rotund form of Mary Rose Groves?

"Brigit, Mother sent this over. She said that you—"

Mr. Streeter took the dish out of her hands and gave it to his daughter. "Please tell your mother that we send our thanks. Now, Mary Rose, you must hurry home, isn't that right?"

Mary Rose started to say something but stopped. "Oh, absolutely."

When Mr. Streeter left the room with the dish in his hands, Mary Rose leaned over and whispered conspiratorially, "I think your father is playing matchmaker."

Brigit groaned. "I am really in for it, then. He is relentless when he gets an idea in that balding head of his."

Mary Rose winked behind her glasses. "Sometimes, Brigit, you have got to admit that he is right. Some matches *are* made in heaven."

Birds twittered and a slight breeze rustled the leaves of the cottonwoods as Peter's horse walked the road to the Streeter home. There couldn't be a nicer afternoon, he thought. This was the Dakota Territory in its sunlit glory.

He spoke softly to the horse and slowed its pace until it stopped. He jumped from the horse and turned around in a complete circle, taking in his surroundings.

God had truly excelled in this land. The sky was an azure arch over his head, reminding him of the vision that far exceeded his own. A faint puff of white, a lone cloud on an astonishingly blue canvas, drifted across the sky. Peter's heart immediately sought prayer.

Lord God of all beings, I thank Thee with all my soul for bringing me to this place of extraordinary beauty. I beg of Thee to let my ears be open to Thy way and my mouth speak only those words assigned by Thee.

He paused and listened to a meadowlark warble its prairie opera, watched a jackrabbit bound across an open field.

The only thing missing was someone to love. . .someone to love him.

He sighed. There was no use in getting philosophical about that in the middle of a country road. Then he smiled and finished that thought. . .especially when love might possibly be waiting at the end of this very road.

He put his foot back into the stirrup and swung himself easily onto the saddle. He clicked to the horse and urged it into a trot. Time was wasting away.

As Peter drew closer to the Streeter home, a wagon passed him. Its driver waved, and he thought he recognized her as someone from the church, although he couldn't remember her name. What a friendly place Archer Falls was!

He was looking forward to this. He really was. His stomach growled in anticipation of the wonderful dinner that was awaiting him.

He'd had enough of his burned stew to last a lifetime.

"He's here."

Brigit's heart leaped up to flutter somewhere in her throat as, from the doorway, she watched Reverend Collins dismount from the horse. He spoke quietly to the animal and then greeted her father, who'd gone out to meet him.

They tended to the animal and returned to the house, and as they did so, she tried to calm herself. She probably had the wrong idea about his feelings for her. To him, perhaps she was simply another parishioner, someone to love only in a godly sense.

He smiled at her as he took off his hat before entering the house. His hair gleamed like coal in the late afternoon sunlight, and his eyes were as dark as warmed chocolate.

"Miss Streeter, it's very kind of you and your father to invite me to your house."

She took his hand, trying very hard to remember to breathe. "The pleasure is ours, and please call me Brigit. Let me take your hat, and you go ahead and have a seat, and my father can show you around."

His face lit in a smile. "I'm not sure I caught all that, but I'm delighted to be here with you."

She knew she should let go of his hand, but she couldn't release her grip. The message that flashed from his eyes told her that she hadn't misread anything. How could her heart leap around like this? Why didn't it stay in place in her chest where it belonged rather than jumping from place to place inside her?

At last she came back to her senses and dropped his hand.

"I'm really glad you're here, Reverend Collins."

Somehow she managed to bumble her way through the next few minutes as they got themselves seated and ready to eat.

"Reverend Collins, would you do us the honor of praying over our food?" her father asked.

"It would be my pleasure." He bowed his head and began to pray. "Blessed Lord, Father of all we have been, all we are, and all we will be, have grace upon us this day as we gather to eat the gifts of this fruitful land. Shower our time together this afternoon with joy and caring. We ask this in Thy holy name. Amen."

"Tremendous words," Mr. Streeter commented as he shook his napkin out into his lap.

Brigit beamed at her father and at Peter and at the casserole. Life had rarely been this good.

What they talked about was as simple as how pleasant the weather had been, how the wheat was coming up good and strong this year, how Archer Falls was growing into a real community.

And all the time, Brigit heard only bits and pieces of the conversation. She felt as if she were dreaming the entire event.

The men's voices brought her back to reality.

"And that's why I've decided to stay in Archer Falls," he was saying. "I know I've only been here five weeks, but they've been a persuasive five weeks, enough to convince me to stay. I suspect the presiding elder will let me do so, that is, if the congregation will ask me to stay."

He turned his winning smile on her and added, "I received

a letter from him this week, saying he was satisfied with my work, so I am ever hopeful that he will agree to let me remain."

"You have determined to stay?" her father asked, and there was an edge to his voice that surprised Brigit. It was almost an anxiety that she heard.

"Yes." Reverend Collins looked at her, and his eyes spoke secrets that she'd only dreamed of.

Something was going to happen. The air almost sizzled with it, like the way the air was charged before a lightning storm, when the earth waits for the celestial fireworks yet to come.

"I've grown quite fond of the area," he continued, "and the people."

A nervous smile that she was unable to control twitched around her face. What was she supposed to do? Her romantic contacts had been limited—actually, there hadn't been any—and she was in the dark about what she should do next.

This was the kind of thing that she and Mary Rose had talked about long into the night, and she was sure that Mary Rose had told her what she should do, but as usual, Brigit hadn't paid any attention.

It hadn't mattered then. The idea that she might some day want to attract and keep the attention of a young man had seemed so unlikely. Certainly none of the men in the community had caught her eye. How Mary Rose had ferreted out Gregory Lester was a miracle. The fellow lived across the river, and they'd met through the help of some far-flung distant relatives who were determined to see them married, preferably to each other.

Speaking of miracles, here was one sitting across from her, and he was clearly waiting for a response to something he'd just asked.

She tried to recover and not look flustered and undoubtedly failed at both.

Chapter 5

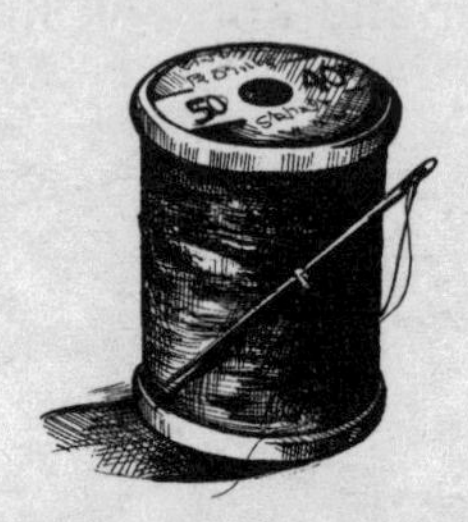

Summer moved along at a clip. Brigit loved the busyness of the season, when the earth seemed to explode with life. It was also the best time to fall in love, with long walks along tree-lined roads and picnics on violet-strewn grass. Brigit and Reverend Collins had just returned from such a walk on a Sunday afternoon.

"Isn't this a glorious day?" she asked, twirling around and sending her bun plummeting down. "What more could you ask for, Reverend Collins, than a day like this?"

His reply was soft. "What I would ask for, Brigit, is for you to stop calling me Reverend Collins. We can't have you calling me Reverend Collins all the time."

"What else would you have me call my minister?" She knew that color was rising in her cheeks, but she was incapable of stopping it.

His voice dropped a level. "You would call him Peter. Or maybe even Dear."

That did it. Her heart flip-flopped its way up her throat and back down again.

Peter. Had there ever been such a beautiful name? *Peter*.

"Nice sermon."

"Excellent."

"Next week."

Peter stood at the church door, staring at his parishioners as one by one they delivered terse compliments and sped out of the small building. They'd never been in that much of a hurry before, he thought. What had it been today? Had the building been too hot and close? Had there been a terrible smell that he hadn't, literally, gotten wind of? Or—horrors!—had his sermon been so awful that they felt compelled to flee from his presence the moment the service ended?

He watched them leap into wagons or onto horseback and hurry away. This was very odd. He leaned against the door frame and absently swatted away a persistent horsefly.

Maybe he shouldn't have come across so strongly about the gifts of heaven. Had the congregation interpreted his message as looking for increased donations?

"Going over your sermon again?" Brigit asked from behind him. "Trying to figure out what you could have said about the loaves and fishes that would be offensive?"

"Can you read my mind that easily?" he asked, only partially teasing.

"I can when your thoughts are written across your forehead." She laughed. "Actually, I can explain this odd behavior in one word: harvest."

"Really?" Peter was fascinated. This was another angle of farming he knew nothing about.

"Oh, don't get me wrong. They're not going home to work in the fields. No, they'll sit in their living rooms and think about their crops and the future. For them, each tiny seed that goes into the ground is a life, and they'll bring it through with prayer.

"They'll become preoccupied and worried and jubilant all at the same time. Remember, they've been looking forward to this day ever since that May morning when the first shoots curled up through the slumbering soil, changing winter to spring overnight."

She made it sound like a poem, he thought, and when she spoke, it was easy to forget how hard the process was, how capricious the weather could be, how much of a struggle the farming life was.

"We live for this," she continued, and he noticed how the sunlight behind her lit her hair into golden strands. "We even dream about the harvest."

"I hadn't realized it was so all-consuming."

"It is," she replied adamantly. "But don't expect much of a drop-off in attendance. We know who gave us these crops. We know who made the miracle of the plant inside the seed. We know, and we must praise Him."

At that moment, he knew what his next sermon would be on. Genesis 8:22 had long been one of his favorite verses. How could he forget it? "While the earth remaineth, seedtime and harvest, and cold and heat, and summer and winter, and day and night shall not cease."

The loving continuity of the Lord—it had been a theme that had sustained him throughout his life, and it continued to support him now. But he'd never seen it through the eyes of farmers, how their very work echoed the promise of the Lord.

How could he, who had been carefully schooled in the seminary, have missed that? He'd needed Brigit with her honest faith and her instinctive understanding of God's love to bring it to him. And now he needed to bring this message to his congregation.

They already know it.

He heard God's voice as surely as if He'd spoken in his ear.

It was a lesson that he, the preacher, was learning from his flock. God was real to them in ways Peter had never thought of and even now only vaguely understood. They saw God's face in the sunflower and heard His voice on the wind.

The yearning in his soul was almost an ache as he thought of what they had—and he didn't. What Brigit felt—and he didn't.

It wasn't that God wasn't very much a part of his life. He was. But Peter longed for the deeply personal relationship these farmers had with God, a deep-seated, internal knowledge that flowed through their veins like blood itself.

Bit by bit, though, Brigit was bringing him closer to his God, and it made him love her even more. Standing there, backlit by the glorious summer sun, her greenish eyes glowed with laughter, and something in his heart sang for the joy of her. She was truly beautiful.

"You're thinking," she said.

"I wish it weren't that obvious," he replied ruefully, dragging his thoughts back to the daily world. "Although I would hope that I'm thinking all the time, not just when it shows."

"Good point. But can I ask what occupied your thoughts so greatly today?" She tilted her head, and some golden-red strands slipped out of the bun and curled into tendrils around her face.

He leaned over and touched her cheek. "Nothing more than a glorious August day and an equally glorious woman. Would you like to go for a walk with me this afternoon?"

"I'd love to."

When Brigit smiled like that, Peter was sure he could hear the angels sing.

⁂

The cottonwoods whispered among themselves, and once in a while a crow cawed a noisy protest about the antics of a lively rabbit.

Inside her small house, Brigit hurried through her meal, barely even tasting the slab of ham her father laid across her plate and gulping down the boiled potatoes mindlessly.

Mr. Streeter watched her silently until at last he said, "Is there a train coming through here that I should know about?"

"A train?"

"I was just commenting that from the way you're wolfing down your meal, there must be a train headed our way."

"Oh, I'm sorry, Papa. No train, just a minister."

He didn't say anything, but from the way his face softened, Brigit knew that her father was fond of Peter, too.

She jumped out of her chair, ran over to him, and threw her arms around his shoulders, trying to ignore for the moment how thin they were. "Papa, dearest Papa, what should I do? About Peter, I mean. We are from two very different worlds."

"Does it matter, Brigit?"

"I believe it does, Papa. You see, I think, I hope, I worry that he is starting to love me. What should I do?"

He held her tightly, and his voice was muffled as he answered, "Love him back."

The afternoon sun was warm on Brigit's shoulders as she and Peter walked down the road leading away from the small farmstead.

"If it weren't for the insects, I think this would be heaven on earth," he said to her, as he smacked a relentless mosquito. "I know our Creator had His reasons for everything on this earth, but I fail to see how the mosquito quite fits into His greater plan."

"They're food for other animals." Brigit sent up an unspoken prayer of thanks for a long-ago schoolteacher who had explained it to her. "Dragonflies, for example, eat them. I remind myself of that whenever the mosquitoes are especially fierce, since I think dragonflies are amazing insects."

"I think the dragonflies had better get busy." He swatted another mosquito. "There's plenty to eat at their table."

"I think it's an uneven battle between them and grossly stacked in the mosquito's favor," she replied. "At least the dragonflies don't go hungry."

A large dragonfly buzzed toward them, its body and wings a kaleidoscope of emerald greens and cobalt blues.

"Isn't it beautiful?" she asked, leaning down to observe it as it paused on a roadside daisy. "God put extraordinary effort into this creature. Look at how it shines! And the wings are so transparent and thin, you'd think they'd tear in the wind, not keep this beauty aloft."

She stood up and smiled at him. "I'm sure I'm not telling you anything you don't already know. I don't know how anyone could not believe in God from simply looking around the everyday world. The perfect symmetry of a snowflake. The perfume of freshly laid straw. The delicacy of a newborn kitten's nose."

"That's right," he said almost to himself. "This is truly God's world."

"Sometimes I have to tear myself away from it or I'd be spending all my time looking at the miracle of a daisy." She touched the flower as the dragonfly flew away. "Here I am, a farmer myself, trying to make plants grow where I want them to, and at the moment, I can't think of a better place than right here for this daisy to grow. God decided that, and His mind was perfect, as always."

"I've never heard it put quite that way." His voice was barely above a whisper.

She felt herself redden. Of course he hadn't. Her views of God must seem mighty simple compared to the theology he had learned in the seminary.

"Do you know what surprises me the most about the Dakota Territory?" he asked, and before she could answer, he said, "The colors. Everything is so intense. The sky is so blue, the wheat is so golden, the trees are so green."

"Listen to this." Brigit pulled a shiny leaf off a poplar and bent the green heart in half. She blew into the bottom edge of it, and the shrill whistle from the folded leaf pierced the air.

She grinned as a squirrel overhead scolded her for breaking the peace of the afternoon.

Peter laughed. "Let me try it."

He plucked a leaf and folded it in half. After a futile attempt at producing any sound at all, he relinquished it to Brigit.

"You are a silly goose. I thought a minister was educated and knew everything."

"Is making a poplar leaf into a whistle part of the curriculum of a seminary now? If so, I must have skipped class that day," he teased her.

"Let me show you. You fold it like this, and then you kind of purse your lips a bit, and then you—"

"Kiss."

"What?" Brigit stopped, the leaf still in her fingers. "I said, you. . .I mean, you. . .that is, why. . .oh, dear."

"It certainly sounds to me like you were describing perfectly how to kiss. But I'd rather kiss you than a poplar leaf. May I?"

For once in her life, Brigit was speechless. She could only nod.

He leaned over, and she raised her lips. A memory of how she and Mary Rose had practiced kissing their pillows shot into her mind and she almost laughed, but then his lips touched hers. There was nothing pillow-like about Peter Collins's lips.

At last he drew back, but he held her lightly around her waist. "I've been wanting to do that for a long time. Brigit, I—"

"Is that Reverend Collins?" Mr. Farnsworth's voice boomed

across the landscape. "It is! Good! I want to talk to you about the men's meeting next Tuesday."

Peter leaned over and whispered in her ear, "Apparently the only way I'll get to kiss you in private is to marry you."

She stood in the shade of the poplars and stared at him as he grinned at her. He squeezed her hand quickly and went to talk to Mr. Farnsworth. She couldn't have heard him right. He must have said he would *tarry* her. *Carry* her. Or even *bury* her.

Peter lounged against the Farnsworth wagon. He didn't seem to look like a fellow who had just proposed. Or not.

She ran the words through her mind again. He hadn't said, "Brigit, will you marry me?" Actually, he hadn't asked her a question at all. It was probably a joke—not a good one, but a joke nonetheless.

The hope in her heart evaporated except for one stubborn bit: *He wouldn't have said it if he didn't mean it.*

The two men talked at the wagon, oblivious to the turmoil in her soul.

What did she want? Did she want Peter to love her? The answer shot back, clear and pure: *Yes.*

Did she want to be his wife? Again the answer was: *Yes.*

Could she be a minister's wife and mingle with church dignitaries and hold teas and serve fancy dinners? The answer this time was no.

She was the kind of woman who knew how to make poplar leaf whistles and could bring in a field of wheat by herself. These were not the talents asked of a minister's wife.

Peter motioned her over to the wagon. "I hate to cut our afternoon short, but I need to get back into town. There's a telegram from the presiding elder that's marked *Urgent.* Mr. Farnsworth has volunteered to drive me in. Can we drop you off on the way?"

His eyes pleaded with her to understand, and she did. She shook her head. "No, but thank you just the same. I believe I'll walk on home."

"Are you sure? Then I'll pick you up tonight around six thirty for the pie supper at church?"

She nodded. "I'll be ready. But don't worry about my walking. It's such a nice day, and as we all know, such warmth is fleeting in Dakota. All too soon it will be cold, and I'll be pining for this heat."

Besides, she added mentally, *I need some time to work out my feelings about you.*

But it wasn't, she acknowledged as she walked slowly back to her home, that she had to sort out how she felt about him. She knew that. She loved him with every bit of her being.

She just had to determine what to do about it.

Peter straightened his tie yet again in the mirror. He wasn't a vain man, but he lamented his inability to center his tie. No matter what he tried, it simply wouldn't stay in line.

He was really looking forward to the evening. Pie suppers were apparently great fun. But that wasn't why his tie had to be straight. No, it was because of a young woman with wild strawberry blond hair who would be there, too.

His heart warmed at the thought.

Clearly, Lord, she is the one Thou hast intended for me. I had no idea that my soul was capable of such love. It seems to grow, to expand inside me. I must thank Thee, O Lord, for bringing her to me.

Tenderly, he touched the daisy that she had picked for him earlier that day. How could he have never noticed the delicate white petals, the velvety yellow center, the texture of the slender green stem?

He grimaced one last time at his reflection and gave the recalcitrant tie one last tug, which sent it completely askew. Peter resisted the temptation to rip the offending item off entirely and jerked the tie back toward the center. By the time he got to the Streeter house, the ride would knock it farther out of line.

The clock in the hallway bonged six times, and he ceased his struggle with his tie. If he was going to get to the Streeter house, collect Brigit and her father, and bring them back into town without being late, he had better get going.

He bolted down the stairs and out the door singing. It was going to be a good night whether his tie was lined up or not.

Some of his joyous mood was, he had to admit, due to the contents of the telegram. He touched his coat pocket where the paper crinkled reassuringly. Yes, it was real. He couldn't wait to share the news with Brigit.

Peter sang all the way to the Streeter farm despite the loud objections of the squirrels and crows along the way. He was no musical prodigy, that was sure. It was a good thing tonight's show did not require audience participation, he thought wryly.

Brigit was in the barn. He could see her outline against the open door. He couldn't wait to see her reaction to his news. That was the best part of love: being able to share joy like this.

Chapter 6

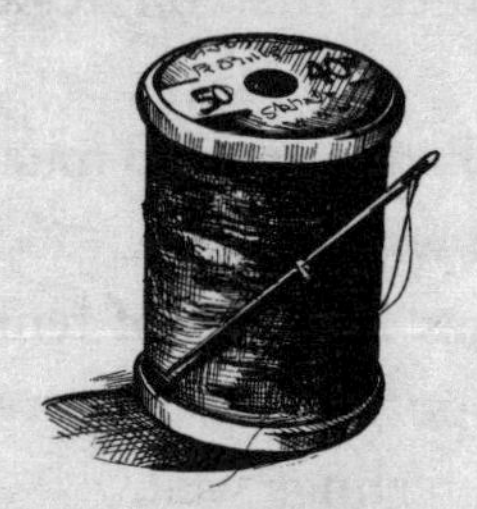

Brigit!" Peter tore into the barn, startling Fulton, who reared up slightly in protest. "Oh, sorry there, Fulton. Brigit, guess what! You'll never guess! Just guess!"

She leaned against the stable door and studied the man she loved. "Why don't we spare us all the pain of my trying to guess something I'll never guess, and you just tell me?"

"Oh, right. Let me take a deep breath. Is he going to be all right?" Peter shot a concerned glance at Fulton, who was watching the minister warily.

"He's fine. What's the news?"

"Reverend Armstrong, the regional presiding elder of the church, is coming right here to Archer Falls!" He reached into his pocket and withdrew a crumpled piece of paper, which he waved in front of her. "That's what the telegram was about!"

Why this was such exciting news was beyond Brigit, and she said so, with polite modifications.

"He's coming here for a visit, Brigit, to see us!"

"To see you and me? Why?"

"No, to see all of us. To see the church and how it's doing.

How I'm doing. He was my mentor when I was in seminary."

"You're not worried, are you?" she asked him.

"I suppose I am a bit," he confessed, "but mainly I'm excited to have him meet the congregation and to see how blessed I am."

He grew serious. "I've learned so much from all of you, and I'm eager to share you with him."

She studied his eyes for signs of tension and saw none. If she were in the same spot, she'd be a nervous wreck. Maybe he was simply hiding his feelings well.

"Is there anything I can do to help?" she offered.

His face lit up. "Interesting that you should ask that. There is. Reverend Armstrong's wife would like to meet the ladies of Archer Falls."

Her smile froze. She couldn't meet someone as important to Peter's career as the presiding elder or his wife. She was only a farm woman.

"I'm thinking a tea would be good." He ducked his head and cleared his throat. "I don't know how much trouble something like this would be—I'm not exactly sure of what one would even have to do to have a reception of this sort. So tell me if I'm asking too much. Could you put together a tea for her?"

Could she put together a tea for the presiding elder's wife? Could she flap her arms and fly to Minneapolis? Of course she couldn't.

Her brain knew that, but her heart knew something else, and her mouth apparently had a mind of its own. "Of course I can."

Was she out of her mind? Frantically she sought a way to

take back the words. "I mean, I can't. . .I don't. . .I. . ."

But the expression on his face stopped her. What she saw there wasn't just gratitude; it was also relief. And then it struck her: he wanted her to do it.

That alone was enough to stem her objections.

She, Brigit Streeter, was putting on a tea.

"Mary Rose, what do you know about teas?"

Brigit's friend turned her nearsighted gaze at her as they sat in the yard of Brigit's house. "I like strong black tea the best. One and a half spoonfuls of sugar or a quick slurp of honey to sweeten it. No cream. Why?"

"No, not that kind of tea." Brigit shook her head. "I'm supposed to put on a tea for Mrs. Armstrong, the presiding elder's wife, and I have no idea how to start."

"A tea? You, hosting a tea?" Mary Rose laughed uproariously. "How did that happen?"

Brigit picked a clover blossom and shredded it. "I'm not really sure. I certainly meant to say no, but somehow I said yes."

Mary Rose nodded knowingly. "Ah. I understand. When is this tea?"

"In two weeks."

Her friend frowned. "I can't help you then. I'm going to St. Paul with my mother to pick out the material for my wedding gown. Did you see the pattern we found? It looks a bit like Queen Victoria's. . ."

Brigit paid only minor attention as Mary Rose launched into the details of her wedding preparations. It wasn't that she didn't care. On the contrary, Mary Rose was her best friend ever. But things like patterns and dresses ranked quite low with her.

Right down there with hosting teas.

"And Reverend Collins said he would," Mary Rose finished with a triumphant beam.

Brigit had no idea what Mary Rose was talking about, but her mention of Peter brought her back to the conversation. "Peter said he would do what? I'm sorry, but I got lost in my own world there for a minute."

Mary Rose laughed. "I do tend to go on and on when I get to talking about my wedding. I was just saying that Reverend Collins agreed to officiate at the wedding in September, depending on how the harvest is going. I want my honeymoon to be far away in Minneapolis, in a big fancy hotel, not in a wheat field here in Archer Falls."

Suddenly the import of what Mary Rose had been saying these past three months since her engagement to Gregory struck Brigit. Mary Rose would be going away to live with her new husband.

What a day this had been!

Some days crept by, thought Brigit, and others simply tore past. It had been fourteen days since Peter had spoken to her about the tea, but she had managed to put off even thinking about it.

That was, until Peter mentioned it from the pulpit in church. "Reverend Armstrong will be visiting us this week. He and his wife are, in fact, arriving around noon today, and I'm looking forward to introducing all of you to them through some very special occasions. I'd like to remind you again that there will be a ladies' tea this afternoon to honor Mrs. Armstrong."

He smiled at her, apparently oblivious to the turmoil that churned in her stomach.

They were arriving today? She hadn't done anything about the tea. What on earth should she do? Why hadn't she given this any thought? Why did she always put things off until the last minute?

These were excellent questions, she realized, but they didn't help her at all. She was still stuck, completely and totally stuck, in a dire predicament.

"Where shall they meet, Brigit?" Peter had spoken from the front of the church and was looking at her expectantly.

She had no idea where they could have this thing called a tea. She ran through the options. The church? Not with the pews. Her house? There were only two chairs. Peter's house? If he'd wanted that, he would have offered.

She wanted to put her head down and cry. Peter would think—rightly so—that she was terribly inept. Again, the differences between them were brought vividly to light. In the same situation, he would have known what to do and, furthermore, done it right away.

Brigit did the only thing she could. She smiled brightly and said, "Let's meet at the front of the church, and we can walk."

Peter's sermon was undoubtedly superb, but her thoughts flew around in her head like unsettled sparrows. She had to find a solution.

The worst part of it all was that it wasn't only about her. This was about Peter and his career in the ministry. If she in any way made his situation perilous with the presiding elder, it could change his life's work—and the countless souls he might yet touch with the Lord's Word.

There was only one thing to do. Pray.

God, I am really in a pickle here. I don't know what I can do, but I know I have to do something. Please help me out, God. Please!

Somehow she got through the service and was trying to slide out the side door when Peter caught her. "The plans for the tea must be going extremely well," he said. "I haven't heard of any problems at all with it. I suppose you decided on having it at the school. There really isn't any other place. . ."

He chattered on happily while Brigit breathed a quick prayer of thanksgiving. How a tea held in a school could be elegant was beyond her, but she'd have to make it do.

She began to relax. Perhaps this tea was not going to be all that difficult.

As soon as she could gracefully slip away, she darted outside and ran across the square to the schoolhouse. She pulled on the handle. It was locked.

"Well," she said to herself, "when a door is locked, you must find a key." It was one of her father's sayings, and she'd heard it often enough when growing up to have it ingrained in her brain.

A key. She needed a key. Who had the key? Her thoughts tumbled around each other like baby puppies, impossible to settle down.

"Brigit!" Her father called to her from the wagon. "Are you coming?"

She ran to him. "Papa, I need to get into the school. I have to set up the tea in there."

"You're having the tea in the school?" From the expression on his face, she knew it wasn't her best choice. Sadly, it was her only choice.

"Yes, I am, and I haven't got a lot of time to set it up."

He studied her face solemnly for a moment and then asked, "Have you prepared at all for this, Brigit?"

She shook her head. "No, Papa, I haven't." Quick tears sprang to her eyes. "And to make it worse, I can't even get into the schoolhouse. Peter will think I'm dreadfully disorganized because. . .because. . .because I *am*!"

Wordlessly, he leaped from the wagon and walked to the school and unlocked the door and returned to her. "You're a fortunate young lady, Brigit. The only reason I could let you in is that I mended the window sashes in there yesterday and neglected to return the key."

She dropped a kiss on his weathered cheek. "Thanks, Papa. You are a dear." She dashed to the schoolhouse and in the front door.

The room itself was quite tidy but horribly inappropriate for a tea—at least what she knew of such functions. The first order of business was to move the desks out of their orderly rows.

She pushed. She shoved. She pulled. She tugged. The desks would not move. They were nailed to the floor.

She sank to the nearest chair and put her face in her hands. This was terrible. Just terrible. What was she going to do?

A sound outside reminded her that the guests would be soon arriving, and her chaotic thoughts scattered even more. What could she do to make the room more presentable?

The teacher's desk was clear. Maybe a centerpiece would make it seem less. . .desk-like? Was there any way to salvage this?

The presiding elder and his wife wouldn't see the beauty of the prairie, she thought sadly as she looked around the room. If only she could show them—

That was it! She knew what she could use as a centerpiece. She leaped out of the chair and ran outside, nearly running into a cluster of women who were standing by the steps of the school. "Oh, I'm sorry. Last-minute details, you know. Be ready in a minute!" she caroled to them as she tore past.

She knew exactly where to go. Behind the church, there was a stretch of even land where she and her father had often picnicked. Right now that area was flush with wildflowers. She scooped up as many daisies as her hands could hold, and she raced back to the school. This would have to do.

Well, she still had at least an hour. Even as she formed the thought, she knew it wasn't good. Having a tea wasn't the same as having tea. Why hadn't she asked for help earlier?

An hour, an hour. It had to be enough time.

She came around the corner of the church and found herself facing Peter and an older couple.

"Brigit, this is Reverend Armstrong and his wife, Mrs. Armstrong," he announced proudly.

"I'm pleased to meet you," she said, not knowing if she should curtsy or bow or shake their hands. *They were early!*

Mrs. Armstrong smiled graciously at her and said, "Oh, my, those are lovely flowers. Are they for me?"

Brigit stared, horrified, at her erstwhile centerpiece, and

said the only thing she could. "Of course."

Mrs. Armstrong took the flowers and smiled. "Daisies are my favorite. I have no idea how you knew this, but thank you so much. Dear, we have a few minutes before the tea. Would you mind showing me around the town a bit? I'd like to stretch my legs after that long train ride."

There went any shred of a chance Brigit had to remedy the tea. *I'm sorry, Peter,* she said silently to him. *I'm really very sorry.*

Mrs. Armstrong was very kind as she and Brigit strolled through the small town, so much so that Brigit felt comfortable confiding as they returned to the school, "This tea isn't going to be nearly as grand as what you're used to. I do hope you won't think badly of us when you—"

Her words froze in her throat as they entered the school. The ladies of the church were all gathered there. The desks were still in their utilitarian rows, but they were all graced by spring-hued napkins. Marie Farnsworth was setting out a bowl of grated sugar. Sarah Bigelow was arranging the last teaspoon. Mary Rose Groves winked at her from behind the tea urn, and Brigit realized what she had totally forgotten—tea! Yet somehow the tea was brewed, and there were even assorted cookies on a tray.

"Why, this is lovely," Mrs. Armstrong said. "Absolutely lovely!"

Brigit introduced Mrs. Armstrong to the church women and pulled Mary Rose aside. "How did. . . ? Who did. . . ? I mean, what. . . ?"

Mary Rose smiled. "You can thank your father and the very organized ladies of the church. He just sent out the word, and they showed up, ready to help. All they were waiting for was someone to ask them."

Brigit nodded, too overcome to speak. But when the time came to introduce Mrs. Armstrong, she thanked the members of the church for all their work. What would she ever do without them?

And so she—and Peter—had been saved again.

That evening, Peter and Brigit walked through the dusty streets of Archer Falls. "This town feels like home," he said to her. "I'm very comfortable here, and I really do want to stay."

He turned to her and asked suddenly, "Have you ever wanted to live somewhere else?"

"Do you mean like Chicago or Rome or London?" She looked at the line of houses all built so close together that they almost seemed to be standing shoulder to shoulder against the prairie wind. "Maybe only for a moment. In my heart of hearts, I think I always want to live in Archer Falls. Why?"

He turned to her and took her hand. "This isn't exactly the way I'd intended to do this, Brigit. Well, the truth is that I didn't have anything planned. I couldn't decide how to—"

"How to what?" She'd never seen him at such a loss for words.

"Do you remember when we were out walking, and you were talking to me about daisies and kittens' noses, and I kissed you?"

Her breath stopped in her throat. How could she ever forget that? She nodded, and he continued.

"And Mr. Farnsworth interrupted us? And do you remember what I said to you then?"

"That if you wanted to kiss me. . ." Her voice trembled.

"I'd have to marry you."

"Yes." It was just a whisper.

"Will you, Brigit? Will you marry me? I can't offer you much, just all of my love, which, to be honest, is quite a lot."

"Peter—"

"I know what I want. I want to live here in Archer Falls with you and raise a family." He took her hands and said earnestly, "I think God brought me to this place to meet you. Until I met you, I was incomplete. You are the other half of my soul. Of my heart. Of my mind. Will you marry me and be a minister's wife?"

She swallowed. "Yes. Yes. Yes."

There was never, she thought, a more inappropriate match. And yet there was never a more perfect match.

"Yes."

Brigit's father smiled happily at her as she waltzed into the small house. "You look as if someone has crowned you queen of the summer!"

She plopped down beside him. "I think someone has. Papa, Peter asked me to marry him."

"And you said yes, I hope."

"My darling father, of course I did." She ran her hand over his work-worn fingers. "But there is something I must ask you. What will you do about the farm? Can you do it without me?"

"You worry too much." He leaned back and frowned slightly. "Has this been worrying you?"

She nodded, unexpected tears gathering in her eyes. "I love

Peter, but I want to farm here with you, too."

"The land is in your blood, isn't it?" he asked.

"It is."

"Ah." He leaned back and shut his eyes. The conversation was abruptly over, but he was smiling.

Chapter 7

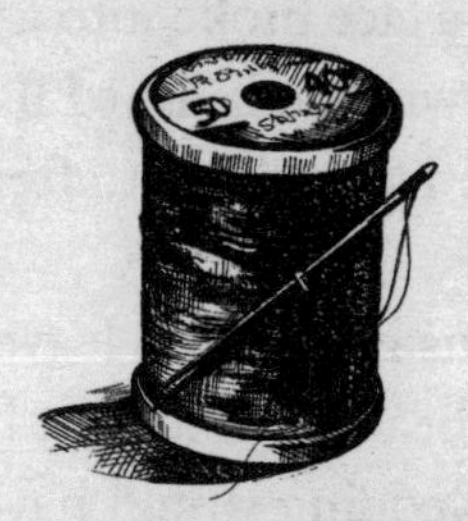

Peter awoke the next morning surprised that the sky was overcast. How could it be this dreary when his heart was so happy?

The Armstrongs met him at the church after breakfast.

"You seem especially happy this morning," the presiding elder said to him.

Peter tried to keep the grin off his face, but it kept popping back into place. "Yes, I am."

Mrs. Armstrong smiled. "Could it have anything to do with the charming woman we met yesterday?"

"Yes, it could." Peter straightened the already neat altar banner.

"If you'd like to share something with us. . . ," she began.

"She said yes!" he interrupted happily. "She said she'd marry me!"

"Lovely choice," Mrs. Armstrong said, and her husband agreed.

A thought came to him—a wild, crazy thought—but maybe, just maybe. . . "Would you do us the honor, Reverend

Armstrong, of performing the wedding? My parents, you might remember, have gone on to be with the Lord. Having you perform the ceremony would mean so much to me."

The presiding elder's face broke into a wide smile. "Why, I'd be honored." His brow wrinkled. "But I'll be out of the country for the next year. We're leaving right after we return from this visit."

"Could you marry us before you leave?"

"Well, I could. But bear in mind that I'm only in this region for two weeks, so this wedding would have to take place soon."

Peter briefly considered that. Certainly he and Brigit hadn't known each other long, and he hadn't given any thought to a quite abbreviated engagement, but an early wedding shouldn't present any problem.

"We can do that," he said.

Mrs. Armstrong tugged on her husband's sleeve. "Might I suggest something?" she asked softly.

"Of course," Peter answered.

"Could we discuss this with Brigit? She might have something to say about it. A woman does only have one wedding in her lifetime, you know." Her eyes lit with a soft love for her husband as she looked at him.

"Did I hear my name?" Brigit spoke from the doorway of the church.

Peter's heart skipped a beat at the sight of her unruly hair, which was, even at this early hour, escaping the pins that vainly tried to hold some kind of a bun arrangement in place. He crossed to the door and took her hands in his and led her to where the Armstrongs stood.

"Brigit, I've told the Armstrongs that you accepted my proposal last night," he began, "and—"

Mrs. Armstrong gave Brigit a quick hug. "I'm delighted for you," she said. Then with a meaningful glance at her husband, she added, "I think that Charles and I would like to take a walk in the fresh air before we return to the dusty world of church records. We'll leave you two alone for a bit."

"But I thought—"

"Didn't you want to—"

Both men spoke at once and were promptly hushed by Mrs. Armstrong, who looped her arm through her husband's. "Come along, now."

Brigit looked befuddled as the Armstrongs left the church, a slightly confused look on the presiding elder's face. "What was that about?"

Peter drew her close and kissed her gently. "I hope you don't mind, but I asked Reverend Armstrong to perform our wedding ceremony."

The thought that he was going to spend the rest of his life with her was almost too much to bear. She was so beautiful, so free-spirited. What a delightful experience life was going to be with her.

"That's fine with me," she said, her voice muffled against his shoulder. "I hadn't thought about it, but I suppose you can't perform your own wedding."

"So it's all right with you to have him officiate?"

"Of course. It would be an honor." She leaned her head back and ran her finger down the side of his face. "Shouldn't we set a date then? I don't know anything about weddings, but

I can ask Mary Rose. She's an expert."

Finally his brain clicked into place. Weddings. They took time. "How long has Mary Rose been engaged?" he asked, trying to sound casual, but he dreaded the answer.

"She's been working on it since Christmas, but she's marrying Gregory Lester, and there are Lesters all throughout this part of the territory. Their wedding is going to be the event of the year."

"So our engagement doesn't have to be that long, right?"

"Oh, not at all."

He took a deep breath. "So, how does two weeks sound?"

She jerked out of his arms. "Two weeks? Two weeks?"

"Too long?" His bad attempt at humor warranted golden sparks in her light green eyes.

"Two weeks?" she repeated. "Two weeks?"

Brigit rode down the row of poplars. Fulton looked over his shoulder as if to ask, *Why aren't we running?* But she needed the time to sort through her thoughts.

This was going much faster than it should. She still had to come to grips with being a pastor's wife. Could she do that and get married—in two weeks?

God, I'm turning to Thee again, she prayed silently. *Once again haste is my enemy. I've never paid attention to much in life, just rushed pell-mell forward, and somehow Thou hast always caught me when I might have fallen. What should I do?*

There was no answer except the soft sound of the wind in the poplars and the soft neigh from Fulton as he again questioned why they weren't running.

When she was a pastor's wife, would she have to forgo these cleansing rides on Fulton's back? Or making poplar leaf whistles?

"Come on, boy. Let's go!" She urged him forward, and together they raced against the day.

By the time she had Fulton stabled for the night, she had her answer. She loved Peter, and she was going to marry him whether it was in a year or a day.

Later that evening, she lay in bed wide awake. Too much was happening for sleep to come. In less than two weeks, she'd be married to Peter. She'd be Mrs. Collins, Mrs. Peter Collins! Brigit Collins. She tried the name on for size and found it fit very nicely.

She sat up in bed, startled, as a sudden thought came into her mind with the force of a prairie whirlwind. Getting married in two weeks wasn't going to be a problem. She couldn't be expected to put on a fancy wedding with that little time. She and Peter would quietly get married with no folderol.

Life was good, very good.

⁂

The Armstrongs handed their baggage to the boy loading it onto the train. "We'll be back in two weeks for the wedding then," Reverend Armstrong said.

"I've enjoyed this visit," Mrs. Armstrong confided to Brigit, "but the wedding is going to be joyous indeed."

She handed Brigit a small, tissue-wrapped package. "I hope this can make the day a bit brighter for you."

"What is it?"

"Open it, dear, and find out."

Brigit unwrapped the packet, and a neatly folded length of material spilled across her hands, as soft and delicate as a baby's breath. "It's lovely." The words didn't begin to express how much the gift touched her.

Mrs. Armstrong smiled and held the material against Brigit's face. "As I thought. The green matches your eyes."

Impulsively Brigit threw her arms around the older woman's shoulders. "Thank you so much!"

"I never had a daughter of my own," Mrs. Armstrong said, "only one boy, and he's not big on spring green dresses. It would be an honor if you would wear a dress made out of this fabric on your wedding day."

"I will, I will," Brigit promised, nearly beyond words as she held the incredible material. "I will."

Mrs. Armstrong dropped a kiss on Brigit's cheek. "I'll look forward to seeing what you do with this. I just know that any woman Peter has selected will be a true Proverbs 31 wife."

Proverbs 31 wife? What did that mean?

She watched the Armstrongs board the train and numbly waved good-bye as the train pulled away, its wheels chugging out the message: *Two weeks, two weeks.*

Peter hooked his arm around hers, and together they walked back to Fulton and the wagon. She couldn't linger today, for the harvest was in full swing and her father needed her help.

"What did Mrs. Armstrong give you?" he asked.

She showed him the swath of fabric. "She thinks it would make a lovely dress to be married in, and I agree. What do you think?"

He squeezed her hand and helped her into the wagon. "I think you'd be the most beautiful bride in the Dakota Territory if you were dressed in Fulton's feedbag."

Brigit laughed. "Now that's something the people of Archer Falls would be talking about for years!"

Mr. Streeter was hard at work in the field, and he motioned to Brigit. "Mary Rose came by to see you. She'll stop by tonight after supper. Meanwhile, can you take over here? I have to run into town to get a part for the baler."

She loved the harvest. The smell of the wheat as it fell to the blade, the warmth of the sun upon her shoulders, the glorious azure sky overhead—all of these made this time exciting.

Plus it gave her time with her thoughts. This year she had plenty to consider. She was about to marry the man she loved. What was she supposed to be doing? There had to be something besides making her wedding dress.

The thought nearly stopped her mid-step. Making her wedding dress? It was insane. She couldn't sew. She couldn't!

She was the only young woman her age who couldn't sew. Whenever something needed mending, her father actually took up needle and thread.

As far as her dresses went, her friends' mothers had always taken pity upon the poor motherless child and tried to help her with making her dresses. But despite their best efforts, Brigit had never learned. Was there ever a duller subject? While the enterprising mothers had talked of needles and seams and selvages, she'd daydreamed of racing Fulton through the fields.

Oh, why hadn't she paid attention—not just to sewing, but

to the whole realm of the household arts? She was getting married in two weeks and had only the vaguest idea of how to cook a dinner and certainly no concept of how to entertain or make a dress or even mend a ripped seam.

What a foolish choice she was for Peter. There was no way for her to learn what she didn't know in two weeks.

That evening she unfolded the delicate material and spread it out. How long she sat there, the material around her like a pool of pastel green, she had no idea. At last a sound at the door made her look up.

"Daughter, what are you doing?"

"I'm making a dress." She didn't sound at all convinced of the fact, but she bravely smiled for her father.

He came and knelt beside her. "Where's your pattern?"

"Pattern?"

"You're going to need a pattern to tell you where to cut. What is this material for, anyway? Why don't you wait for one of the women in town to make it for you?"

She buried her face in her hands. She was not a crying woman, and she wasn't about to start now, but this project had vexed her beyond her capabilities.

"Why are you doing this?" he repeated.

"It's my wedding dress. Or it's supposed to be."

Mr. Streeter smoothed her tangled hair, as if by doing so he could smooth her tangled thoughts. "I think you should wait for someone to help you."

"How can I?" She looked up at him with worried eyes. "They're all busy with the harvest. I barely have time as it is to work on it myself. Mary Rose is in Chicago this week, looking at shoes of all things. That's what she wanted to see me about today, to tell me that. So she can't help me."

"I can help."

"Papa, I need to make the dress myself. Mrs. Armstrong expects, and Peter expects, and I—"

"And you expect," he finished for her. "I understand. Might you take some advice from an old farmer? The wheat grows straighter if you line up the seeds."

Brigit gaped at him. He had clearly spent too much time in the sun.

"Plan before you cut, dearest daughter. Plan before you cut."

She studied the cloth a bit more. She could see the imagery. The fabric as the land. The scissors as the plow. The needle and thread were like planting.

Her soul began to rise, ready to take on this next challenge. She could do it.

After all, how hard could it be to make a dress?

Chapter 8

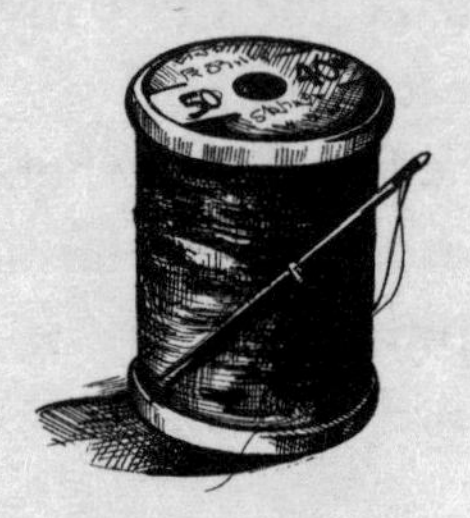

The next day, Brigit stared at the material and pondered what to do. This, like farming, would take some planning. It wouldn't be right to just cut into the cloth, willy-nilly. She had to be in the right frame of mind, ready to focus.

The fields called to her, a ready excuse. The harvest needed to come in. That couldn't wait, whereas a dress—oh, how long would it take to sew some seams together?

The next day, she wasn't prepared to cut into the material, nor the next day, nor the next.

"How are the preparations for the wedding going?" Peter asked her as they strolled down past the poplars once again.

She couldn't meet his eyes. "Fine," she lied, and then, because she couldn't bear such dishonesty, changed from an outright lie to a little fib. "There isn't much that can be done, not with such short notice. The ladies of the church are putting together a reception, and they're decorating the church with some flowers. That will be about it."

"I've asked Reverend Armstrong to read Proverbs 31 as

one of the scriptures. It reminds me of you."

Proverbs 31 reminded him of her? Was she misremembering it?

"You have such talents," he continued, "like cooking—that was a wonderful dinner you made when I first came to town. You're superb at entertaining as I saw with the tea. Plus, you're making your wedding dress, and I'm sure it'll be breathtaking."

Yes, she thought, *it easily could be.*

She needed to stop him, to tell him the truth, but she couldn't. She loved him so much that she couldn't imagine not spending her life with him.

He hugged her waist. "I'm counting the hours until we become man and wife. When you walk down the aisle toward me in your green dress."

Her mind guiltily fled to the pile of green fabric on her bed. Every day she had duly spread it out, and every day she had packed it back up.

Tonight she would begin.

"At some point, you will have to cut the cloth," her father said gently that evening.

"I'm afraid," she said, her voice barely audible. "I'm afraid I will make a mess of it, just as I made a mess of the dinner, and the tea, and everything else. And now I've waited so long that I can guarantee you it will not work out at all well, and the Armstrongs will think I'm not good for Peter, and what's worse, Peter will know that I won't be a good wife."

"What have you done about it?" he asked.

She shook her head, and half of her bun came unpinned. "I

don't know what you mean."

"Who have you talked to about it?"

"Mary Rose, of course. And, well, you."

"Ah." He leaned back in his chair. "Have you talked to God about it?"

"God isn't going to sew my dress, Papa!"

"No, but He has certainly helped you out before, hasn't He? It seems to me that the dinner went fine. The tea was a success. Why don't you trust Him now? Ask for His help. At least do that."

She picked up the well-worn Bible. "For a woman who's marrying a minister, I certainly have been wrapped up in my own worldly issues, haven't I?"

"Brigit." He stopped.

"Papa?"

"I never told you what your mother said to you with her last breath, did I?" His words were thick and his eyes moist.

She could only shake her head no.

"She kissed you and. . ." His voice broke. "She told you why she chose Brigit as your name. It means strong. She wanted you to be strong. Brigit, she would have been so proud of you. You're strong and capable, and I know that you've made your mother very proud in heaven."

She stood up, and as she dropped a kiss on the top of his head, a few tears mingled in. "Thanks, Papa."

⁂

By the next afternoon, it was quite clear to Brigit that God was not going to step in and save her. She had already taken apart her favorite dress to use as a pattern. The first lesson she'd learned about sewing was that she had to lay the pieces out carefully or she'd run out of room.

One arm of the dress was going to be spliced from two end pieces, thanks to her carelessness in not laying the pieces out neatly.

The second lesson was that she should cut slowly. The collar looked like it might end up lopsided, because there were some scraps of the pattern dress laying on the floor, and she knew that wasn't right.

The third was that fabric was very slippery and should be pinned or held down while being cut. Pieces that were supposed to be the same certainly didn't look the same.

The fourth lesson had to do with seam allowances, and the fifth and final one was that it was always a good idea to know what piece went where. She had long thin bits that could be sleeves, or they could be—well, she didn't know. But she couldn't be sure they weren't sleeves.

The needles pricked her fingers mercilessly, and she was forever swabbing blood droplets from the pale fabric.

People do this for a living, she thought with amazement. She'd rather muck out pigpens than do this.

Someone knocked at the door, and she smiled. This was the help that God was going to send her, at last. Mary Rose wasn't due back until the evening train, but perhaps she had gotten home early.

"Come in," she sang out.

"Brigit, Rever—" Peter's voice stopped midword as he surveyed the scene in front of him. Behind him, the Armstrongs stepped into the room, and she could see the shock in their eyes. The room was chaotic, and she was not better.

She leaped up from the floor where the pieces of the dresses were strewn about, and as she did so, the pins holding the bun on the back of her head sprayed out, and her hair, tangled and curling wildly like a madwoman's, showered around her shoulders.

"It's good to. . . Please excuse the. . . I'm a bit. . ." She couldn't pull the words together.

"It looks like we've caught you at a bad time," Mrs. Armstrong said. "Is there, uh, anything I can do?" She looked at the disarray doubtfully.

Brigit summoned a smile. "Oh no. Just last-minute things. I'll be fine. See you tomorrow!"

She didn't dare look at Peter for fear of what she might see in his eyes.

She probably pushed them out the door rudely, she thought, but other things were more important, like making the pieces turn into a dress.

Proverbs 31 ran through her mind endlessly. Everything God expected of a wife was right there. She got the Bible from the table and read through it again with a sinking heart. Peter was wrong: this was everything she was *not*.

Brigit looked at the destruction around her. "She maketh fine linen," but Brigit cut it up. "She maketh herself coverings of tapestry," but Brigit couldn't get the needle threaded. "Strength and honor are her clothing," but Brigit had been living a lie to Peter.

She shouldn't marry him. He needed a wife who wouldn't be an embarrassment to him.

She heard his voice outside. Her father had come home, and Peter and the Armstrongs were still there.

Brigit gathered up the bits of the soft green cotton and called to him from the door. "Peter, please come here. I–I have something I must say."

The sunlight glinted across his hair as he turned to her, and from the way his smile flashed at her, she knew that whatever else might be wrong in her life, he was the one thing that was right. She loved him. He loved her. They needed to be together.

Nothing else mattered.

"Brigit, did you want to say something?" Peter asked as he came back to the house from the wagon.

She smiled at him. "I love you. Just that, I love you."

Reverend Armstrong called from the wagon, "We'd better go, Peter. The poor girl has enough to do without our interference. Remember, she's getting married tomorrow!"

Brigit stood in front of the altar of the small church, and it all seemed like a reverie. Reverend Armstrong read the marriage ceremony, and from somewhere in a dream, she heard herself saying, "I do," and saw Peter's warm gaze.

And then it was over.

The congregation surrounded them with good wishes and congratulations. Even Milo Farnsworth, although he seemed puzzled by the whole matter, shook Peter's hand heartily and nodded awkwardly at Brigit, clearly not sure what to say and finally settling for a vague, "Yes, yes, excellent."

Mary Rose, though, knew exactly what to do. She hugged her good friend. "Mrs. Collins! Who knew you'd be able to marry for love!"

"The dress is lovely on you," Mrs. Armstrong said, when the crowd had thinned.

"Don't look too closely at it. If I take a deep breath, the seams are likely to spring apart," Brigit said confidingly.

"We do what we need to do," the presiding elder's wife said wisely, "and we learn. My dear, I have one more gift for you—a sewing basket. Life is going to give your heart more rips and rends than a simple silver needle pulling thread can fix, but it's a start. God bless you, dear."

Brigit hugged Mrs. Armstrong, wondering if the woman had any idea how inapt the gift was. Already the seams of the green dress were loosening, but it didn't matter.

The dress, Brigit realized as her handsome new husband joined them, was just outerwear. It was the love that she and Peter shared that was important.

Her father's eyes were suspiciously red as he approached them. "Peter, she's my girl. She's always been my girl, and she always will be. I have just one request of her."

"Yes, sir?"

"She's part of this land, you know. She was born in Dakota and raised here, too. Farming's in her blood."

Peter smiled as Mr. Streeter continued. "So I think we should tell her what the surprise is."

Brigit's new husband turned to her. "I've been living in a rented house. It's small and cramped and no place to raise twigs."

"Twigs?" she asked blankly.

"Twigs, on our family tree," he explained. "Children."

The thought of their children warmed her heart.

"Your father is building us a house on the farm," he went on. "We can live there and farm together, all of us, your father, you, me, our children—"

"Our twigs," she added laughingly.

Chapter 9

Peter, can you come here, please?"

He put down his book and joined Brigit by the back door where she was washing clothes. Life with her was sweeter than he'd ever imagined. "Yes, my dear?"

Brigit dipped her hands into the washtub again and again, pulling out piece after piece of sodden green cotton. "Look at this, Peter. Do you know what this is?"

He shook his head. "Stockings? Gloves? Towels?"

"No," she said sadly, retrieving yet another bit of cloth from the water. "This is my wedding dress. It came apart when I washed it."

He bit his lip, trying to stop the inevitable quivering.

Brigit went on. "I'm a terrible cook, and I can't organize a tea, and I have never sewn a dress before in my life, and when I did sew it, look what happened."

He bit harder on his lip.

"I'm not a Proverbs 31 wife," she continued, "not at all, but I love you, and I want to be with you always."

Peter gave in to his laughter. "Darling Brigit, I don't care about cooking or teas or sewing. All I care about is that you love me."

She studied the damp pieces of what had been her wedding dress. "Peter, do you know what I'm going to do with these? I'm going to use these to teach myself to sew. I'm going to put that sewing box Mrs. Armstrong gave me to good use, and I'm going to make a quilt. I will teach myself to be a Proverbs 31 woman."

He held her closely. "Don't you remember what else is there? 'A woman that feareth the LORD, she shall be praised.' You, Brigit, my dear, are already truly a Proverbs 31 wife."

He kissed her roundly and soundly while the green scraps dripped, unheeded, onto the floor.

Epilogue

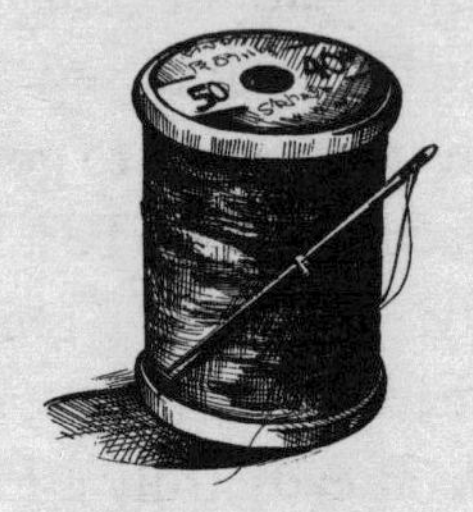

My dearest son,

This quilt is the story of your family and the love that binds us together as truly as the threads that hold together these pieces of cloth.

I began this quilt as a new bride. I didn't know any more about sewing than I did about being a wife, but I knew about love. The pieces of my wedding dress are in here and form the center block. They are the delicate spring green swatches. It's the same green, by the way, you'll see when the first wildflowers poke their brave stems through the winter-worn earth.

There are a few patches of white in this quilt. They are cut from the shirt your father wore when we got married. Ah, John, what a fine figure he presented that day! I can still see him in my mind, so elegant, so handsome, so sure. . .and so very much in possession of my heart.

The little patches were once your blanket. This was the first earthly fabric that touched your newborn skin. Yellow-spotted flannel looked so warm against your infant skin, like God had poured sun around your tiny body. It was cold the night you were born—so cold the doctor's breath froze midair—but you quickly warmed our hearts.

As our family grew, so did our love—and the quilt. Notice how the stitches get more even and practiced on the outer patches. I was just learning in the center section, but the patches, straggly though they may be, are still holding together after many years of hard use.

Love is like that, John. At first, it's all very new and awkward, but if you're willing to put your heart into it, it'll hold steadfast. There aren't any silk or satin or velvet pieces in this quilt, but to me, its beauty far exceeds the grandest coverlet. Even the littlest, most mundane pieces of life make an extraordinary tapestry when united by love. . .these scraps of love.

Your loving mother,
Brigit Streeter Collins

JANET SPAETH

Janet Spaeth grew up on the prairie and enjoys writing about it. She's the mother of the two best children in the world (and she has pictures to prove it). Besides writing, her favorite pastimes are reading, baking, and—above all—spending time with her family. She finds writing inspirational romance to be fulfilling because of her deep belief in God—and in love.

Mother's Old Quilt

by Lena Nelson Dooley

Dedication

To my two best friends, Rita Booth and Aleene Harward.
They have prayed for every book I've written,
every proposal I've sent in, and every meeting
at which I was the speaker.
I love you both from the bottom of my heart.
You have added a special dimension to my life.
I'm glad God tied our heartstrings together.
The book is also my small tribute to John Collins,
a wonderful youth minister and strong man of God
who is now at home with the Lord.
As with every book, it is also dedicated to my husband,
James, who has helped our family create
a colorful tapestry of love.

Chapter 1

Wayzata, Minnesota—Early March 1905

"If one more thing happens, I think I'll scream."

Maggie Swenson trudged through snowdrifts on the way from her house to the barn. The tops of her boots didn't come above the snow, so the cold stuff spilled over, wetting her thick, wool socks. Before she had to come out here again, she needed to borrow some of Valter's trousers. She knew it wouldn't be ladylike to wear her brother's long pants, but it would be better than dragging a woolen skirt that grew heavier and heavier because of the damp snow clinging to it.

It had been so long since she had any time to herself. Only six months ago, both her parents died when the buggy they were riding in smashed against an outcropping of rocks because something startled their horse, making it run away. Maggie and her brother, who at twenty-one was two years older than she, inherited the farm their parents had worked hard to sustain through summer droughts and harsh Minnesota winters. Now Maggie tried to run the farm all by herself. Valter lay in the house with a high fever, growing weaker every day no matter what she did for him. She feared he had the dreaded influenza that was taking such a toll this year.

Just as she reached up to unlatch the door to the barn, Maggie heard a soft moan followed by a pain-filled whine. She glanced around, and the sun glinting off the white world around her stabbed her eyes. As she squinted, her gaze traveled over the landscape around the barn. The few bushes were laden with snow, as were the trees in the pasture and beyond. When she heard the sound again, she determined that it came from the side of the building. Maggie plunged into the drift that had blown against the wall of the secure structure. Now her long underwear was wet up to her knees. If she didn't go inside soon, she might get as sick as Valter.

With her curiosity stronger than the desire to get out of the biting wind, Maggie rounded the corner of the barn in search of the origin of the sound. She almost stumbled over a warm lump in the snow. Horror filled her mind when she realized what it was.

"Rolf!"

She fell to her knees and lifted the head of her beloved dog. His thick, light brown coat was clumped with dampness, and a red stain spread across one shoulder and down his leg. Already his eyes were glassy, and he didn't seem to recognize her.

"Rolf." Ignoring the damp snow, she sat back and pulled his large head into her lap. "What happened?" Maggie whispered against the wet fur and wished her pet could answer. While she held him, crooning encouragement into his ear, his head went limp in her hands and his labored breathing ceased.

An icicle fell from the edge of the roof, shattering on the crust of the snow behind her. Silence surrounded her, broken only by the irregular click of icy tree limbs tapping a staccato rhythm in the cold wind.

Maggie looked beyond the lifeless body and noticed a bloody trail in the snow, leading toward the woods that ran from the back of the barn all the way to the creek a couple of miles away. She knew Rolf liked to romp in those woods, and she had allowed him that freedom. After all, it was on their property, so the animal should have been perfectly safe.

What had Maggie been thinking a few minutes ago? *If one more thing happened. . .* Well, it had, and she didn't have the strength to scream, so she dropped her face into both upraised hands and sobbed—deep, wrenching sobs that shook both her body and her soul.

When John Collins emerged from between the trees, he saw a girl or woman hunched over. Although she appeared to be a woman, she was tiny. She looked as though she was crying as she sat in the snow beside a barn, an animal stretched out beside her, half in her lap. John's heart almost stopped beating. He knew he was the reason she cried. Why hadn't he been more careful? He had been so sure that the patch of light brown fur he glimpsed between the trees was a deer or an elk that he had taken aim and pulled the trigger. If only he had waited until he was close enough to be completely certain.

John took pride in the fact that he shot so accurately from a distance. Pride made him risk the shot, knowing he wouldn't hit anything except the patch of brown fur he sighted down the barrel of his rifle. He shifted slightly to allow for the wind and squeezed the trigger. Immediately after the loud boom of the gun stopped echoing in the trees, the animal dropped behind the underbrush.

It had taken John awhile to climb the fence and find a place to cross the creek without getting wet. Then he worked his way to the spot where he was sure he would find the deer or elk to dress. The meat would be a welcome addition to the larder at the boardinghouse where he lived, and he planned to give some of it to the preacher's family. Before he reached the spot, John pulled his hunting knife from its sheath so he could make quick work of field dressing the animal.

Instead of the game he expected, he found an impression in the snow where an animal had fallen, but it couldn't have been a deer. The path through the snow told its own story. Paw prints surrounding the bloody trail where an animal had dragged its body were evidence that John had shot something besides wild game. Probably someone's guard dog or pet—or both. His heart sank. Heaviness fell over him like dusk on a winter evening in North Dakota. He followed the trail to find the heartbreaking sight before him.

Reluctantly, John trudged across the open space between himself and the woman. When he was about three feet from her, he stopped. He knew she wasn't even aware of his presence. Tears ran down his own cheeks as he studied her. Although she was bundled up against the cold, she appeared to be almost as old as he was. Blond curls peeked from the edge of the multicolored knitted cap she wore pulled down around her ears, and tears made streaks on cheeks rosy from the winter wind. John wished he could relive the last half hour. He constantly battled his pride. This time, pride won, and this woman paid the price.

John cleared his throat. "Ma'am, I'm sorry."

He stepped forward, and after sliding the animal to the ground, he pulled her up into his arms. John hadn't held anyone this way except his mother and sisters, but he wanted to comfort this woman. She cried so hard that she didn't seem to be aware of much, but she let him pull her into his embrace. She continued to sob as if her heart had shattered.

He looked down at the lifeless animal, and silently he called himself all kinds of uncomplimentary names. At that moment, he never wanted to shoot his gun again. All the warnings his father had given him while teaching him to hunt ran through his mind in a cycle, the chants magnifying just how far he was from heeding them. John felt helpless. Was there any way he could ever undo the damage?

When Maggie became aware of the warmth surrounding her, she pulled back and looked up into the face of. . .a stranger. The tall man wore a heavy coat with a scarf to ward off the cold, but she noticed dark curls peeking from under the brim of his hat. The clear green eyes that gazed back at her held sympathy and great sorrow, and traces of tears stained his cheeks.

Maggie looked at her gloved hands grasping the front of his coat. Quickly, she let go, and his arms dropped to his side. She stepped back, never taking her gaze off her gloves. They were stained with Rolf's blood. She stared at them before looking down at the lifeless body at their feet.

"I'm really sorry."

Maggie glanced up at the man and realized he had apologized two times to her. What did he have to apologize for? Who was he?

She must have voiced the last question, because he answered it. "I'm John Collins, the new stationmaster in Wayzata."

Maggie continued to stare at him. What was the stationmaster doing beside their barn?

"I was hunting, and. . .I must have shot your dog by mistake." His gaze dropped to where Rolf lay on the cold ground. "I followed his trail through the woods."

Maggie didn't have to look where he gestured to know that he had come from her woods. Why would anyone kill her dog, even by mistake? Rolf was her companion during the long, hard nights. He stayed near her feet while she sat in the rocking chair beside Valter's bed. Just last night, Maggie had tried her best to stay awake, but she had been so tired her head dropped against the high back of the chair. Exhaustion brought a deep sleep. She wasn't even aware when Vally began struggling to breathe. But Rolf knew. He managed to wake her up. Because of their dog, she had been able to keep Vally from dying.

While these thoughts ran through Maggie's head, she became aware of the cold. Realizing she had become chilled to the bone, she stamped her feet, trying to get her blood to circulate in her nearly frostbitten extremities.

"Can we at least go into the barn to get out of this wind?" Mr. Collins's words brought her attention back to him.

She nodded and led the way. Being a well-built barn, it had no cracks where the wind could swirl through. With two workhorses, two riding horses, and three cows inside, the temperature felt almost warm.

After the man latched the door, Maggie turned her fury on him. "What were you doing hunting on our property anyway?"

He took a step back and pulled his hands in front of his chest as if to ward off her attack. "I didn't realize it was anyone's property."

"You won't find many places this close to town that aren't owned by someone." She placed her fisted hands on her hips the way her mother had when she was upset. "We don't mind if people hunt here if they ask permission. . .and as long as they don't kill our animals."

The man stuffed his hands in the pockets of his heavy coat. "I know I made a mistake. What can I do to make it right?"

"You can never make it right!" Maggie knew she shouted at the man, but she didn't care. She was very near losing all control. "Just get off my property and don't ever come back!" She pointed toward the closed door.

The man shifted his weight from one foot to the other. "I want to do something to help you. You're not all alone out here, are you?"

Maggie wondered if the man was some kind of monster who preyed on lonely women. "No! My brother's in the house." She put her shaking hands under her arms. "Now please, leave." She started toward the door.

The man didn't move from his place, blocking her exit. "I'll take care of the dog for you."

Rolf! Maggie hadn't even considered what she would do with his body. The ground was too frozen for her to bury him by herself. Maybe she should let Mr. Collins do it. At least he could do that much.

Maggie slowly nodded. "Okay. Then leave our farm and don't ever come back." She stepped around John Collins and reached for the latch.

"I'll go to town and get a wagon." His baritone voice held sympathy she didn't want to accept. "I won't be long."

Without turning her head, Maggie nodded again, then exited the barn.

John's heart broke for the woman he left at the farm. He hadn't even asked her name. When he stepped into the brightness of the wintry sun reflecting off the snow, he squinted to watch her walk toward the house. Her shoulders sagged and shook. She probably sobbed as she went. He wouldn't be surprised if her brother came looking for him after he heard about the fiasco. John hoped he wasn't a violent man.

Because his father was a preacher, John had been taught to be honorable, but he felt anything but honorable right now. He would rent a wagon from the livery and drive back to pick up the dead dog. Perhaps his new pastor would tell him what to do with it. He couldn't just drag it off into the woods where some wild animal would devour it. The dog meant too much to this woman. However, John knew that just disposing of the animal wasn't enough. He had to do something more. Maybe he should go out and talk to her brother. Help him with the chores or something like that. Of course, he could pray and ask God to show him what needed to be done to make up for what he destroyed. John's heart sank within him as he made his way toward his new home.

After Maggie shut the door, she slumped against it. The heaviness of disease hung in the house, filling it with a palpable feeling of misery. Even this room, which had been warm and cheery before her parents died, looked and felt dreary. After a moment, she took off her coat, hat, and gloves and went into Valter's bedroom. She sank into the rocking chair beside his bed. He slept soundly. She pulled her arms tight across her abdomen and gently rocked the chair. What was she going to do if her brother didn't get well soon?

"Please, Valter," Maggie whispered as she leaned close to his ear. "Your name means 'strong fighter.' Live up to that name. Fight this illness."

As the sound of her last word died, his eyes fluttered. Soon they opened, and he looked at her. When he spoke, the words crackled through his dry lips. "Margareta, our pearl, you've been so good to take care of me."

His words scared Maggie. They carried the sound of finality with them. She pushed his hair back from his face. His hot skin felt like delicate parchment, making her afraid she would hurt him just by touching him.

"Vally, dear brother, you're going to be okay." With her words of assurance, his eyes once again closed, and he fell into restless slumber.

Maggie stood and paced around the room. *Oh, God, please don't let Vally die. I need him so much. Our parents are gone, and Thou didst not prevent their accident. Now Rolf is gone. I can't take much more.*

She opened the door to the kitchen and slipped into the other room. The fire in the fireplace burned low, so she went out on the back porch and brought in another armload of wood. The woodpile had really dwindled in the last few weeks. When Vally cut all the wood and loaded it onto the sheltered porch, he told her it should last all winter, but now Maggie feared it wouldn't. She would have a hard time cutting more wood.

After the fireplace once again warmed the room, she went back to get more fuel for the kitchen stove. Mother had been so proud of the new cookstove. Father bought it only a few months before their deaths. Every time Maggie looked at it, she remembered how happy Mother was when he brought it home. When he finished setting it up, Mother grabbed him from behind. He turned around and danced her across the kitchen, and their shared laughter filled the house. At the time, Maggie thought they were crazy. Now she would give anything to have them back, even if they did dance around like children. It had been a long time since she felt happy about anything, and she wasn't sure she ever would again.

Chapter 2

John had left his mare tied in a grove of small trees with plenty of underbrush to protect her from the biting wind. He hurried back there. Quickly he mounted and rode into town. When he reached the livery stable, he found a note tacked to the door. It said that Henry had gone to Rose's Café to have coffee with the preacher. John led his horse into the stable and rubbed her down before going down the street to find the livery owner.

When John stepped out of the stable, the wind had died down, but the air still felt nippy. He blew out a deep breath and watched the cloud it formed dissipate around him. He had lived through many cold winters. In North Dakota where he grew up, the weather was even colder than in central Minnesota. Halfway to the café, John wished he hadn't forgotten the gloves he shoved into his saddlebags before he rubbed down his horse. He stuffed his hands into the pockets of his suede coat. At least it had a warm wooly lining.

More than a block away from the café, the tantalizing aromas of biscuits and bacon met him. His stomach growled. He hadn't taken time for more than a cup of coffee at dawn. Maybe he could eat a quick bite while he talked to Henry and Pastor Martin Hardin.

The preacher was a young man, barely older than John, and they became friends soon after John moved to town. Since John grew up in a parsonage, it helped him understand what a man of the cloth had to contend with.

When John stepped through the door of the eating establishment, warm, moist air made him shed his heavy coat. He hung it on the coat tree by the door, noticing that all the windows were completely steamed up, adding a cozy but cutoff feeling to the room. He leaned across the counter so the cook could hear him.

"Rose, can you scramble me two eggs? And if there are any of your wonderful biscuits left, I'd love to have a couple."

The two men he was looking for sat alone at a table at the far end of the room. They looked up when they heard John. Martin waved him back.

John dropped into a vacant chair at the table. "I wanted to talk to the two of you anyway."

Both men leaned toward him expectantly. "What's on your mind?" the livery owner asked.

John tried not to show how emotional he felt. "A couple of things." He cleared his throat. "I went hunting this morning."

"Did you kill anything?" Henry raised his bushy eyebrows at the end of his question. John noticed he often did that.

"Well, yes. . .and no."

A thoughtful expression covered Martin's face, much like John's father often looked. It must be because they were both preachers. "What exactly do you mean?"

John countered with a question of his own. "Whose farm is directly northwest from the edge of town, about half a mile or so?"

"You mean the Swenson place." Henry shook his hoary head. "It's sad, really."

John's interest piqued. He leaned his arms on the tabletop. "What's sad?"

Henry looked at Martin as if expecting him to answer.

"The farm is owned by Valter Swenson and his sister. Her name is Margareta, but we all call her Maggie."

John couldn't see anything sad about that.

"Last summer their parents died in an accident. It's been hard on Maggie and Vally. Now Vally is very sick, and Maggie is trying to run the farm by herself, as well as take care of her brother."

Can things get any worse? He had added to the pain the woman was already dealing with. A huge lump settled in his chest, right beside his heart, making it hard to breathe.

"Well, I killed her dog this morning." The shocked expressions on the faces of his companions added to John's distress. "It was an accident, but. . ."

"Here's your breakfast, John." The grandmotherly woman who owned the café set a steaming plate in front of him, then retreated to wait on another customer.

John looked at the food, and his stomach congealed. He knew he wouldn't be able to eat more than a few bites, if that. He didn't want to offend Rose. She had been good to him since he came to town, so he forced some eggs and a bite of biscuit past the boulder inside him.

Pastor Hardin studied John. "What kind of accident would kill her dog?"

John took another bite before he answered. The food seemed to grow larger in his mouth, so he picked up his glass of water to wash it down. "I thought I was shooting some game."

Henry gave a snort. "That dog is big enough to be a deer or elk, but he didn't look anything like either of them."

John rested his fork on the edge of the plate. "I know it was a stupid mistake, and it's one I'll regret for a long time."

Martin nodded. "I'm sure you will."

"I told Miss Swenson that I would take care of her dog's body." He turned toward the owner of the livery. "It's a pretty big animal, so I want to rent a wagon to pick it up."

The grizzled man shook his head. "Won't need to rent it. Just take what you want. Bring the body back here. I'll start a fire near the stand of trees a ways behind the stable to soften up the ground a little. When you get back, I'll help you dig the grave."

When John stood, so did the pastor. "Would you like me to go with you?"

John nodded, and the two men headed toward the livery stable.

The horses plodded down the rutted road toward the farm. Cottony clouds scudded across the blue gray sky. A rabbit hopped across the snow-covered meadow beside the road, leaving a thin trail behind it.

John had been silent for a while before he turned to the pastor. "Is anyone helping the Swensons?"

Reverend Hardin, who had been staring at the road ahead, looked at John. "We try, but they're proud people. They think they can do everything by themselves, so we let them. I've been keeping an eye out for any way their neighbors can help, but they've done a good job. . .until the boy got sick."

"Just how old are they, anyway?"

Martin gave a wry laugh. "I guess I shouldn't call them boy and girl. Vally must be at least twenty or twenty-one, and Maggie isn't far behind. They're adults doing an adult job. But she's had her hands full since Vally got sick. At least it's winter, and there isn't so much outside work to do. Doc told me that all their stock is in the barn. Maggie just has to go that far to take care of them. It'll be a different story when spring and summer get here. I hope Vally gets well soon, but Doc doesn't hold out much hope at this time. He tries to go out there every day or two."

Maggie heard the wagon rumbling down the road. She walked to the window and peeked through the curtains while the two men took Rolf away. Maggie almost opened the door and asked where they were taking him, but she wasn't ready to face anyone yet. She had cried so much that her face looked all blotchy, and her eyes were swollen.

After the two men left, Maggie went back into the bedroom to sit beside her brother. Earlier she had spooned broth between his pale lips. She wasn't sure how much he swallowed. It took her awhile to clean him and his bed up from all that spilled. Her strong playmate and protector was now helpless. She spent most of the night with her head leaning against his bed, napping when she could. Two times she had to prop him up so he could just get a breath.

Maggie didn't want to put a name to the icy fear that gripped her heart. She was so tired she could hardly hold her eyes open. She knew she should go out and check on the stock again. First she sat in her mother's rocking chair by the fireplace to rest just a few minutes. Her head nodded, and she sank into the oblivion of slumber.

Thwunk! Maggie jumped awake. How long had she slept, and what was that noise? The clatter of falling wood followed another large thump. She hurried toward the back door. The disturbance came from that direction. Not taking time to put on a wrap, she pulled the door open and peered out. A tall man placed a large piece of wood on the chopping block. Although he looked wiry, he must have been all sinews. When he raised the ax and brought it down on the thick slice of a tree, he made it look easy. With precision and using only one stroke, he placed the blow to split the log into the right size pieces for the fireplace. But why was he cutting wood in her backyard? Didn't the man understand anything about private property? This was the second time today that he had trespassed on her land.

Realizing she felt chilled, Maggie shut the door and went to get her coat from its hook. She quickly threw it on and pulled a warm knitted cap down over her hair and ears. After turning up the collar of her coat, she jerked on gloves before opening the door again.

"Mr. . . .Collins, isn't it?" Maggie tried to rein in her anger.

The man leaned against the handle of the ax. "At your service, Miss Swenson." He removed a handkerchief from his hip pocket and swiped it across his forehead. He must have been working awhile to sweat in this weather. His cavalier behavior reignited her anger.

"What do you think you're doing?" Maggie didn't care that she shouted.

"I thought that was obvious." His smile dampened Maggie's wrath. "I'm chopping wood."

She stomped through the snow toward him. "Why are you doing it *here*. . .in my backyard?" Maggie felt as if her world had tilted and nothing made sense.

"To fill your wood box. It's nearly empty." He reached to place another piece of log on the chopping block. When he lifted the ax, Maggie finally realized that although he wore a heavy woolen shirt, he didn't have a coat on.

"Mr. Collins, I don't need your help." Maggie stomped her foot for emphasis, and pain shot through her foot. Why did she do that? It didn't accomplish anything.

"That's all right, Miss Swenson." He started toward the back porch, his arms loaded with wood. "I need to do this for you."

Maggie didn't know what to reply, so she turned and hurried back inside. Maybe the man would work off his penance with this one good deed and leave her alone after that. This stranger wasn't the answer to her loneliness.

It didn't take long for Maggie to find out that chopping wood wasn't the only thing he planned to do for her. John Collins often came to the farm. No matter how many times she told him she didn't need his help, he kept coming back.

One day when her best friend, Holly Brunson, sat with Valter so Maggie could go to town for supplies, she found John working in the barn when she got home. He must have heard her drive up in the wagon, because he came out and helped carry things into the house. Then he took the wagon to the barn and unhitched her horses. She could talk until she was blue in the face, telling him she didn't need his help, but Mr. Collins didn't listen to a word she said. The man was almost a nuisance. Almost. . .but not quite.

At least his assistance allowed Maggie to spend more time with her brother. Not that it did much good. Each day, she thought he couldn't get any weaker, and every day, he did. The doctor often came out from town to check on Valter. Maggie did everything Dr. Morgan said to do, but she began to think Vally wasn't going to make it. Everything inside her screamed against the idea whenever it dropped into her mind.

One morning in early April, John Collins came out of the barn just as Maggie prepared to check on the stock. She felt bad for always telling him not to come. The pain of losing Rolf was receding, and she had finally forgiven him for shooting the dog. Maggie couldn't remember if she had ever thanked him for all his help. She stepped out on the porch.

"Mr. Collins!"

He untied his horse from the hitching post, then looked up at her. "Yes, Miss Swenson?"

Maggie tried to smile, but her lips stayed flat beneath the weight of her fatigue. "I don't think I've thanked you for all you've done."

His eyes narrowed, and he studied her as though trying to figure her out. "That's all right. No thanks are needed."

"Yes, they are. I do appreciate all you've done for me. . .for us."

He tipped his hat and turned back toward his horse. Just as Maggie shut the door, she became aware of a different sound coming from her brother's room. She rushed toward the door. Vally was breathing in a strange rattling way she hadn't heard before. His body made a slight jerky movement with each breath.

Maggie raced out the front door. John Collins was just turning his horse toward town.

"Mr. Collins! Please get the doctor out here right away!"

John rode as fast as he could. It didn't take the doctor long to hitch up his buggy. John followed him as he drove as fast as the buggy would go down the road toward the farm. He wasn't sure Miss Swenson would want him to be there, but he had to know what was happening. He would stay out of the way and pray while the doctor took care of his patient.

No one answered the doctor's rap on the front door, so he opened it and went in. John was right behind him. The cabin's large main room stood empty, so Dr. Morgan headed toward one of the other doors. John followed him, but the doctor stopped in the doorway.

When John saw Maggie, his heart ached. She sat beside the bed, mechanically rocking the chair and staring at some unseen spot across the room. A sheet covered the face of the man in the bed. A man John had never met.

The doctor went to Valter and pulled the sheet back. He listened to the patient's chest with the stethoscope and felt for his pulse. Then he replaced the covering.

John felt helpless. He wanted to do something for the vulnerable young woman who looked to be in shock. Maybe he should have become a minister the way his parents wanted him to. Then he would've learned how to help those in need. Especially Margareta Swenson.

Doc turned toward John. "Please go to town and ask Holly Brunson to come out here. She's Maggie's best friend."

John nodded before he strode through the silent house. Shouldn't Maggie be crying? Maybe she'd already cried before he and Doc arrived. John hoped so.

It didn't take him long to find out that Holly Brunson lived about a mile out of town in the opposite direction. When he inquired at the café, Rose told him that Holly had only been married a few months. He hoped she would be able to come to the Swenson farm with him.

When he knocked on the door to the farmhouse, a young woman about the same age as Maggie answered the door. Her dark blue eyes contained a question as she stared up at him. "My husband has gone over to a neighbor's because his cow is having a hard time birthing a calf. He'll be back later."

John removed his hat and held it with both hands in front of him. "I didn't come to see your husband. Are you Mrs. Brunson?"

She moved a little farther behind the door. "Yes, I am. What can I do for you?"

This wasn't going to be easy. "I'm here to ask if you can come with me." When her eyes widened and a frown veiled her face, John cleared his throat and tried again. "I've just been at the Swenson farm. Margareta's brother passed away, and Dr. Morgan thinks she needs you."

Quickly, Holly wrote a note telling her husband where she

was going. She packed a valise while John saddled her horse. Then she rode beside him. They didn't talk. There didn't seem to be anything to say.

When they entered the house, John followed Holly as she went straight to the room where her friend sat.

"I'm here."

Maggie jumped up from her chair and threw her arms around Holly. Then she burst into tears.

John knew they didn't need him, so he went to the wood-pile and picked up an armload to feed the fire. It was the only way he could help Maggie right now.

Chapter 3

Maggie couldn't have made it through the last three weeks if it hadn't been for Holly. Even though they hadn't been married very long, Hans Brunson insisted that Holly stay with Maggie. He ate his meals with them, so Maggie didn't feel so bad about taking her best friend away from him.

As soon as the neighbors heard about Valter, they let Maggie know that she wouldn't be alone. Besides providing a big meal the day of the funeral, they made sure food arrived on time for dinner and supper every day for the next two weeks. Maggie told everyone they didn't need to do that, but she was thankful they did. Managing the farm and nursing Valter had drained her more than she realized.

Holly pampered her during those weeks, taking care of the house so Maggie could rest. She was surprised by how much Maggie slept. While Maggie was asleep, Holly searched through the trunk and found the dresses her friend had worn after her parents died. She even hemmed a black dress that had been Maggie's mother's so she would have something new to wear during her mourning.

Now, though, Maggie was ready to do more. After thanking Holly and telling her to go home to her husband, she found herself alone for the first time since her brother died. She tried to turn her thoughts away from all her sorrow. If she ignored it, maybe it would go away. Many of her friends from the church had told her to pray, but Maggie wasn't sure she could trust God anymore. Hadn't He taken away everything dear to her? If He hadn't caused it, at least He had allowed it to happen.

When she went out to the barn, Maggie couldn't believe what she found. Neighbors had come every day to care for the livestock. She assumed they had only fed the animals. But when she entered the stable, it was clean. The stalls had been mucked out and new hay placed down. Maggie had dreaded all the back-breaking work it would entail to get the barn in good shape.

She walked to the stall where her mare, Stormy, stood munching grain. The horse looked up and shuffled over to Maggie, playfully nudging her shoulder. Maggie threw her arms around the mare's neck and crooned words of love into her ear.

"You're all I have now, since Vally and Rolf are gone." Maggie had told all her secrets to her dog. Now she would have to talk to her horse instead.

Every few days since Vally had been buried, Maggie had made the trip into town to visit her brother's grave at the cemetery by the church. She wiped off the plain wooden cross that marked his place. Maggie often talked to him while she was there.

That day, she dropped to her knees on the cold ground. "You'll never believe what happened today. I went into the barn, and someone had cleaned it up for me." She rubbed her finger over the carved letters that spelled Valter Swenson. "Vally, why didn't you fight the disease harder?" A sob escaped her throat. "I miss you so much."

When she stood, tears streamed down her face. She wiped them away, but others pooled in her eyes, making it hard for her to see as she turned toward her horse tied outside the cast-iron gate. She almost bumped into someone standing close behind her. Strong hands took her arms to steady her, and she looked up into light green eyes filled with sorrow.

"Mr. Collins?" Maggie pulled away. "What are you doing here?" She straightened her shoulders and stood taller.

"I wanted to make sure you were all right." The sound of his rich baritone voice reached deep inside her, releasing a whisper of something she couldn't define.

"I'm just fine." More tears spilled over as if to deny her claim. She dashed them away with the back of her hands. As she hurried toward her mount, she thought she heard a soft reply.

"I'm sure you are."

Why did the words sound as if he didn't mean them?

John watched Maggie ride away. The more he saw of the petite blond, the more something inside him called out to her. He prayed for her every day. As he prayed, he wondered if she could be the woman God was preparing for him. What else could explain the way he was so drawn to her? But John knew that she wasn't ready for any kind of relationship, and when she was ready, she probably wouldn't look in his direction. He wondered if she would ever forgive him for shooting her dog. They never mentioned it after the day it happened. John expected her to ask him where the grave was, but she never had.

He feared that Maggie was mad at God. The only time he saw her at church was at her brother's funeral. When people consistently stayed away from services, it usually meant they had a problem with God. John talked to Martin about both Valter and Maggie. He found out that their whole family had been active in church for years, so John prayed for her spiritual well-being as well as for comfort from her sorrow.

Not only did John pray for her, but he also got up before dawn every day. That way, he could go out to the farm and take care of the chores before he returned to the depot for the first train of the morning. And he kept her wood box filled. If he could think of anything else to do, he would have done it, because his heart broke for Maggie and her grief—and for the fact that the first time they met, he added to her already heavy burdens.

John didn't want to awaken Maggie when he rode up to the farm, so he usually left his horse tied in the woods and walked the rest of the way to the barn. He slipped in the door and went about his work without making any noise that could be heard from the house. It hadn't taken him long to make friends with all the animals. They turned their attention to him as soon as he came through the door, knowing they were about to be fed. When he had time, he even curried the horses, gently talking to them as he did.

One Tuesday, John climbed into the hayloft to throw down enough hay to replace what he had taken out of the stalls. Before he filled the pitchfork, the door opened. He glanced down to see Maggie walking toward her horse. He couldn't decide what to do. He didn't want to startle her. While he was trying to figure out a way to let her know he was there, she started talking to the animal. John didn't plan to eavesdrop, but her sweet voice drifted up toward him.

John peeked over the edge of the hayloft. Maggie's arms were around the horse's neck, and he heard every word she said.

"Oh, Stormy, I wish you could come into the house with me the way Rolf did. He was so much company to me when Vally was sick. I talked to him, and I wasn't as scared. Now I'm alone, and the house feels so empty. Sometimes I just climb into bed and pull the covers over my head and cry."

Her voice became more muted, and John could no longer understand what she said. He thought about what he heard. There must be some way he could help her.

When John got back to town, he took his horse to the livery. The proprietor was raking the hay that covered the floor.

"Henry." John dismounted and walked his horse toward its usual stall. "Have you heard about anyone whose dog has had puppies recently?"

The old man took a minute to answer. He scratched his stubbly chin while he thought about it. "Not right off. I'll ask around, though, if you want me to." He leaned his arm on the handle of the rake. "You want a dog, do you? They're a mite o' trouble to take care of, 'specially since you're living in the boardinghouse."

John chuckled. "It's not for me. I want to give it to someone."

Henry stood looking at John as if he wanted to know who, but he didn't ask, and John didn't tell him.

The next day, Martin came by the Wayzata Depot. John was receiving a telegraph message, so the preacher walked around the station, looking at all the information tacked up on the walls. When John finished, he called to his friend.

"Martin, how can I help you? You don't need tickets to go somewhere, do you? It's pretty cold to be traveling."

Martin quickly came to the counter and leaned on its polished surface. "No, but maybe I can help you."

"Help me? I didn't know I needed any."

The preacher smiled. "I heard you were asking about a puppy."

John chuckled. "Oh, that. News travels fast around here. I only asked Henry about it yesterday."

"You know how it is." Martin joined his laughter, his fingers tapping an accompaniment on the polished wood. "He told me over coffee at Rose's Café. Rose heard him, so she asked everyone who came in yesterday and today. It's a good thing she did. There's a family with a farm west of Lake Minnetonka whose dog had puppies a few weeks ago. They were just starting to try to find homes for them. Does it matter what kind of dog it is?"

John hadn't thought about that. "I don't know. What kind are they?"

"Well, the momma is a big, long-haired dog. They aren't sure who the daddy is. Henry said you wanted to give it to someone. Will that person want a big dog?"

John nodded. "A big dog would be just fine." He figured

that a large dog would help Maggie feel safer. When it was grown, it could protect her.

Martin pulled a piece of paper out of the inside pocket of his suit coat. "Here are the directions to their house. You can go today if you want to, but you probably should take something to wrap the puppy in. It's only been in the barn with its momma and the other puppies. The wind is still nippy in the evenings. It might be too cold to carry it far without being wrapped up."

John took the proffered paper and unfolded it. He read the words scribbled on it and studied the crude drawing of a map. "Thanks, Martin. I'll go out there after the last train leaves this evening."

It didn't take John long to pick out which puppy he wanted. While he watched them tumble around their mother, one seemed to have more personality. Light tan in color, it sported irregular white patches around each eye, making it look as if it were wearing a mask. When he picked it up, the puppy jumped higher in his arms and licked his face. Then it settled down against his chest as if satisfied. John held the little dog away from him and studied it all over. If this puppy looked anything like his mother when he was grown, he would have long hair.

Now the wiggly ball of fur was wrapped in an old quilt John's mother had given him when he moved from North Dakota. He had used it to wrap some of the things that could break easily. Since he had been at the boardinghouse, it had remained in the corner where he dropped it after unwrapping the framed photos of his family that spread across the top of the bureau in his room. Sometimes when he undressed, his shoes landed on the quilt, transferring dirt and mud to the surface of the coverlet. He was sure this dog didn't care if the quilt wasn't too clean. Besides, by the time they arrived at the farm, the puppy might have soiled it, anyway.

Maggie carried a bowl of stew to the table. After she set it down, she heard a horse ride up. Although she was lonely in the house by herself, she wasn't sure she wanted unannounced company this late in the evening. On most days, she would have already been through eating and washing the dishes by now, but she had spent extra time in the barn with Stormy. It wasn't that she didn't want to come in the house, but she felt less lonely when she could talk to her horse. She set a pan of hot corn bread on the table and covered it with a tea towel to keep it piping hot. Then she went to the door to peek out between the curtains on the window.

It was so dark that she could see only shapes and shadows. A man was having a little trouble dismounting from the horse. He carried some kind of bundle that moved a lot. Finally, both feet were planted on the ground, but he stood there a minute, looking down. From the soft murmur of a masculine voice she could hear through the door, the man was talking to the bundle.

Maggie hoped he wasn't some kind of lunatic. Her door had a lock on it, but she seldom used it. However, she reached for the skeleton key and inserted it into the lock. Before she had time to turn it, the man started toward the house. His gait looked familiar. Just before he stepped up on the porch, Maggie caught a glimpse of his face in the moonlight. It was John Collins!

She placed her hand on her chest to try to quell the rapid beating of her heart. Lately, every time he came near, she went hot all over and her knees felt weak. She tried to convince herself that she was only responding to his kindness, but she knew that didn't completely explain what she felt.

Maggie took the key out of the lock and hung it on the hook between the door and the window before pulling the door open.

"Mr. Collins, what are you doing here this time of night?"

A smile lit his face. "I brought you a present."

Maggie shook her head. "I can't accept anything else from you."

John pulled the edge of the dirty quilt away from a squirmy mass of fur in his arms. The cutest puppy face she had ever seen peeked over the fabric.

"Maggie, I wanted to replace what I took from you. Please don't say no." He was able to get a good hold on the bundle with one arm, so he removed his hat. "I know it won't be the same as the dog you lost, but he could be a real friend to you if you let him."

Maggie opened the door farther and moved back to give him room to enter. "Please, come in." After he stepped through the opening, she shut the door to keep the cool air out.

How did the man know that a puppy was just what she needed? Maggie guessed it had to be John who came to the barn so early every morning. Yesterday she had tried to get there while he was still working, but when she arrived, he was nowhere to be seen.

"Mr. Collins, you do too much for me as it is."

His eyes twinkled before he answered. "I don't know what you're talking about."

No matter how hard he tried to sound sincere, Maggie knew different.

As if he just that moment realized he still held the wiggling puppy, he looked down and pulled the quilt away some more. He held the little animal out to her.

If Maggie hadn't already fallen in love with it, she would have now. The big brown eyes were full of mischief and affection as the puppy squirmed, trying to reach her face with its tongue.

"If you'll hold him for me, I'll get something to make him a bed." She dropped a quick kiss on the furry head before she deposited the warm puppy back into John's arms.

She went into the room that had been Vally's and returned with a wooden crate. She set it near the fireplace and turned to go get something to line the box to keep him warm. All the time, John played with the puppy, talking nonsense to him. She grinned as she looked at them.

"Why don't you use this old quilt in the box?" John pulled the puppy under one arm and reached down to pick up the cover that now lay on the floor.

"I can probably find something. You need to keep that."

John shook his head. "No, I'm not using it anyway. It's just one of Mother's old quilts."

After Maggie finished making the bed, she asked John if he had eaten supper. When he said he hadn't had time, she offered to share her stew and corn bread with him.

After he was seated at the table, John glanced at Maggie. "Would it be all right if I say grace before we eat?"

Maggie liked the way he talked to God as if He were a friend.

John smiled when she passed the hot bread to him. "I really like corn bread with stew. My father says Mother makes the best corn bread in the whole church."

Maggie handed him the butter and watched him slather it on. "Does she?"

He looked up almost as if he didn't know what she meant, then laughed. "She has as long as I remember." He took a bite and smiled while he chewed it. "This is as good as hers is." He reached for his spoon and dipped it into the fragrant broth. "She always laughs when he says she is a good cook. Evidently, she didn't know how when they married."

Maggie liked the way his eyes lit up when he talked about his parents. "Where are you from?"

"North Dakota. My father is a pastor there, but he also lives on the farm that belonged to my grandfather."

Quiet fell around the table as they continued to enjoy the food, and Maggie tried to think of what else to ask him. "Why did you come to Wayzata?"

"I wanted to venture out on my own. The railroad had been looking for men to train as telegraphers. When I became proficient, the position of stationmaster came open here, and they offered it to me." John put his spoon back into his bowl and trained his gaze on Maggie. "I'm really glad they did."

I am, too.

Later as John started to leave, Maggie couldn't believe that they had found so much to talk about. It almost felt as if they were old friends.

John stopped just before he opened the door. "Thank you, Maggie, for the good food. . .and the congenial company."

Maggie glanced at the crate where her puppy snuggled into the quilt fast asleep. "Thank you for the puppy."

John looked toward the box. "What are you going to name him?"

Maggie thought for a minute before answering. "With that mask on his face and his bright eyes, I think I'll call him Rascal."

"Sounds like a good idea to me." John settled his hat on his head and reached for the doorknob.

"John, thank you for all the work you've done for me, too." Maggie clasped her hands in front of her waist and gave him a tentative smile. "But you can stop. I can take care of things now."

She couldn't interpret the expression on John's face, but when he went out and the door shut behind him, she said to herself, "You're a good man, John Collins. A very good man."

Chapter 4

Before she went to bed, Maggie played with the puppy on the rug in front of the fireplace. Then she took him outside until he finally did his business in the yard behind the house. When they came back inside, she sat in the rocker and watched the fire as it died down, all the time rocking the puppy as it snuggled close against her heart. After she put him in the box and covered him with the quilt, Rascal slept.

Maggie was surprised that she slept so peacefully that night. Since Rascal was in a strange place, she had expected him to wake her several times during the night, but it didn't happen. Instead, Maggie woke early and jumped out of bed, looking forward to taking care of her new puppy. He gave her an added purpose in life, a purpose that had been missing since she'd lost her brother a month ago.

John Collins was a good man. But Maggie had already decided that, hadn't she? How could any man understand what she needed and meet that need for her? Yet John had done that very thing. This puppy filled a void in her heart.

Maggie needed to concentrate on something besides the

never-ending work. Spring had arrived, and she didn't like to think about what that meant. After growing up on the farm, she understood just how much work it involved. Since she was old enough to know what was going on, she had watched her parents fight the forces of nature to keep their land. Through good seasons and bad, Momma and Daddy had worked, and now the farm was something to be proud of.

If only her parents hadn't met their sad end. They had been traveling to Minneapolis to look at new homes. They planned to get rid of their snug cabin and purchase a two-story house. After the double funeral, it was all she and Vally could do just to keep the farm going. Now it was up to her, and she felt alone in the face of almost insurmountable odds. She didn't want to think about the possibility of having to sell the farm until she tried her best to keep it. Just having Rascal to talk to gave Maggie the feeling that she could make it.

After she took the dog back outside, she fixed breakfast for both of them. She pulled Rolf's tin pans out of the bottom cabinet where she had put them after he died. She filled one with water and the other with bread soaked in milk and set them on the floor near the table. While she ate, she talked to the darling puppy. Every time she spoke, Rascal turned those big brown eyes toward her and looked as if he understood every word she said. By the size of his paws, Maggie knew he was going to be large when he grew up. Although his puppy fur was short, it was thick and wooly. She felt sure he would be a long-haired dog when he was grown.

When she went out to the barn, Rascal darted around her, jumping and nipping playfully at her skirt until she found herself laughing into the fresh spring air. Maggie had forgotten how good it felt to laugh. Because she often went to see about the animals, the path was dry and packed down. At least the little dog wouldn't pick up mud to track into the house.

While Maggie checked on things, Rascal became acquainted with every nook and cranny of the building. He even made friends with all the livestock. She and Rascal didn't stay very long, because, as usual, John must have taken care of the chores. Maggie decided that she would get up really early tomorrow so she could insist that he not come anymore. The thought caused an unhappy catch in her heart. She liked knowing he was around, even when she didn't actually see him, but she felt odd about it. He had more than compensated for Rolf's death. His constant penance made her feel guilty, as though she were taking advantage of his kindness.

Maggie turned the animals out into the pasture to spend part of the day, but she returned before it got too cool and herded them into the shelter. The night wind was still sharp, and she didn't see any reason to make the animals stay out when she had a warm barn for them. Every time she entered the barn, she pictured the man who often worked there. She was sure his dark curls fell across his forehead while he worked. She had seen them there on many occasions. Her hands itched to reach up and push them back so she could see the sparkle in his eyes, which were the color of the leaves on the trees in the pasture.

The next morning, Maggie did awaken before dawn. Quietly, she stoked the fire and dressed in front of it, but Rascal woke anyway. She watched as he rose up on his front legs and stretched his neck. One eye opened and looked at her. Then he hopped up and gave a happy yip. Maggie decided to take him with her to meet John in the barn.

This time she caught him. He didn't hear her come in because he was singing:

"What a Friend we have in Jesus, all our sins and griefs to bear!
What a privilege to carry everything to God in prayer!
O what peace we often forfeit, O what needless pain we bear,
All because we do not carry everything to God in prayer.

"Have we trials and temptations? Is there trouble anywhere?
We should never be discouraged; take it to the Lord in prayer.
Can we find a friend so faithful who will all our sorrows share?
Jesus knows our every weakness; take it to the Lord in prayer."

The lyrics sung in his strong baritone resonated through the lofty structure. Maggie stood inside the door and listened, enjoying the texture he added to the words. When John paused before going on to the third verse, Rascal yipped and tumbled toward him, stirring up the straw on the floor as he went.

John turned. "Maggie." The sound of her name spoken in such a tender tone made her breath catch.

His gaze sought hers, and they connected for a moment before the little puppy jumped up on his legs, seeking attention. For an instant, Maggie wished she was adorable like the puppy and could snuggle in John's arms. While he knelt and picked up Rascal, Maggie shook her head, trying to clear it of the crazy thoughts.

John stood with the puppy in his arms. Rascal pawed at him and tried to reach John's face with his tongue. "What are you doing out here so early, Maggie?"

She took a step closer. "I wanted to tell you that you don't need to do my chores anymore, John. I appreciate all you've done for me, but you don't owe me anything," she ended on a whisper.

John's gaze never wavered from her face. "I want to come, Maggie. Although my father was a pastor, I grew up on a farm. Since I live at the boardinghouse and work at the depot, I miss the physical labor. It's a blessing for me to have a place to get all this exercise." Rascal succeeded in reaching John's chin with his tongue. John raised his head a little higher. "Besides, I need to check on this little mutt." He gave the puppy a big hug while he scratched it behind the ears.

A week later, the desire to do a thorough spring cleaning filled Maggie with restlessness. After going to the barn and letting the animals out into the sunshine, she headed toward the house. She pulled all the quilts off her bed, then went into the room that had been Valter's. There was no need to change his. Evidently Holly had washed the linens during the three weeks when she had stayed at the farm. Maggie hadn't even realized that.

While the water heated on the stove, Maggie glanced toward Rascal. The puppy slept on the rug in front of the fireplace. The quilt John had wrapped around the dog was pretty dirty, so she went to the box and lifted it out. She hadn't paid much attention to it when she made the bed the night John brought Rascal to her. Maggie looked closer at the places on the quilt where it wasn't soiled. This wasn't just some old quilt as John said. Someone had worked hard to piece beautiful fabric together into a lovely pattern.

Maggie spread the large cover on the floor. Running her fingertips over one clean area, she appreciated the predominantly light green pattern that made up the center section of the quilt. The fabric had a fine texture. Many patches were made of this color. The other patches were a variety of lovely hues that coordinated with the green. Strips of creamy fabric surrounded each block, framing it. The small squares on each corner of the frame were flannel with yellow dots. Maggie held up a corner of the coverlet. This quilt was a work of art.

Maggie had learned to sew by helping her mother make many of the quilts her family used over the years. This quilt was not some haphazard job. It had been well planned. Did John realize how much work went into making this coverlet? Maggie hated to see it ruined or mistreated by a rambunctious puppy. She went to the cedar chest and searched for an old quilt that had seen better days. After putting it in the dog's bed, she lovingly washed the one John had brought.

As she finished washing each quilt, she hung it across the clothesline in the backyard to dry. Once John's quilt was spread out in the bright sunlight, Maggie saw the exquisite beauty that had been hidden under all that soil. While she handled it, she noticed several places where the stitches had pulled apart. Maggie decided to restore the quilt and return it to John. It should stay in his family. The idea of doing something nice for him filled her with a sense of excitement. After all he'd done for her, this was the least she could do.

When she went back into the house, Maggie took out the

sewing basket. It had been awhile since she'd thought of replenishing these supplies. She needed more thread and needles. After lunch, she put Rascal in his box for a nap. The puppy had worn himself out chasing butterflies and grasshoppers around the yard while Maggie had washed the quilts.

After Rascal fell asleep, Maggie saddled Stormy and headed into Wayzata. Each time she went into town, she noticed many changes. It amazed her how quickly they took place. Because of Lake Minnetonka, people from other places often came to their city. The streets bustled with activity. Today, strangers in one of those new motorcars made their way down the main street. Maggie had to keep a tight rein on Stormy. Those noisy contraptions made the horse a little skittish. She tied the animal to a hitching post on a side street and walked to the mercantile. Maggie hoped those people would keep their vehicle on the main thoroughfare and not venture anywhere near her mare.

While Maggie was choosing thread, Holly walked up behind her. "Maggie, it's good to see you in town."

Maggie turned and gave her friend a hug. "I'm glad I ran into you, too."

"I've been planning to go out to the farm to see you." Holly picked up a couple of spools of thread.

"Why don't you come tomorrow?" It would feel good to have company again. "I'll fix lunch, and we can make a day of it. Hans can come over for lunch if he wants to. I'm restoring a quilt John Collins left at the house."

"I would love to help you." A speculative gleam twinkled in Holly's eyes. "You can tell me all about why Mr. Collins would do such a thing."

When Holly arrived the next morning, she carried a basket over her arm. The tantalizing aroma of cinnamon wafted through the room even before she removed the towel covering the food.

"I baked these this morning." Holly went to the cabinet and removed a couple of plates and took them to the table where she forked two of the hot rolls onto them. "Hans likes pastries for breakfast. I thought I'd share them with you. By the way, Hans won't be coming for lunch. He's going to town to have some horseshoes replaced. He's planning on eating at Rose's with Henry."

"My mouth is watering already." Maggie lifted the dish containing her roll and took an appreciative sniff. "I set a pot of tea to steep only a few minutes ago."

After they finished eating, Maggie went to Valter's room and picked up John's quilt, which she had spread across Vally's bed. She brought it out and laid it across the settee. "Isn't this lovely?"

Holly studied the handiwork. "Now tell me why he brought this to you."

When Maggie finished the story about John bringing Rascal wrapped in the quilt, Holly asked where the puppy was.

"I put him in the barn. We wouldn't get much work done without him tearing things up. I'll introduce you to him when we take a break."

Maggie sat at one end of the quilt and Holly at the other. While they talked, they worked their way around the cover, repairing every place that had pulled loose.

"Tell me about Mr. Collins." Holly didn't waste any time getting to the point.

"Well, first he killed my dog."

Holly's eyes widened, and her work dropped into her lap. "I wondered what happened to Rolf. You never did say."

"It was an accident, and John has been coming out and doing chores before I get up in the mornings. Then last week, he showed up with Rascal. What a blessing that little puppy is! I'm not as lonely or as fearful as I was before."

At lunch Maggie brought Rascal in so he could eat at the same time they did. Holly enjoyed the exuberant puppy as much as Maggie did. After they finished their meal, both women sat on the floor and played with him. When Maggie put him in his box for a nap, she and Holly went back to working on the quilt.

"Maggie." Holly looked up from her stitching. "I've been missing you at church. People ask about you all the time."

Maggie had expected this question to come sometime, but she dreaded it. If she had to explain how she felt to anyone, she was glad it was Holly. They had been friends most of their lives, so she should understand.

"I haven't even read the Bible since long before Vally died."

Instead of the shock that Maggie expected, Holly's expression contained only sympathy. "Why not, Maggie?"

"I can't understand how a loving God could let all these things happen to me." There, she had finally said the words out loud. "I'm not sure I even trust Him anymore."

Holly put the edge of the quilt down and stood. She looked around the room. Then she turned to Maggie. "Where's your Bible?"

"It's on a table by my bed."

Holly marched into Maggie's room and returned with the book in her hands. She sat in the rocking chair and leafed through the pages. Finally, she started reading silently. Maggie tried to ignore her, but she was aware of every move her friend made. With renewed vigor, Maggie worked on the quilt, making tiny, almost-invisible stitches.

"Here it is."

When Maggie looked up, Holly held the Bible with her finger marking her place.

"I read this chapter just this morning, and I wanted to share a portion with you. It's from Psalm 51: 'Make me to hear joy and gladness; that the bones which thou hast broken may rejoice. Hide thy face from my sins, and blot out all mine iniquities. Create in me a clean heart, O God; and renew a right spirit within me. Cast me not away from thy presence; and take not thy holy spirit from me. Restore unto me the joy of thy salvation; and uphold me with thy free spirit.' "

Maggie listened to the words her friend read. She often felt as if God had broken her bones. That was why she didn't know if she trusted Him or not. But this passage said a lot more. She put the quilt down and went to stand behind Holly so she could read over her shoulder. Holly pointed to verse eight, and Maggie started reading there.

"I really like verse twelve." Holly handed the Bible to Maggie, then went over to the quilt and lifted the edge, running her fingers over a place that had been badly torn. "See how we're restoring this. God wants to restore your relationship with Him in the same way. . .if you'll let Him."

Chapter 5

Finally, summer arrived. John had always thought that North Dakota was lovely in summer, but Wayzata had a special beauty that touched his soul. Working at the train depot added to his blessings. To see the most spectacular panorama, all he had to do was look out the window. The rippling waters of Lake Minnetonka reflected the blue of the clear sky. Tall trees framed the picture postcard scene. Occasionally he would glimpse the *City of St. Louis* as the side-wheeler traversed Minnesota's largest lake, carrying passengers to various towns scattered along its banks. Other times, small fishing boats bobbed like corks on the surface.

Whenever John feasted his gaze on the soothing water, his thoughts returned to Maggie Swenson. Her eyes often flashed the same shade as the deep water outside his window. Of course, lots of things reminded him of Maggie. Since he took Rascal to her, Maggie had changed. Sometimes when John saw her, he detected the remnants of sorrow in her expression, but she was finally moving on from the devastating sadness she had experienced after the death of her brother.

John continued to go to her farm and do chores early in the morning, but he no longer tried to keep from waking Maggie. Often, she and Rascal joined him in the barn. He enjoyed those times with her working beside him. John wondered what it would be like if he had her waiting at home when he finished work every day. John knew that he wanted her to always be a part of his life. If she had some family left, John would ask her father or brother if he could court her. He wasn't sure what the proper move would be under the circumstances, and he knew his mother would expect him to do what was proper. Maybe he should ask Pastor Hardin about it.

One thing still bothered him. Maggie hadn't come back to church. John yearned to talk to her about it, but he hadn't felt the time was right to bring up the subject. He didn't want to hurt her or push her away with his questions.

Maggie wearied of wearing black. She had been dressed in the depressing color off and on for most of the last year. Although she still grieved over losing both her parents and her brother, she now realized that life must go on.

The next time she went to town, she bought fabric for a new dress. Tiny light blue flowers with dark green leaves scattered in uneven clusters across the deep purple background, making it a good choice for moving away from mourning clothes. In the evening, after taking care of the chores, she worked on the dress.

Things on the farm weren't as bad as she anticipated they would be. In addition to John Collins doing chores in the mornings, several neighbors helped her plant fields of wheat and corn, as well as her kitchen garden. About once a week, one or more of the men came to lend aid as she cared for the crops. Their assistance reinforced Maggie's belief that God hadn't forgotten her.

She started reading her Bible again. One Saturday when Hans and Holly came to help her, they asked if she would accompany them to church. Even though they lived in the opposite direction from town, they offered to pick her up. Probably Holly realized it would be easier for Maggie to return to church if she didn't have to go alone.

The next day as Maggie patted her hair and pushed a hairpin to hold a curl more securely, she heard the buggy approaching. She quickly used a long hat pin to anchor a straw hat on her upswept hairstyle, then pulled on her new white gloves. After picking up her handbag and Bible, she arrived at the door just as Hans knocked.

"Maggie, what a pretty dress. Is it new?" Holly asked when Maggie sat beside her in the buggy.

Maggie nodded. "I made it this week."

"The color really darkens the blue in your eyes."

The trio carried on a lively conversation all the way to town. As they approached the church, Maggie's gaze was drawn toward John Collins, who stood under a tree talking to a farmer. Just looking at him took her breath away.

When John saw her, he walked up to the buggy and extended his hand to help her alight. "You look lovely today, Maggie."

Coming from him, her name sounded like a caress. Warmth rushed to her cheeks.

"Thank you, John." She couldn't keep her voice from sounding husky. Maggie cleared her throat. She hoped he hadn't noticed the blush she felt move up her cheeks.

John accompanied the three of them inside. When they sat, somehow he ended up beside her. Maggie wondered what people thought about her sitting with John. It made them look as if they were a couple. Not that she minded the thought, but it wasn't true.

It felt good to be back in fellowship with other believers. Maggie wondered why she had stayed away so long. The singing warmed her heart and caused a few tears to make their way down her cheeks. Before she could pick up her handbag to search for a handkerchief, John reached into his pocket and retrieved his own. He pressed thc white cotton against her palm.

She patted the tears away, enjoying the scent that clung to the pristine white square. John's scent. Woodsy, spicy, masculine. For a moment, all other thoughts fled her mind, and John filled every crevice. When she finished with the hanky, she folded the square and placed it in her handbag. She wanted to wash and iron it before she returned it to him.

After the service, John accompanied her to the Brunsons' buggy.

"Mr. Collins." Holly smiled up at him. "Would you join us for dinner?"

"I wouldn't want to impose, ma'am."

"I have plenty of food. We often ask people to eat Sunday dinner with us, so I prepare extra." Holly put her arm around Maggie's shoulders and pulled her closer. "Maggie is going home with us, too."

John's gaze sought Maggie's. "Then I would be delighted."

All the way to the Brunson farm, Maggie couldn't get John's words out of her mind. What about her delighted him? The warmth in those clear green eyes ignited something deep inside her.

Although she enjoyed the afternoon spent with Holly, Hans, and John, Maggie felt a restlessness she didn't understand. Long into the night, she relived every moment of the day, repeating in her mind every word John said. What was it about the man that touched her so deeply? After she went to bed, it took her a long time to fall asleep.

On Monday Maggie slept later than usual. John had already been to the barn and gone by the time Maggie went out. She sensed the shadow of his presence in the building when she entered, but she missed his substance. She pictured him as he was the last time he was there, muscles rippling under his shirt with the sleeves rolled halfway up his forearms. Maggie wished he would be there every day for the rest of her life.

Father God, why do I feel this way? What am I going to do?

That evening after she fed Rascal and sat down to eat her dinner of cold chicken and biscuits, Maggie heard horses riding up outside the house. It was rather late for company. She peeked out. Two men were dismounting. One was John, and the other one looked a lot like Pastor Hardin. Neither man had ever come to her home this late in the evening. Maggie went to the looking glass and checked her hair. She swept a few stray wisps away from her cheeks and neck and anchored them with hairpins.

When the knock sounded, she paused a few seconds before she moved toward the door. She didn't want them to think she was watching from the window, even if it was true.

"Come in, Pastor, John."

Rascal pushed past Maggie, and John hunkered down to pat him. She offered to make coffee or tea, but the two men declined. After she ushered them to the settee, she sank into the rocking chair and folded her hands in her lap.

Pastor Hardin cleared his throat. "John asked me to accompany him out here tonight. He wanted to talk to you."

Maggie glanced at John. She still didn't understand what was going on. Why did he need to bring someone when he wanted to talk to her?

John stood and shoved his hands into his pockets. He walked closer to where Maggie sat and looked down at her.

"I didn't know what else to do. You don't have a father or brother, so I talked to Martin." John gestured toward the other man. "Pastor Hardin."

Maggie had never seen John so ill at ease. She wondered where this conversation was headed.

John hunkered down by her chair as he had earlier for Rascal. The dog came over and laid his head on John's leg. John absently stroked Rascal, but he kept his attention trained on Maggie's face.

After taking a deep breath, he continued. "Maggie, I want to court you. . .if you'll let me."

Court me? The thought grabbed Maggie's imagination. She looked down at her clasped hands. *Court me.* She hadn't thought about anything like that. She had been too busy. But she wanted to be courted. A strange fluttering sensation started in her stomach.

She raised her eyes to John's face and smiled. "That would be nice."

He looked relieved. He nodded and stood, never taking his eyes from her. A smile lit his face like one of those electric lightbulbs at the hotel. Maggie felt as if the sun was shining on her, even though it was far past sundown.

John whistled as he rode toward the depot. He had gone to do Maggie's chores extra early today. She came to the barn just in time to tell him thank you before he left. Since he had started courting her, John made sure they weren't alone for very long. He didn't want anyone talking about them. Protecting Maggie's reputation was essential to him.

This courtship progressed better than he had dreamed it would. He escorted Maggie to church every Sunday. Often they went to the Brunsons' for dinner. A time or two, he took her out to eat at the restaurant in the hotel. Once, he and Maggie accompanied Hans and Holly to Minneapolis to see a stage play. Every minute he spent with Maggie made him grow more in love with her. He wanted to be with her and protect her.

Because of all her losses, Maggie had developed depth and strength of character. But John rejoiced that she had been able to move beyond her sorrows. He loved standing beside her at church as they sang hymns. Her rich contralto harmonized with his voice. He wanted to sing with her forever. Each time they parted, it became harder to leave. John yearned to take her in his arms and press his lips against her sweet, bowed mouth and pour all his love for her into the caress. But John knew he couldn't start kissing her. He wasn't sure he would be able to stop.

When he finished work that evening, he and Maggie would take a ride on the *City of St. Louis*. Equipped with electric lights, the boat often floated across the lake in the evening. The day couldn't end soon enough for him. The anticipation of being with Maggie again colored every moment.

Right after he arrived at the depot, his telegraph machine started clicking. He grabbed the pad and pencil and began to decipher the dots and dashes. When the message stopped, John sat back in his chair and smiled. Wait until he told Maggie. He hoped she would share his excitement.

Maggie stood at the railing and watched the huge wheel turn on the side of the boat. With every revolution, the large vessel slid through the tranquil waters of Lake Minnetonka. The day had been windy, but the breeze died down as dusk settled over Maggie and John while they rode in a buggy toward the pier where the *City of St. Louis* waited for passengers. She was glad there wasn't any wind tonight. Even though it was late June, a strong breeze on the lake would have blown chilly air across the deck. Maggie pulled her crocheted shawl higher around her shoulders.

John stepped closer, almost touching her back. "Are you cold?"

All she could do was shake her head no. She forgot everything around them, lost in his nearness. Even the fascinating electric lights paled in comparison to John Collins, the man of her dreams. Noise from a party inside the cabin seeped into the quiet that surrounded them. People talked and laughed while a piano player filled the air with the latest tunes. But out here on the deck, tranquillity prevailed.

Maggie wondered what John would do if she leaned back until she was in his arms. She knew a lady wouldn't do that, but right now she didn't care if she was a lady or not. It was as if John were a magnet and she a piece of iron. It took all her willpower to fight the force that tried to pull their bodies into contact. How Maggie wished her mother were still alive. Did other women feel this way, or was she just wanton?

John shifted to stand beside her and held onto the rail with one hand. "What are you thinking about, Maggie?"

She wondered if he would be shocked if she told him. After a moment of silence, she murmured, "It's beautiful out here on the lake. Thank you for bringing me."

She looked up into green eyes that had deepened in the soft light. Something dark and mysterious called out to her, and for a moment, she thought he was going to kiss her. She wished it were proper for him to do that very thing. Would his lips feel soft or hard like his muscles? She couldn't even imagine what a kiss would feel like, but she really wanted to find out—and soon. Maggie turned back toward the water.

John wanted to pull Maggie into his arms and kiss her. Truthfully, John had never felt this way before. Here he was, twenty-four years old, and he hadn't stolen a kiss from any girl. But every time he looked at Maggie's lips, he desired them above everything else in the world.

He needed to get his mind off that subject. "I received an interesting telegram today, Maggie." How he enjoyed the feel of her name in his mouth.

That caught her interest. "From whom?"

"My father." John still had a hard time believing it. "My parents have never traveled since they had children, but now they're coming to Minnesota to visit me."

Maggie laid her hand on John's arm. "That's wonderful! When are they coming?"

John placed his other hand on top of her fingers, hugging them close. "They'll be here for the Independence Day celebration."

"But that's just next week."

"I know." He gave her hand another squeeze. "They'll arrive on Monday and stay until Friday." John released her fingers and slid one arm around her waist. "I can hardly wait for them to meet you."

Maggie wanted to meet them, too, but she was a little anxious. What if she wasn't what they had in mind for their son? What if his mother could tell what she was thinking? Maggie needed someone to talk to about all that was happening. Maybe Holly could help her.

When Maggie told her best friend what she had been thinking on the boat, Holly laughed. "Oh, Maggie, you're so funny."

The two women sat in the parlor at the Brunson farm. Maggie picked up a decorative pillow from beside her on the sofa. She hugged it close. "I don't see anything funny about it."

Holly got up from the rocking chair and came to sit beside Maggie. "What you're feeling is perfectly natural." She put her arm around Maggie. "That's what a courtship is. Getting to know one another and letting your feelings for each other grow. It wouldn't be natural if you didn't want to touch John and have him touch you."

Maggie smiled. "I really want him to kiss me, even if it wouldn't be proper. On the boat when he put his arm around me, I felt as if I were melting inside. I wanted to stand on tiptoes and kiss him if he wasn't going to kiss me first."

Holly laughed again, even longer this time. "Do you love John?"

"I'm not sure what love for a man is, but I can hardly stand the waiting when we're apart. Even while I'm working around the farm or sewing or taking care of Rascal or the other animals, all I think about is John. The last time we were together. The next time we'll be together. Is that love?"

Holly gave a secret smile. "I know. That's how I felt about Hans. . .before we married."

"And now?"

"Oh, Maggie, that love just grows and grows, and the touching gets better all the time." A blush stained Holly's cheeks. Maggie wondered exactly what she was talking about, and she hoped she would soon find out for herself.

Chapter 6

It had been months since John had last seen his parents. Although he came from a close-knit family, he hadn't realized how much he missed them until he received the message that they were coming to Wayzata. He went to the depot early so he could finish most of his work before they arrived. He planned on taking the rest of the day off so he could show Mom and Dad around town. Not many trains came through on Monday. The eastbound they rode came through about three p.m. It was the last.

When it was almost time for the train to arrive, John shoved his hands in his pockets and paced the wooden platform that connected the depot to the railroad tracks. The breeze that blew fluffy clouds across the sky brought relief from summer's heat. He wondered what his parents would think about Maggie. He dismissed the question from his mind. How could his family not love the woman he planned to wed?

The next few days would be busy. Tomorrow was the Independence Day celebration, and Wayzata already was decked out in patriotic colors. Bunting hung around buildings and at intervals across the street along the parade route. Not only were Wayzata's citizens planning on participating, but many people from Minneapolis and St. Paul who spent part or all of the summer in cottages on the banks of Lake Minnetonka would be present as well.

The last time John passed the ice-cream parlor, he noticed a sign advertising a red, white, and blue sundae made with vanilla ice cream, strawberries, and blueberries. He planned to take Maggie and his parents to get one. Both Maggie and his mother would especially enjoy the frozen treat.

The whistle of the approaching train brought him out of his musings. John moved back and leaned against the wall of the depot, striking a relaxed pose.

The engine chugged into the station accompanied by the squeal of brakes as it slowed to a stop. John scanned the windows, trying to catch a glimpse of his parents. He spotted them in the third passenger car, so he hurried toward that one where the conductor hopped down from the steps. John's father followed the man, then turned to offer his hand to John's mother, who stood on the bottom step.

John drank in the beauty of her face. She looked younger than she had the last time he had seen her. When her feet touched the platform, he pulled her into a bear hug and whirled her around. John was glad he was tall like his father instead of being short like his mother.

"John, put me down." Mom whispered into his ear while she held her straw hat on with one hand and hugged him back.

After John settled her on the wooden platform, he shook

hands with his dad, then the two men clapped each other on the shoulder.

"Let's get the two of you settled in your hotel room before supper." John picked up the two valises the conductor set on the platform beside them.

John and Maggie ate dinner at the hotel with his parents. It didn't take her long to fall in love with them. His father was as tall and slim as John. Evidently, John had inherited his dark hair. Maggie was sure John would look just as distinguished as his father did when his hair silvered at the temples. John's eyes, though, had come from his mother. Not only were hers the same light green, but they contained a sparkle similar to the one that usually lit his.

Maggie already knew a lot about his parents. How his mother hadn't learned a lot about being a housewife and mother before his parents met. John told her about being a young boy and loving to brush the tangles out of his mother's long strawberry blond curls. She enjoyed letting the children take turns brushing her hair. The woman who sat across the table from Maggie had her hair arranged in a Gibson girl hairdo. The smooth pouf let only a few wisps touch her cheeks and neck. To achieve a style like that, she must have learned how to manage all the curls John talked about.

"John has told us a great deal about you." Mrs. Collins's smile went straight to Maggie's heart. "We're glad he has a good friend like you."

John had told Maggie about his two sisters. Esther was only two years younger than he was, and she had married recently.

Miriam was four years younger than John. At ten, their brother, Matthew, was the youngest. The lively conversation around the table contained many references to John's brother and sisters. Maggie imagined that life had been interesting in the Collins's home in North Dakota. She often wished for more brothers and sisters when she was growing up.

"Where are Miriam and Matthew staying?" John asked his mother.

Maggie could tell from the tone of John's voice and the smile on his mother's face that the two of them had a special relationship. She remembered the wonderful relationship Valter had with their mother. Maybe someday she would have a son to love the same way. For a moment, she saw a little boy with dark hair and John's green eyes laughing up at her with love in his expression. It brought the heat of a blush to her cheeks. She hoped no one noticed.

"They're with Esther and Levi. They're the first guests to stay with them in the new house Levi built for Esther before they married." Mrs. Collins straightened the silverware on the table in front of her. "He's such a nice young man. We're glad he and Esther got together."

John's father cleared his throat. "We're sure God put them together, aren't we, Brigit?"

Mrs. Collins turned a loving glance toward her husband and nodded. Then she looked back toward John. "So what are we going to do tomorrow?"

"There's a parade in the morning at eleven o'clock. Then we'll have a picnic. The city has a park down by Lake Minnetonka. That's where most of the activities will take place." John looked at Maggie and paused, giving her a chance to add to what he said.

"There'll be races and games like horseshoes and baseball. I think you can even take a ride on the side-wheeler if you want to. Lake Minnetonka winds around in many directions, and that's the best way to see it."

Mrs. Collins started to say something, but the waitress arrived with their food. After the woman left, John's mother leaned toward Maggie. "It sounds like a lot of fun."

"I'll prepare a picnic basket for us." Maggie looked down at the huge steak sizzling on her plate. She wasn't sure that she would be able to finish it.

"Would you like me to return thanks, son?" John agreed, and his father spoke a few words of blessing over their food.

When John arrived at the farm to pick Maggie up on Tuesday, she had everything prepared for the Independence Day festivities. He went into the house to help her carry the picnic basket. She also handed him a quilt they could spread on the ground under one of the shade trees. Maggie accompanied him to the buggy. Besides her handbag, she carried a large parcel wrapped in brown paper and tied with twine.

"Would you like me to get that for you?"

"No, it's not heavy." Maggie placed the package in the floorboard beside the basket.

"What is it anyway?" John couldn't contain his curiosity.

"You'll see later. It's a surprise."

John placed his hands on Maggie's waist when he helped her up into the vehicle. He liked the feel of her trim waist.

"Who is it for? My parents?"

"Aren't you the curious one?" Maggie laughed and didn't give him any more information.

When they arrived at the hotel, John stopped the buggy at the back door and tied the horses to the hitching post. He took the picnic basket in and left it in his parents' room so it would be out of the sun during the parade. Maggie waited in the hotel lobby for him to return with his parents. The proprietor had placed chairs on the boardwalk in front of the building so his customers would have a comfortable place to watch the parade. When the Collins family arrived in the lobby, they accompanied Maggie to choose where they would sit. A canopy over the boardwalk in front of the hotel protected them from the bright sunlight.

Soon after they sat down, the parade started. A band led the procession, playing "Stars and Stripes Forever." Maggie enjoyed the lively march, tapping her toe in tune with the beat. She had read about how John Philip Sousa wrote the march on Christmas Day in 1896 while on an ocean voyage. After his return to the United States, the song became very popular. Now it was a welcome addition to Independence Day celebrations all over the country. The song made Maggie proud to be an American, too. Her parents hadn't been born in the United States, but she and Vally had been.

Soldiers who fought in the Spanish-American War followed the band. Maggie didn't like the idea of war, but this one lasted less than a year. It gave Cuba independence from Spain and made Guam and Puerto Rico part of the United States. It also ended Spanish rule in the Philippines. She understood why the soldiers were proud of the victory they won. As they marched in perfect precision, they often saluted the citizens lining the path of the parade.

Aoooga! Aoooga! Maggie turned her head to look behind the last of the soldiers.

"What is that awful noise?" Mrs. Collins craned her neck as she searched for whatever was causing it.

"It's the horn of a motorcar." John patted his mother's hand.

Maggie watched the mayor of Wayzata as he slowly drove down the street while squeezing the bulb on the horn of his automobile. His wife sat beside him. The open vehicle was painted red with lots of gold accents. "I'm not sure if I really like those things. They make a lot of noise, and my mare shies away from them."

"They cause many of the horses to be restless," John added. "One even ran away with its rider last week. It was the talk of the town for a day or two."

"Thankfully, no one near us has one yet." Mr. Collins frowned as he watched the contraption go down the street away from them.

Following the mayor, several young men rode their bicycles, which they decorated with red, white, and blue streamers. They rang their bells in no particular sequence, but the cacophony wasn't unpleasant. Maggie wondered if it would be hard to ride a bicycle. She liked riding her horse. They were partners in the balancing act, but how could you balance on thin wheels?

Mrs. Collins started laughing at the antics of three clowns who followed the cyclists. One did flips and walked on his hands as he moved down the street; another floated along on tall wooden stilts; and the third rode a unicycle. Maggie had heard about these one-wheeled cycles, but this was the first time she had seen anyone riding one.

With the end of the parade, people started making their way toward the park. John escorted Maggie and his mother to the buggy while his father went to the room to retrieve the basket of food.

When they alighted from the buggy at the park, John led the way to one of the tall trees that spread shade across the lush grass. He chose one on a little rise so they could observe all that went on around them. John noticed that Maggie once again carried the mysterious parcel. However, she set it aside while they had lunch. After they ate their fill of the baked chicken, fresh tomatoes, and chocolate cake, the two women packed all the dishes and utensils back into the basket, and John carried it to the buggy. When he returned, he dropped onto the quilt beside Maggie. His mother was sitting nearby, and his father lay with his head in her lap. Although there were many people in the park, groups were scattered far enough away from each other so it felt almost private.

Maggie looked up at John. "I have a surprise for you." She thrust the parcel into his hands and waited wide-eyed for him to open it.

When he pulled back the brown paper, he uncovered a quilt. "Did you make this for me?"

"My quilt!" His mother leaned close and rubbed her hand gently across the folded cover before she glanced at Maggie.

"How did you get my quilt?"

Maggie studied John. "I know you said it was just an old quilt, but when I washed it, I could see that it was special."

"It certainly is!" his mother exclaimed. "I told you all about it in the letter I packed with it when I gave it to you."

John's brows knit in a confused expression. "There wasn't a letter with it."

"I don't understand. I wrote it so you would understand." She gave John a loving pat. "It's all right. You didn't know. I learned to sew while making this quilt using my wedding dress. That's where this green fabric came from." Once again, her hand caressed the coverlet in John's lap.

Mr. Collins sat up and watched them.

"I made my wedding dress, but it fell apart the first time I washed it." She took the quilt from John and spread it out so they could see all the blocks. "This white fabric I used in several blocks. It was the shirt Peter wore for our wedding." She caressed another block with her fingertips. "This was from a gown Mrs. Gladney made for John when he was a baby. She was a member of our church. And this flannel came from one of John's blankets. That's why I gave the quilt to him when he moved."

Maggie had been intently watching John's mother. "I knew the quilt had to be special, but I didn't know how special. It pulled apart in several places after I washed it. My best friend, Holly Brunson, and I restored it. It was actually when we were working on the quilt that my relationship with God was restored, too."

John knew that statement would catch his father's attention.

"Why was your relationship with the Lord damaged?" he asked.

"I pulled away from Him after I lost both my parents and my brother. Holly told me that God could restore my relationship with Him the same way we were mending the quilt. After I had time to think about the idea, I understood what she was talking about. I started going back to church, reading my Bible, and praying. My life completely changed."

John's mother touched his arm. "You haven't told us why Maggie had your quilt in the first place."

"It's kind of a long story." John swallowed a lump in his throat. He felt guilty for not realizing the importance of his mother's gift to him.

"We have plenty of time." John's mother leaned back against the tree and crossed her arms.

John knew she wouldn't leave him alone until she had the whole story, so he told her all about killing Maggie's dog by mistake and taking Rascal to her wrapped in the quilt.

When he finished, Maggie added to the story. "I don't know what I would've done without John's help. . .or without Rascal to love. That puppy filled a void in my life. I'm thankful John brought him to me."

Brigit patted Maggie's arm. "I'm glad he did, too."

Chapter 7

John's mother told him to come by the hotel after he took Maggie home. He figured she would chastise him for not taking care of the quilt. She hadn't told him how important the thing was when she gave it to him. He just remembered it being around the house most of his life. All the way back to town, he rehearsed different ways to apologize to her for what he had done.

His mother answered his knock. "Come in, John."

She didn't look upset. In fact, her bright smile and twinkling eyes warmed his heart. She pulled him into a welcoming hug.

After the embrace ended, John studied his mother. "What did you want to talk to me about?"

"Why, Maggie, of course." The answer contained a lilt of excitement.

John's thoughts jumbled, since he was prepared to apologize and defend his actions but his mother introduced an entirely different subject. "Why do you want to talk about Maggie?"

His father stepped up behind her and placed a hand on her shoulder. "Just what are your intentions toward the young lady?" His eyes also twinkled.

"I'm not trifling with her emotions, if that's what you're asking," John stammered. He wasn't sure what to expect next.

Father shut the door and ushered John to a chair. "We just don't want you to hurt the girl by leading her on. She's very nice, and she deserves more than that."

"I plan on asking her to marry me," John blurted out, almost feeling like the boy he had been when he often got in trouble for all his mischief and had to face his parents.

His mother clapped her hands. "Good! When are you going to do it?"

John felt as if he had stepped into a stage play in the middle of the second act and hadn't seen the script. "I'm not sure. . .uh, soon."

Mother sank into a chair and modestly arranged her skirt. "She doesn't have any family, does she?"

John stood up and paced across the floor, rubbing his hands together. Then he thrust them into his pockets so he could keep them still. He wasn't exactly comfortable talking about this with his parents. "No, but I took Martin. . .uh, Pastor Hardin with me when I asked her if I could court her."

A sweet smile lit Mother's face. "I'm glad you're doing things the proper way. I tried to raise you right."

Father placed a hand on his shoulder. "If you plan on asking her to marry you sometime soon, maybe you could do it while we're here. If she doesn't mind getting married quickly, I could perform the ceremony. It would be a privilege, son."

John felt as if a whirlwind had picked him up and was slinging him around in a dizzy circle. He wished it would deposit him back on the carpet that stretched almost from wall to wall in the room. He needed a firm foundation under his feet so he could think straight. "I'm trying to plan something special for the day I ask her."

That was all Mother needed. He could almost see her creative mind go to work as she jumped up from the chair, reminding John of what she had been like when he was younger. So full of life, meeting every challenge head on. "Maggie enjoyed the ride on the side-wheeler."

John nodded.

"You could take her tomorrow night." She move closer to John. "If she says yes, we'll telegraph Esther and Levi, telling them how much longer we'll need to stay."

Maggie worked in her garden all morning. She had an abundance of produce, which she didn't want to take the time to can. When John had come to help with the chores that morning, he'd asked if she would like to go on a boat ride after they ate supper with his parents. She looked forward to the evening and didn't want to spend the afternoon slaving over a hot stove. She wanted plenty of time to get ready for the outing.

After lunch, Maggie went into town and delivered all the vegetables to the parsonage. Elizabeth Hardin gladly received the bounty. Then Maggie went to the mercantile to purchase ribbons to match her favorite blue dimity dress. All the way home, she planned the hairstyle she would wear and how she would wind the ribbons through it.

When John arrived to pick her up, Maggie was glad she went to all the trouble. The way his eyes lit up when he saw her made the effort worthwhile.

After supper at the hotel, Mr. and Mrs. Collins accompanied them to the pier where the *City of St. Louis* gently swayed in the water. As the boat moved away from the wooden platform, twilight was falling over the water. Lights along the bank reflected in the ripples, and stars appeared one by one in the sky. Maggie started counting them in her head until there were too many. She and the Collins family stood by the railing and watched the summer night unfold before them accompanied by the gurgle and splash of the water as the wheel lifted it up and poured it out. By the time the boat moved around the first bend in the lake, the inky sky twinkled as though covered with a field of diamonds. A three-quarter moon cast its path across the water, beckoning Maggie to some unknown, enticing place. She knew God had created this spectacular display. Her heart filled with praises.

Before long, people drifted into salons on the boat, where music played and porters served refreshments. Maggie wanted to stay right where she was, beside the man she had come to love with all her heart. John stood so close she could feel the heat radiating from his body, but he didn't touch her. They didn't talk, but instead enjoyed the movement of the boat and the wonder of the night that surrounded them.

When John finally spoke, Maggie turned and noticed that they were alone. Even his parents weren't beside them any longer.

"What are you thinking about, Maggie?"

His quiet voice sounded like a caress. Maggie could only wonder how a real caress from John would feel.

She peered up into his beautiful green eyes, which sparkled in the moonlight. "I was praising God for providing us so much beauty."

A look of disappointment crossed his face for a moment. "Yes. . .it is beautiful." He turned and gazed across the expanse before them.

"And I was thankful that He brought you into my life," Maggie whispered.

John's expression brightened as he turned back toward her. "I am, too, Maggie." His fervent declaration touched her heart.

He moved closer and slipped his arm around her waist. Maggie looked up into his face, studying the lines and planes outlined in the moonlight, all the time aware of the weight and warmth of his arm around her.

"You're lovelier than anything out there." He gestured toward the lake.

Tears pooled in her eyes, and she glanced down at the bright trail across the water. Through her tears, the ripples along the surface looked extra sparkly.

"Maggie, I love you so much my heart feels as if it might burst."

John's words whispered against her hair arrowed to her heart, then she heard him breathe in her scent. She knew what he meant. She felt the same way about him.

"I brought you on this boat ride for a specific purpose."

Maggie didn't know what he meant, but it intrigued her. "And it was. . . ?"

John turned her toward him and gently held her upper arms. "Will you marry me, Maggie Swenson?" His intense gaze almost consumed her. He had spoken the most wonderful words she had ever heard.

"Yes." The syllable slipped out on a whisper. "Yes." This time she made sure John could hear her answer.

He gently cupped her face in his hands and studied her as if memorizing her expression. His eyes stopped their journey on her lips. He slowly lowered his face toward hers but stopped a hairbreadth away.

Maggie slipped her arms around his waist and closed her eyes, lifting her lips willingly to him. When their mouths touched, Maggie couldn't believe the sweetness that enveloped her. The love that poured into her heart and soul was so much greater than she had ever imagined. She became lost in the wonder of it.

John could hardly believe how easily the words had poured from him. He didn't know why he worried about it all day. He asked her to marry him, and she said yes. Twice. Her lips tasted better than John had ever imagined. He wasn't sure whether the kiss lasted for a second or an hour. Whichever, it wasn't long enough. A lifetime of kissing Maggie might be long enough, and he was going to find out. He planned to kiss her several times a day for the rest of their lives. The very thought lit a fire deep inside him. A fire he knew would be hard to keep under control. His father's idea of a swift marriage sounded better all the time.

When their lips parted, he gazed into her eyes and read the love there, but she spoke the words anyway. "I love you, John Collins, and I will until the day I die."

He pulled her against him, holding her so that their hearts beat in one accord. She rested her cheek on his chest, and the intimacy of the moment overwhelmed him.

"When, John? When should we get married?"

He pulled back but didn't take his arms from around her waist. "Would it be all right if we get married really soon?"

"How soon?"

John sighed. "I would like to get married before my parents go home. That way my father could perform the ceremony."

Maggie took a deep breath, then let it out slowly. "That is soon."

"I'll understand if you want to wait longer. Of course, they can stay a week or two while we make wedding plans." John pulled Maggie's head back against his chest. He loved the feel of her against him. The perfume of her essence filled him with heady anticipation. How he hoped that she would agree to marry quickly.

Maggie took a few minutes to answer, but she didn't pull away. John watched the ripples dancing in the moonlight, feeling as if his heart was dancing right along with them.

"One of us should have family at the wedding. I don't have any left, and it's a long way from North Dakota. I wouldn't ask your parents to return later when there's no real reason the wedding can't take place right away." Maggie smiled up at him. "Do you think it'll be all right with them?"

John leaned his forehead against Maggie's, and their breath mingled. "I told them I planned to ask you to marry me. They thought it was wonderful. It was their idea to stay until the wedding if we get married soon."

Saturday, July 15, dawned bright and sunny, but a breeze blew welcome relief from the high temperature. Holly spent the night with Maggie, helping her finish making her wedding dress. They had found a bolt of silk the same shade of light green that John's mother wore when she married. They adorned Maggie's dress with an abundance of lace, and Maggie found her mother's lacy veil in one of the trunks. Including the traditions of both mothers in her wedding attire made the day more special.

Holly went out in the late morning and picked wildflowers. With them, she fashioned a bouquet for Maggie to carry. Scraps from the lace they used on the dress surrounded the blossoms.

The wedding was more elaborate than Maggie first thought it would be. All their friends at the church pitched in, planning a wedding supper for after the ceremony. These people provided the food and decorations. Maggie felt blessed to have so many people around her, supporting her.

At four thirty, Pastor Hardin and his wife came to the farm to get Maggie and Holly. White fabric streamers decorated the buggy he drove. He had offered to stand in for Maggie's father and walk her down the aisle. The church was already full when they arrived. John, his father, and Hans waited at the front of the church. John and Maggie had asked Hans and Holly to be their attendants.

All Maggie saw when she walked down the aisle was the face of her beloved. She knew that later she would try to remember every detail, but everything happened so fast. Soon

Mr. Collins pronounced them man and wife. *Mr. and Mrs. John Collins.* The fervent kiss John gave her made her blush.

After the new couple exited the church, John's mother came to hug both of them. "Welcome to the family, Maggie. I'm officially making you the keeper of the quilt."

John laughed. "She'll take better care of it than I did."

Once again he kissed his bride, and Maggie welcomed it with all her heart.

Epilogue

By late August, Maggie had settled happily into married life. Sharing a home with John fulfilled many of the dreams Maggie had had as a young girl. She already knew what an honorable man John was, but she never dreamed how much fun he could be. When he came home, he filled the house with laughter and love.

Early in the month, John hired the son of a neighbor to help with the work at the farm. Because he enjoyed being stationmaster and telegrapher, he didn't want to quit his job. But the farm demanded a great deal of time when he got home, and he wanted to spend his evenings with Maggie and Rascal. It was just one more thing for Maggie to love.

One day at noon when he came home for dinner, he carried a package wrapped in brown paper. "I picked up the mail, and this is for you."

Maggie turned from the stove where she stirred gravy. "Who is it from?"

"My mother." John set the parcel on the end of the table. "It's probably a wedding gift."

"Should I open it now?"

"I can't stay long today." John came up behind Maggie and slipped his arms around her, dropping a kiss on her upswept hair. "Open it after we eat. You can show it to me when I get home this evening."

Maggie stepped from his arms, picked up the skillet, and poured the gravy in a waiting bowl. "Okay. Dinner is ready."

Pleasant conversation punctuated the meal, but Maggie couldn't keep her eyes from straying to the package sitting on the other end of the table. After John left, she made herself wash the dishes before she opened it. When she finished, she swiped her hands down the front of her apron before removing it and hanging it on a hook near the sink.

When Maggie unwrapped the brown paper, she found two wrapped bundles. The first parcel contained linens—sheets, pillowcases, and kitchen towels. According to the notes pinned to two pairs of pillowcases decorated with delicate embroidery, Miriam had made one pair and Esther the other. John's mother created a set of pillowcases in cutwork embroidery, outlining the flowers and leaves in many colors. Seven kitchen towels, one for each day of the week, were also decorated with needlework.

Maggie laid them aside and opened the other package. She uncovered a sewing basket. When she opened the top, she found two envelopes on top of the contents. The words *Read this first* were written on one of them. She tore it open.

Dear Maggie,

The time Peter and I spent with you and John was special, and we welcome you into the family. His sisters and I hope you enjoy using these items as much as we enjoyed making them for you.

I must admit I was amazed that John hadn't realized the significance of the quilt, because I wrote him a note explaining it. After I returned home, I searched my sewing basket and found it stuck in the side. It's in the other envelope. I must have neglected to attach it to the quilt when I gave it to John.

My daughters are better seamstresses than I will ever be. They now make my clothing, too. I gave each of the girls her own sewing basket for her birthday when she was twelve years old. Since my sewing basket is lined with some of the same fabric that I used in the quilt, I wanted you to have it.

We hope you and John can come to North Dakota to visit the family soon. The girls are eager to meet you.

Love,
Brigit Streeter Collins

Maggie put the paper down and carefully opened the other envelope.

My dearest son,

This quilt is the story of your family and the love that binds us together as truly as the threads that hold together these pieces of cloth.

I began this quilt as a new bride. I didn't know any more about sewing than I did about being a wife, but I knew about love. . . .

As Maggie continued to read the words, tears pooled in her eyes. Soon they streamed down her face. After she finished reading, she dashed them from her cheeks with the backs of her hands.

She bowed her head and thanked God for allowing her to become a part of this wonderful family. Maggie was confident that she, John, and the wee one she suspected she was carrying would add to the tapestry of love her mother- and father-in-law had begun.

LENA NELSON DOOLEY

Lena Nelson Dooley is a freelance author and editor who lives with her husband in Texas. During the twenty years she has been a professional writer, she has been involved as a writer or editor on a variety of projects. She developed a seminar called "Write Right," and she hosts a writing critique group in her home. After working several years on a church support staff, she currently works full-time as an author and editor. She has a dramatic ministry, an international speaking ministry that crosses denominational lines, and an international Christian clowning ministry. She and her husband enjoy taking vacations in Mexico, visiting and working with missionary friends. She has written six **Heartsong Presents** titles, and one of her books is included in the Crossings Book Club "Heaven Sent" series volume entitled *Cross My Heart*. Visit her at http://www.lenanelsondooley.com.

The Coat

by Tracey V. Bateman with Frances Devine

Dedication

Special thanks to my mom, Frances Devine.
Not only does she read every word I write,
but she writes with me when I'm in a crunch.
Thank you for being Supermom and saving the day.
You took my thread of an idea and helped me weave it into
a wonderful story I'm proud to add my name to.
Most of the credit for this project is yours.
I love you so much!

Chapter 1

Leah Halliday clutched her pay envelope tightly and held her head high as she walked down the service street behind Rosemont Industries. Arms linked, she and her two best friends marched side by side, their oxfords in silent step. At least misery had company—the proof being the two dozen women who trudged along behind them down the icy street. *Although,* Leah thought ruefully, *I would have preferred to suffer alone in this case.*

At the corner, the trio turned left and headed down the sidewalk, still not uttering a sound except for an occasional deep sigh. Two blocks away, they walked into Simon's Café. Simon's had been their special coffee klatch hangout for nearly four years now. This was where Susan had sobbed out her misery the day she received the "Dear Jane" letter from her sailor fiancé. It was the place where Janie Brown had shared her doubts about ever being published when the seventeenth rejection letter had arrived in her mailbox. And it was here that Janie and Sue had sat in stunned silence while Leah, trembling and dizzy, told them the news about Bob's death.

Leah hardly noticed the scent of freshly brewed coffee and sweet buns as they walked back to the last booth. She sighed heavily and dropped onto the seat. Sliding over, she made room for Janie.

"They didn't even give us notice! And two weeks before Christmas!" Janie burst into tears and flung her purse onto the table. Grabbing a handkerchief from the open bag, she blew her nose loudly and pressed her lips together.

"I know, sweetie. But ever since the boys came home, we've known it was just a matter of time. At least they gave us two months' severance pay." Leah patted her friend on the shoulder and gave a wobbly smile that wouldn't have fooled anyone.

They ordered Cokes from the waitress and, in silence, listened to the blaring of the jukebox as the Andrews Sisters sang the last roistering chorus of "Boogie Woogie Bugle Boy."

Susan Ryan, the petite blond sitting across from them, blew a strand of hair from her face. "Are they ever going to stop playing that song? Don't they know the war is over?" When none of her friends answered, she frowned, squinting her blue eyes. "Can you believe Mr. Kites—complimenting us on a job well done as we 'held down the fort for the boys in uniform'? Then to say he just knew we would all be happy to give the jobs back to our husbands and fathers. Well, I, for one, don't have a husband or a father, and I need to pay the rent."

Leah bit her lip and stared at the saltshaker that had fallen over on the table. She understood her friend's dilemma; the same war waged inside of her.

"And what about you, Leah? How are you going to take care of Collin?"

"I don't know, Sue. I'll manage somehow. I'm sure another job will turn up." Leah breathed a sigh of relief that she had already bought Collin's Christmas gifts.

"Well, I don't know how you can be so sure." Janie dabbed at her eyes with a clean handkerchief. "After all, everyone's going to be hiring the *returning heroes*. Of course we can always clean houses or wait tables, I guess." She stopped, a look of remorse flashing across her face. "I don't mean to sound like I'm ungrateful for what the boys did. I don't begrudge them their jobs back—" Her voice broke, and she shook her head.

Neither of her friends spoke. There was nothing to be said. Nothing to be done. As many other women in the country were discovering, their usefulness to industrial America had come to a screeching halt the second the first wave of returning GIs stepped off the ships. Leah sipped her Coke, staring glumly at the fizz, and despite her optimistic facade wondered how on earth she and Collin would make it through the winter.

Later, as Leah waited at the corner for her bus, her back turned to the cold December wind, she tried to weigh her options. Since Bob's death, she hadn't had time to think about the future. She fell into bed exhausted most nights, and her days off were spent cleaning and shopping and trying to make up to her ten-year-old son for not having a dad.

But now she had to think about it, and unfortunately, there didn't seem to be any options unless she wanted to sell the house. The thought ripped through her like a jagged piece of glass, but she couldn't rule out the thought that it might eventually come to that if the time came when she had no choice. Their house wasn't fancy, but at least it was a comfortable, roomy place for Collin to grow up. She didn't want to raise him in a three-room flat if she didn't have to.

At the thought, Leah's whole body tensed. Her breathing quickened as the fear she had held at bay for the last four years reached out and wrapped its tentacles around her heart.

Hot grease popped and sputtered as Leah added potato slices to the sizzling iron skillet, then dashed on a bit of salt and pepper. Just as she placed the lid on the skillet, the front door slammed. Her lips curved into a smile while she waited for her reason for living to join her in the kitchen. When too much time passed, she frowned at the silence. Not even Collin's usual "Mom, I'm home" greeted her ears. Grabbing a towel, she wiped her hands on the way to the living room. "Collin?"

Her son stood at the end of the overstuffed sofa, his head down.

"Honey, what's wrong?" Her throat tightened as he raised his head and looked at her with mournful eyes.

Blood trickled from his quivering bottom lip, and dirt smudged his cheeks and forehead. She gasped and hurried to him.

"What happened?"

Looking down at the floor, he shook his head. "Nothin'."

Her heart constricted. "It doesn't look like nothing to me.

Come into the bathroom so I can get you cleaned up, then you can tell me, okay?"

He nodded and went with her without saying anything. Getting cotton and gauze from the medicine cabinet, she cleaned the cuts and scrapes, then leaned back and scrutinized his face.

"Hmm, it doesn't look so bad now that you're all cleaned up. Want to tell me what happened?"

He shook his head.

"Were you fighting?"

His silence answered her question. "All right. Go upstairs, and when you're ready to tell me what happened, you may come back down." He preceded her into the living room, then started to head upstairs, still wearing his coat. For the first time, she noticed he was clutching his arm.

"Honey, is something wrong with your arm? Why are you holding it like that?"

Collin swallowed loudly and blinked his eyes. "Nothin's wrong with my arm, Mom." Avoiding her eyes, he started to climb the stairs.

"Collin, get back down here and let me see your arm."

Sighing loudly, he turned and came back. He looked at her sadly. "Mom, it's my sleeve. It's ripped almost all the way off."

Leah felt her forehead wrinkle up with worry and consciously smoothed it out. "Let me see."

Obediently, he lifted his arm and showed her the sleeve. It was ripped along the seam the length of the sleeve, but Leah sighed with relief when she saw it could be fixed. The thought of having to spend money on a new coat almost made her ill. Worse still was the reality that if the coat had been ripped beyond repair, she couldn't have bought him a new one.

"I think I can mend it, honey. Don't worry. Now, who were you fighting with?"

"Just one of the guys at school."

"Do you want to tell me why?"

"I dunno. Guess he said some mean stuff. Then he grabbed me."

"What did the teacher do?"

Collin widened his eyes in disbelief. "Mom! I'm ten. A fella doesn't squeal."

Leah reached over and brushed back a lock of dark, ash blond hair from his forehead. When had her baby turned into this boy? When had he begun to think of himself as a fella?

"Okay, Collin. I'll let it go this time. But I don't want you fighting anymore. If you can't avoid it any other way, you'll just have to tell a teacher. If you don't, I'll go to the school and report it myself. Now, put your things away while I stir the potatoes. Supper is almost ready."

Collin stood slowly and started to walk away. Suddenly he spun around and ran back, throwing his arms around Leah's waist. "Mom, can't I just go back to my old school? I hate it here. Those Rosemont kids are nothing but a bunch of stuck-ups."

"Listen to me, Collin. You know Rosemont Academy is a much better school, academically and in every other way. They have up-to-date books and equipment, and it will look so much better on your records. We were blessed that you won that scholarship." She wiped a tear from his cheek. "You'll get used to it. And I'm sure you'll make new friends soon. It's only been a month. Give it time. Won't you do that for me? You know I only want what's best for you."

"Okay, Mom." Collin's expression crashed, and he was obviously trying hard to hold back tears as he headed up the stairs. Leah got up from the sofa with a sigh and walked to the kitchen.

Didn't God even care?

Leah sat in the wooden rocker with her grandmother Collins's sewing basket on the table beside her. Tears of frustration poured down her cheeks and onto Collin's coat. While she'd examined the sleeve earlier, she'd failed to notice the lining inside the coat was ripped to shreds. Beyond repair. What in the world was she going to do? The money from her paycheck added to what little savings she had would have to last them for food and utilities until she could find another job. And there was always the possibility of medical emergencies. She wouldn't dare spend any of their meager funds on a new coat or even fabric for a new lining.

Lord, what am I going to do? It's too cold for Collin to go outside without a warm lining in his coat. The thought was there before she even realized what she was doing. Leah hadn't prayed since Bob died. Why should she? God hadn't seen fit to answer her prayers to keep her husband safe. Apparently He hadn't cared that her son would have to grow up without the love and companionship of his dad. So why bother to pray? Yet, there it was. Leah grew still. Would He answer or would

He ignore her as she'd ignored Him?

Wiping her eyes with both hands, she got up and went to the kitchen to put the kettle on for tea. As she walked back through the dining room with the fragrant brew in her hand, her eye caught a splash of color in the moonlight streaming through the window. She stopped and stared, then inhaled sharply. No, it wouldn't be possible. Or would it?

Leah set the cup on the dining table, and walking over to the window seat, she picked up the patchwork quilt. It was a family heirloom, passed down to her on her wedding day. It was very old and, according to family tradition, had some extremely interesting stories connected with it. She held the quilt close to her and caressed the cool, soft fabric. Did she dare rip it apart? Would her ancestors turn over in their graves at the thought of her pulling out their stitches? Or would they understand that she had no choice?

Still clutching the quilt, she walked back into the living room and sat back down in the rocking chair. Reaching into the loose lining of the sewing basket, she carefully pulled out a slip of paper, now yellowed with age. With a sigh, she read the words she knew by heart.

My dearest son,

This quilt is the story of your family and the love that binds us together as truly as the threads that hold together these pieces of cloth.

I began this quilt as a new bride. I didn't know any more about sewing than I did about being a wife, but I knew about love. The pieces of my wedding dress are in here and form the center block. They are the delicate spring green swatches. It's the same green, by the way, you'll see when the first wildflowers poke their brave stems through the winter-worn earth.

There are a few patches of white in this quilt. They are cut from the shirt your father wore when we got married. Ah, John, what a fine figure he presented that day! I can still see him in my mind, so elegant, so handsome, so sure. . .and so very much in possession of my heart.

The little patches were once your blanket. This was the first earthly fabric that touched your newborn skin. Yellow-spotted flannel looked so warm against your infant skin, like God had poured sun around your tiny body. It was cold the night you were born—so cold the doctor's breath froze midair—but you quickly warmed our hearts.

As our family grew, so did our love—and the quilt. Notice how the stitches get more even and practiced on the outer patches. I was just learning in the center section, but the patches, straggly though they may be, are still holding together after many years of hard use.

Love is like that, John. At first, it's all very new and awkward, but if you're willing to put your heart into it, it'll hold steadfast. There aren't any silk or satin or velvet pieces in this quilt, but to me, its beauty far exceeds the grandest coverlet. Even the littlest, most mundane pieces of life make an extraordinary tapestry when united by love. . .these scraps of love.

Your loving mother,
Brigit Streeter Collins

Leah's heart nearly broke as she read Brigit's letter to her son, John, Leah's own father. She knew what the quilt had meant to her family members. What would they think?

Leah lifted her chin and pressed her lips together. Collin's health and comfort were more important than a quilt, even if it was a family treasure. And inside she had a feeling that if they could see her from heaven, the grand old ladies would agree.

Max Reilly rubbed frost off the ice-cold, second-story window and peered through at the snow-covered schoolyard below, searching for the taunting voices that had drifted to his office. He located the origin of the noise directly below his window and scowled. A cluster of boys in their early teens stood jeering and occasionally shoving a much smaller boy who stood defiantly in the middle of the circle.

Indignation clutched at Max. He wheeled around and headed for the nearest staircase, taking the steps two at a time until he reached the first floor. Max charged through the double front doors and headed for what had now become a scuffle, as the younger boy had somehow found the gumption to defend himself.

Max pressed through the ring of bullies. Their young victim pulled himself off the ground, his face scrunched up in a valiant effort to keep from crying.

"What's going on here?"

At the sight of the angry headmaster, the boys scattered. Max managed to grab two of the culprits, making a mental note of the ones who were running off.

"No, you don't. Whoa there. Stay right where you are, Mason and Carlisle."

Mason had the grace to look ashamed of himself, while he sputtered, "We were only having some fun. We didn't hurt him any."

"Um-hmm. We'll see about that later. You two get yourselves to my office right now. Sit down, and don't move until I get there."

Shaken by the sternness of their usually good-natured headmaster, both boys obeyed instantly, heading for the building.

Max turned to the younger boy, who was clutching his coat tightly around him and shivering.

"Are you hurt, son?" He knelt down in front of the boy, who tried unsuccessfully to wipe the tears away with his bare hands.

"Here, take my handkerchief. I promise it's clean." He grinned. The kid took the hanky and wiped his face, then blew his nose loudly.

"You're Collin Halliday, the new boy, aren't you?"

Collin nodded. Max picked the boy's hat up from the ground and brushed off the snow. "Here, better put this on. It's mighty cold out here. What was the ruckus about?"

Collin took a ragged breath and bit his bottom lip. "I'm not squealing."

"I understand. But bullies like that don't deserve to be protected. If they get by with treating you like this, they'll do it again to other boys, too. You don't want that, do you?"

A frown furrowed the lad's brow. He shook his head. Looking straight into Max's eyes, Collin said firmly, "No, sir, I wouldn't want that. But I just can't squeal."

Max nodded, wondering how to handle the situation. He had witnessed enough to know that the boys were teasing Collin about something, but unless he knew what it was so he could try to take care of it, the teasing was bound to happen again.

The boy stood shuffling from foot to foot, obviously in a hurry to go.

"All right, Collin. You may go now. But I want to discuss this with you further."

"Yes, sir. Thank you, sir."

Max grinned at the look of relief on the boy's face as he turned to go, but his grin faded as Collin's coat fell open, revealing a multicolored lining. *What in the world?* What kind of mother would line her son's coat with something that looked like a patchwork quilt? Surely she could have found something less conspicuous. Maybe she didn't realize how cruel children could sometimes be to anyone different. This was one reason Max had pushed for uniforms—overcoats included. Unfortunately, the board had overruled him on that.

Max knew what it was like to be the victim of bullies. Being the grandson of Templeton Rosemont, the founder of the academy, hadn't sat too easily upon his own small shoulders when he was a lad in this very school. And the fact that his father, James Reilly, had been the chairman of the board hadn't helped, either. He wasn't sure what he could do to help Collin through this tough time in his life, but at least he could take care of the coat situation. That was the easy part.

Pressing his lips together, he walked with determination back toward the building. First, the boy's tormentors had to be dealt with.

Chapter 2

Leah pursed her lips as she searched through her spice rack for cinnamon, cloves, and ginger. Setting each one on the table, she grinned triumphantly at her son. "Yes, I have everything we need for gingerbread men. Hooray!"

She'd already calculated the cost. Butter and sugar were precious commodities and had cost her more than she should have spent, but after the month they'd just endured, she couldn't say no when he'd asked her to make the treat.

Collin let out a war whoop and jumped off the wooden stool. "Call me when they're done! I'm going to play cowboys with Billy."

Leah shook her head and stared after her son, hands on hips, as Collin grabbed his coat and hat, then headed out the back door. So much for this being a joint effort. Apparently baking cookies with Mom was not Collin's top priority on a Saturday morning.

She walked into the pantry and took out the flour, sugar, and other ingredients she would need. She was just stirring the dry ingredients into the creamed mixture when the doorbell rang.

Leah wiped her hands on her apron and went to open the door.

Max Reilly, headmaster of Collin's school, stood there holding his hat in his hands. He looked down at her with the deepest blue eyes she had ever seen.

"Mr. Reilly?" Her voice almost squeaked, and she cleared her throat. "Is something wrong?"

"Mrs. Halliday, I'm sorry to intrude without sending a note home, but I really need to speak to you if you have a few moments."

Leah frowned. "Collin's not in trouble, is he?"

"No, no, nothing like that." He shuffled his hat from one hand to the other. "But there was an incident in school yesterday that I'd like to discuss if you don't mind."

"Of course. Won't you come in? Here, let me take your coat."

He shrugged out of the wool overcoat and handed it over.

Feeling dwarfed by the size of the headmaster, Leah cleared her throat and angled her head to meet his gaze. "I have fresh coffee on. May I offer you a cup?

"Thank you. Just black, please."

He smiled, and Leah's heart nearly stopped. A dimple winked at her from each cheek, and his black hair and thin mustache reminded her of Rhett Butler.

"Is everything all right, Mrs. Halliday?"

Leah blinked. "Huh?" Then she noticed the amused grin. Heat seared her cheeks. Apparently this man was accustomed to making women lose their ability to speak. "Of course. I'll just hang this up and bring in the coffee. I won't be a minute."

"Take your time."

Oh, that smile again.

Leah walked to the coatrack, caressing the material. The quality was evident, and she carefully hung it up, smoothing imaginary creases. She went into the small kitchen and pulled two cups and saucers from the cabinets. Why did some people have so much while others had nothing? The price of Mr. Reilly's coat alone would have paid for every item of clothing Collin needed and then some.

She pushed back the tears and, squaring her shoulders, returned to the living room with the steaming coffee. Mr. Reilly still stood in the middle of the room, looking ill at ease, his hat between his hands.

"I'm so sorry. You must think me awfully rude. Please sit down." She motioned toward the sagging, worn sofa and pushed back niggles of shame that she had nothing better for the headmaster of the elite boys' school to sit on.

With a wistful sigh, she dropped into the wooden rocker across from him. She crossed her ankles gracefully and sat with her hands clasped in her lap, dreading what must be coming. After the week she'd had, it could only be bad news.

"What brings you all the way over here on a Saturday, Mr. Reilly?"

He leaned forward and placed his cup and saucer on the coffee table. "I don't know quite how to tell you this, but there was a scuffle on the playground yesterday. Some of the older boys were teasing Collin and shoving him around a little bit."

"Again?" Indignation bit a hole in Leah. She sat up straight, leveling her gaze at him. "This is the second time in a month! Isn't it your duty to keep this sort of thing from happening?" She stood, took a deep breath, then stepped back and dropped her arm as she realized she had been shaking her finger almost in the headmaster's face. She sighed and gave him an imploring look. "Why would anyone want to tease a kid like Collin? At his other school, everyone liked him. He had dozens of friends."

Suddenly she noticed that he was looking uncomfortable.

He stood up, and then cleared his throat. "Boys can often be cruel. They don't always see things—clothes, for example—as adults do."

Leah's eyes grew wide as understanding dawned. Why hadn't she realized? "His coat?" she whispered. She had been so concerned with keeping her son warm it had never crossed her mind.

"Yes. They were teasing him about the lining. Which is one of the things I wanted to talk to you about." He paused for a moment, then rushed on. "I, uh, took the liberty of purchasing a coat for Collin. Considering—"

A gasp escaped her throat. Her legs felt weak; humiliation burned her cheeks. "I–I appreciate your thoughtfulness, Mr. Reilly, but I am perfectly able to provide for my son. Just because the president of Rosemont Industries believes only the returning soldiers need to provide for their children doesn't mean I am so destitute I would take charity from a stranger."

He blinked in surprise, and a flush washed his handsome face.

Leah's frustration had finally found an outlet, and she planted her hands on her hips. "Perhaps it would be better to teach the boys at your school that just because they come from affluent homes doesn't mean they have the right to bully others who are not so fortunate. Rosemont is a prep school, Mr. Reilly. Prepare them to be good men. That's your job. My job is to teach my son to appreciate what he has. Even if that means wearing an old coat lined with a family heirloom because it was all I had."

Anger fueled her courage, and she walked, straight-backed, to the door. "I am sorry that you had to come all the way over here for nothing. In the future, please confine your attention to Collin's education, and let me take care of matters that are none of your business."

Max's shoes clicked brusquely on the wood floor as he took the bold hint. "Mrs. Halliday, I apologize for offending you. But I do hope you'll reconsider. It's admirable that you want to provide for your son, admirable even that you don't want to accept charity. But sometimes having too much pride is simply foolishness." He gave a curt nod and slipped through the door, which she quickly slammed behind him.

Unable to hang on to composure for another second, Leah threw herself onto the sofa and allowed the tears to flow. Wrenching sobs erupted from a hurting place deep within. When gradually they began to subside, she sat up, wiping furiously at the tears streaming down her face. The audacity of the man. What was he thinking?

She gasped, and her hands flew to her cheeks. Never mind

what he was thinking. What had she been thinking talking to him that way? *Let me take care of matters that are none of your business?* Had she really said that? What had she done? Would he expel Collin after her outburst?

The mantel clock chimed noon. Leah had to pull herself together before Collin came home.

Collin! She'd forgotten all about his gingerbread men.

Trembling and heartsick, she got up and forced her legs to carry her to the kitchen. She had to think. She had to find a way to undo what she had just done.

Max drove home in a state of self-condemnation, despite the fact that she'd thrown him out without giving him his coat back. How could he have been so stupid? Why hadn't he at least asked before buying that coat? He just hadn't thought. He simply saw a need and took care of it, just as he had done so many times before. Looking over Collin's records, he had noticed that Mrs. Halliday was a widow and employed at one of his grandfather's factories. What he hadn't known was that she had been let go. Of course she would be angry. He hadn't meant to be insensitive, but the hurt and humiliation on that lovely face were evidence that he had been.

He sat in his living room later that day trying to figure out how to mend the situation, but all he could think of were those soft brown eyes filled with anguish just before she exploded and let him have it with both barrels. Not that he blamed her.

And he never did get to mention his other idea, which was probably a good thing. He rather doubted she would have wanted him to take her son under his wing. If she had realized his grandfather was the one who signed her compensation check and fired her along with the other women who had held down the fort during the war, she probably would have booted him down the steps rather than simply slamming her door on his back.

All in all, Max, you made a big mess of things.

Still, he couldn't help grinning at her spunk. He'd find a way to make it up to her. Somehow, he'd break through that iron will of hers and convince her to allow Collin to have the coat.

The heavy wooden doors shut behind Leah, and she stood for a moment looking down at the gray-painted concrete floor of the long hall. Lifting her chin and taking a deep breath, she stepped to the first door on the right and entered the school office. A middle-aged woman at the front desk looked up from her work and smiled as Leah came through the door. She eyed the man's coat draped over Leah's arm.

"May I help you?"

"Yes, my name is Leah Halliday. Would it be possible for me to see Mr. Reilly?"

"I'll see if he's available."

Leah turned away, looking at the prints on the wall as the secretary spoke into the receiver.

A door at the back of the room opened, and Max Reilly stood, smiling as though he'd been expecting her, which she knew he hadn't. Leah's heart did a strange flip, and she breathed deeply. *I'm just nervous because I don't want him to expel Collin.*

Still, those eyes were every bit as deep and intense as she remembered.

"Mrs. Halliday. Please come in."

He ushered her into his office and pulled out a chair in front of his desk. She sat stiffly on the leather-cushioned chair as he went around and sat down behind his desk. "You, um, forgot your coat."

"It was thoughtful of you to bring it down here. You could have just sent it with Collin."

"I didn't want him to get it dirty." Leah felt like an utter fool. All those thoughts about his gorgeous eyes and broad shoulders. Silly girlish thoughts about a man so far out of her reach he might as well be Rhett Butler.

"Mr. Reilly. . ."

"Mrs. Halliday. . ."

They both stopped.

"After you, please," Max said.

Leah swallowed and started again.

"Very well, then. I'm here to apologize for my actions on Saturday. You were only being kind, and I overreacted. It was inexcusable of me, and I hope you won't hold it against my son." She gathered a shaky breath. "It would break my heart if he were expelled from Rosemont due to my outburst and—"

"Whoa, there. Wait a minute." Max stood up and walked around the desk. He sat in the chair next to her, giving her a look of earnest appeal. "You did nothing wrong. I'm the idiot who needs to apologize. In fact, I'd intended to do just that at the end of the school day. I had no idea how the gift would affect you. When the boys told me about the other fight and Collin's coat getting torn, I felt it was the responsibility of the school to replace it. This whole thing was my fault for not consulting you first."

She averted her gaze to her hands. "Oh, Mr. Reilly, now I feel even more foolish. I should have given you a chance to explain." She lifted her chin and looked into his eyes. "To be quite honest, when I made the new lining, I wasn't thinking about anything but my son's warmth and health. Until I find another job, I'm afraid new coats aren't in the budget, so if you still have the one you offered us, I would very much like for Collin to have it."

Max's heart lurched as he stared at the brimming eyes of the young woman beside him. He would have given almost anything to remove the embarrassment she was so obviously feeling. He stood up and leaned against the desk.

Clearing his throat, he said, "There's another matter I'd like to talk to you about."

"Yes?" She looked up at him, a question in her eyes.

His heart jumped again. Making a quick decision, he glanced at his watch. "Look, it's about lunchtime. If you don't have plans, could I take you to lunch and talk about it there?"

"I suppose that would be all right. Or I could just come back."

"No, no," he said quickly. "After all, we both have to eat, so why not take care of this other business at the same time?

Nodding, she permitted him to take her arm and guide her toward the door. Max left a few brief instructions with his secretary, then he escorted Leah to his car. They drove to a nearby restaurant.

After giving their order to the waiter, Max sat back in his chair and looked across at Leah Halliday. The artificial light in the room brought out gold highlights in the soft brown waves that caressed her shoulders. And her lovely eyes sparkled like stars. He shook his head, wondering where he was getting such poetic notions.

Clearing his throat, he began. "Mrs. Halliday, I hope what I'm about to propose won't offend you or sound strange in any way."

A little frown appeared between her eyes, and he hurried to continue.

"As you may or may not know, Rosemont Industries has begun a program for the sons of soldiers who died in the war."

"What kind of program?"

At the suspicion in her tone, he hurried on.

"It's simply a way to show appreciation for the sacrifices of our soldiers and their families. Of course there is no way we could ever replace a boy's father, but we can try to do things with him that his dad would do if he were here. Fishing trips, baseball games—those sorts of things. And most important, we provide a listening ear. No matter how close a boy is to his mother and how wonderful a mom she is, sometimes he just needs a man to talk to and hang around with."

"I see." She looked down at the plate that the waiter had just put on the table.

She's being too quiet. I've blown it again.

"I think it sounds like a wonderful idea. And I would love for Collin to have a friend like that." She studied him for a moment. "But I need to think about it. If I do agree to it, I'd be very particular about who my boy went anywhere with."

"Yes, of course you would. A mother can't be too cautious where her child is concerned. Actually, if you allow Collin to take part in the program, I'd be honored if you'd consider me for his companion."

A look of surprise crossed her face, and she looked at him closely as though searching for some ulterior motive.

"That's very kind of you, of course, and I'm sure as the headmaster of Rosemont, your character is above reproach, but I still need to know you better before permitting my son to spend that amount of time alone with you."

"Well, then, how about the three of us doing some things together first?" *Max, you sound like a rambling idiot. She's never going to agree to this.*

"Let me think about it, Mr. Reilly."

"Of course. I'm sure you want to take time to think it over and pray about it."

"I really need to be going, Mr. Reilly. I have an interview this afternoon."

"But you've hardly touched your food."

"I'm not very hungry. Thank you for lunch. I really must go now."

She stood abruptly, nodded her head in his direction, then walked through the busy restaurant and disappeared out the door.

Chapter 3

Max sat hunched over his ancient oak desk, tapping a pencil on the polished surface. His lunchtime conversation with Leah Halliday kept going through his mind—especially her comment about him being a man of good character. He wondered how she'd feel if she knew about Claudia. Pushing his chair back from the desk, he turned sideways and stared unseeing out through the window.

If only he hadn't decided to spend the summer at the family farm that year. If only Jake hadn't chosen that particular summer to spring his new bride on them. Maybe it would have happened anyway, though. Some things were just inevitable, and no matter how many times he replayed that day in his mind, trying to conjure different scenarios, the ending was always the same.

He could sympathize with the H. G. Wells's character in his novel *The Time Machine.* No matter how many times the poor, grief-stricken slob went back to try to save the woman he loved, she died in every instance. Some things were simply going to happen. As though they were predestined. Still, nearly four years later, Max failed to see how God could possibly want such a thing to happen to him.

The disruption of his ordered life was unforgivable. The accusation that had rocked him to the core and caused the eye of suspicion to rest upon his up-to-then stellar character caused him to squirm with humiliation and regret. He tried to push it aside and get on with life, but during quiet, reflective moments, he couldn't help but wonder, how did things go so wrong? If only his brother had never brought his young bride home that summer of 1942. His mind drifted back, the images playing through his mind as though it were yesterday. . .

"Bruiser! Get down!" Max grabbed the Saint Bernard's collar and yanked him back away from the trembling young woman who stood stock still on the circular, stone driveway. His brother, Jake, turned on him with fury.

"Why can't you control that stupid animal? He's going to hurt someone some day!"

Max looked at his brother in surprise.

"Sorry, Jake. He just gets excited when he meets someone new. Don't you, boy?" Max scruffed the dog behind the ears, earning himself a happy half-moan from the Saint Bernard.

He turned to the lovely young woman, who was looking into a tiny mirror she had pulled from her handbag and patting at the platinum blond locks that had strayed from the roll of hair gracing the top of her head. "Especially when it's someone as pretty as your guest."

The woman glanced away from her reflection and snapped her compact closed. She observed Max as though she'd just noticed his presence. Her arched brow rose with sudden interest that sent a warning signal through Max's midsection.

"I apologize for Bruiser's bad manners. I'm Jake's brother, Max, and you are. . . ?"

"She happens to be my wife." Without another word or look, Jake grabbed one of his wife's mink-draped arms and led her up the path to the house. She followed after him, glancing back over her shoulder at Max. Her full lips curved into a bold smile as her gaze traveled the length of him.

Shock jolted through Max like a lightning strike at her shameless perusal, and as heat crept up his neck and face, he stared after them in embarrassed outrage. What had Jake gotten himself into?

The hiss of the radiator brought Max back to the present. He stood and walked to the window, looking down at the boys on the snow-dusted playground. Most of the students seemed to be occupied in a heated game of dodgeball. Their excited laughter rang out, reaching through the closed window. What innocence. If only life could stay that simple. They say a man controls his own destiny. But Max was proof positive it wasn't always so.

Unbidden, thoughts of the past returned, and he found his unwelcome memories taking him back to that last Sunday in the stable. . .

"Well, Sadie, how's that little girl doing today?" Max smiled and patted the roan mare on the nose, then reached down and ran his hand over the flanks of the new foal. "Seems to be a fine little filly you have here, Mama."

Without warning, slender arms encircled his waist from behind. Jerking loose, he whirled around to see Claudia grinning.

"Don't be so shocked, Maxie. I've seen you watching me. You've wanted to hold me in your arms all summer, haven't you?"

"I don't know what you think you've been seeing, Claudia, but I'd as soon hold a boa constrictor." He stepped past her and waited 'til she followed him, then closed the door to Sadie's stall.

For a moment, anger clouded her eyes, but then her red-stained lips puckered into a pouting smile.

"Don't be so mean, Max. You know I really like you a lot."

Suddenly she reached up and wrapped her arms around his neck, smiling seductively.

Stunned by her audacity, Max couldn't move. Obviously taking his inaction as an invitation, Claudia stood on her tiptoes and inched closer to him. "You like me a little bit, don't you, Maxie?"

"No!" his mind screamed. And just as he was about to throw her from him, she pressed her lips against his in a very unsisterly kiss.

That's when Jake had walked in, and of course he believed every outrageous lie Claudia had come up with. Finally, he had accused Max, before the whole family, of attacking his wife. His parents had not believed it for a moment. Claudia's character had become fairly obvious to them by that time, but a huge uproar arose among the rest of the family, some of whom were quite eager to believe any piece of gossip they heard. Worst of all, somehow word got around their society set, bringing shame to the entire family.

Earlier in the summer, Max had been offered a position helping with war supplies, so shortly after the scandal arose, he left for Washington, turning down the offer of a teaching position at Rosemont Academy. He hadn't been back to the farm since, and he only visited his parents in their Chicago mansion when he knew Jake and Claudia wouldn't be there. By the time he returned from Washington, the gossip mongers had moved on to other, juicier, more recent scandals, and the incident seemed to have been forgotten by everyone but the family.

His father had helped Max to acquire the position of headmaster at the academy, which had always been his desire, so he had managed to create a stable and happy life, even though his brother Jake still thought the worst. Max avoided him and Claudia as much as possible.

Max shoved back the unwelcome memories. He directed his attention once more to the playground and noticed Collin sitting alone on a bench, staring wistfully at some boys playing dodge ball. Max's heart went out to the lonely looking child. He had to think of a way to convince the nervous mother that he would make a good companion for Collin. Suddenly an idea came to him. He returned to his desk and, pulling out a sheet of school stationery, he wrote a short note inviting Leah and her son to attend church services with him on Sunday morning. He would send the note home with Collin after school.

In the meantime, maybe he could get Collin off that bench for the rest of recess.

Leah turned the skeleton key and opened her front door. She

had an hour before Collin would be home. Dinner would be a simple meal of leftover meatloaf and vegetables, so all she really had to do was make a salad to go with it.

She put her coat and hat in the closet and made a cup of tea. Sitting at the kitchen table enjoying the steaming, spicy drink, she thought over her afternoon.

After leaving the restaurant, she had gone straight to her appointment at Seville Toy Company. The interview had gone fairly well, but Leah wasn't at all confident. Mr. Monroe had seemed impressed with her shorthand, but her typing wasn't nearly as fast or accurate as it had been four years ago. The factory job at Rosemont had paid so much better than any of the secretarial positions that she hadn't given a second thought to leaving her skills behind. Now she wondered if that had been wise.

Although Mr. Monroe had promised to consider her application, Leah wasn't sure how she would compare to others with more recent experience, especially with so many being let go from the factories. Jobs were scarce. It would be a miracle for her to land this one. Oh, if only she could come up with enough money to start her own bakery! But that would take an even bigger miracle. And Leah just didn't believe in miracles anymore.

"Mom! I'm home!"

Leah jumped up from the table. "I'm in the kitchen, Collin." How in the world had an hour passed by so quickly?

Leah stood and took the meatloaf and vegetables from the ice box, then stopped and stared at Collin as he came in with a big grin on his face.

"Look, Mom. Mr. Reilly said the school owed me this coat because of my other one getting ripped. He said he talked to you about it. Was it okay that I took it?" Leah looked at the navy blue wool coat that Collin was proudly displaying. Mr. Reilly and Rosemont Academy had obviously spared no expense in replacing the old one.

"Yes, of course. Now, come here and give me a hug."

The boy obliged with a squeeze that almost took Leah's breath away. She laughed and held him away from her.

"Let me get a good look at the new coat. It's very nice, Collin. Much nicer than your old one."

He smiled widely, then suddenly the grin faded and he headed back into the living room, coming back a moment later with a bag containing his old coat.

"I really like this one too, Mom. You did a swell job fixing it. I'll just keep wearing it. I don't need the new one."

Leah looked at her son standing there bravely, willing to sacrifice the new coat to spare her feelings. What could she say to convince him it was all right to keep it?

"You know, Collin, if you don't mind, I'd sort of like to remove that lining and repair Grandma's quilt."

Leah's heart lurched at the look of relief on her boy's face. His expression told her more than any words just how difficult it had been for him to wear the mended coat.

"Sure, I'll just wear the new one then. Isn't it a swell coat? Mr. Reilly's really swell, too. He's an okay guy, not just a headmaster. He came out on the playground at recess and judged us in some races. I almost won the last one." The statement was spoken in such awe-filled tones that Leah struggled to keep from laughing.

"Oh, I almost forgot, Mom—Mr. Reilly sent you something."

"He did, huh?" The thought of "Mr. Reilly" sending her anything raised her defenses. Perhaps she hadn't made it clear that she and Collin weren't charity cases.

Collin reached into his pocket and pulled out a small envelope, which he handed to her.

"Thanks, son. Now run upstairs and change out of your school clothes. I'll just see what Mr. Reilly has to say and get dinner on the table."

The boy headed for the stairs, running.

"Don't forget to wash up," Leah called after him.

She looked curiously at the envelope, hesitating briefly before tearing it open. She nibbled on her bottom lip as she glanced over the note. An invitation to church? They hadn't been to church in years. Not since Bob died. She wandered back into the kitchen, her mind playing scenes of the little wooden church she had attended with her husband before the war had ruined everything.

As she prepared a salad and heated up the leftovers, she thought about her luncheon conversation with the handsome headmaster. Sure, she had wanted to get to know him better before Collin spent time alone with him, but. . .church?

As they ate their supper, Leah glanced over at her son.

"Mr. Reilly has invited us to go to church with him on Sunday. What do you think?"

Collin swallowed a mouthful of milk and grinned at her.

"That would be great, Mom. I kind of miss going to Sunday school."

"You do? Why haven't you said anything before?"

"Well, I sort of started to once. But you got a funny kind of look, so I changed my mind."

"Oh, Collin, I'm so sorry." What kind of a mother was so easily read by her ten-year-old son? "Well, I guess we'll go then."

"Really, Mom? Wow, okay by me. Maybe we could go get a hamburger or something after church, too."

"Now, Collin, Mr. Reilly didn't invite us to dinner, and you know we can't afford to be spending our money on hamburgers right now. Don't say anything about dinner to Mr. Reilly. You promise me now."

"Oh, okay, Mom."

The dejected look on her son's face brought a choking sadness to her heart. She knew it wasn't really the hamburger he was yearning for but the male attention.

"Hey, sport, I've got an idea. How about if we invite Mr. Reilly here for dinner?"

"Really?" Collin's shining eyes were evidence that she had been right.

"Sure, but you have to help me decide what to cook. Deal?"

"Deal!" He reached a hand over the table to shake.

"I already know what you can fix for dessert, Mom. How about some of your doughnuts? All the guys around here say yours are better'n the ones at the doughnut shop."

"Better than, Collin, and I don't know about doughnuts for a dinner dessert."

"Okay, then. Chocolate cake. Everybody likes chocolate cake, and yours is the best, Mom."

"I'm afraid I just don't have enough sugar to make it."

Collin's expression crashed. "Aw." He kicked at the ground.

Leah's heart went soft. "Listen, kiddo. I think I have just enough sugar left for about a half batch of molasses cookies. I know it's not chocolate cake, but what do you say I whip some of those up?"

His eyes brightened. "Swell!"

"Good. Now if you're through eating, you can help me with the dishes. Then I'll write a note to Mr. Reilly while you take your bath."

Max couldn't keep the smile off his face as he read Leah Halliday's note for the third time. Not only had she accepted his invitation to church, but she had extended her own invitation to dinner. That much more time to start building that relationship with Collin. But he had to admit to himself that wasn't the only reason for his elation. The lovely Leah's deep brown eyes and pensive smile had haunted his dreams all night. He'd have to guard his feelings a little better. He certainly didn't need any involvements. Not after what he'd been through. All he needed was a hint of scandal, and even his grandfather's good name wouldn't be enough to keep his job for him. And being headmaster of Rosemont Academy meant everything to him. His heart was here, with the education and upbringing of these boys.

Chapter 4

A soft glow enveloped the sanctuary where Leah sat straight-backed, holding tightly to Collin's hand. The last strains of "Amazing Grace" faded, and the purple-robed choir members seated themselves in the choir loft. The elderly pastor walked to his place behind the pulpit, opened the enormous black Bible that lay there, and smiled out at the congregation.

The pastor greeted the congregation and began to say something about the new addition to the building, but Leah was having trouble hearing him through the loud beating of her heart.

"Mom!" Her son's desperate whisper drew her attention, and she looked down and realized she was gripping his hand too tightly. She gave him a tremulous smile and released it.

"Sorry," she mouthed silently.

"It's okay," he mouthed back, grinning.

She glanced over at Max, who sat at the end of the oak pew on Collin's other side. He smiled, then turned his attention back to the pastor.

Leah closed her eyes and took a deep breath. *Calm yourself down, Leah,* she lectured herself silently. *It's just a church service. You've been to hundreds of them.*

She realized suddenly that everyone was standing, and she quickly rose to her feet and bowed her head as the pastor began to pray.

"Our heavenly Father, first of all we would like to thank You for all the many blessings You have bestowed upon us. Thank You for supplying our daily needs and for guiding us in our walk on this earth. We also thank You, Father, for the boys that You have brought safely home to us. It is such a blessing to see these beloved faces that have been absent from our midst. But, Lord, some of our brave boys didn't come back. We can only accept Your will and ask You to comfort their families and friends. Help us to remember, Lord, they are with You in a better place. . . ."

Is Bob with You, God? Is he really with You? Will we see him again some day? I can hardly remember what he looks like. When I think of him, I see a tall, handsome man in a blue suit standing by me in our wedding picture. But I can't see the twinkle in his eyes or his smile anymore. He loved You. And he taught me to love You, too. But I've strayed away. I can't remember the last time I read my Bible. Does he know about that, God? Does he know I'm not only forgetting him, but that I've just about forgotten You, too?

Leah started as people began to take their seats again. She sat down, wiping tears from her eyes.

The aroma of roasted chicken filled the kitchen as Leah took the lid off the roasting pan. The potatoes were browned to perfection. The salad was already on the table. She put the chicken on a platter and surrounded it with the potatoes and carrots. After placing it on the dining room table, she stepped back and looked everything over one more time. *Perfect.*

Max and Collin didn't even hear her come into the living room. They were stretched out on the floor putting together a model airplane that Leah had unsuccessfully attempted to help Collin with. From the looks of things, it was pretty much completed.

"Hey, anyone hungry?"

Two heads turned and smiled up at her at the same time. Leah blinked hard in an attempt to stop the tears that were rising unbidden to her eyes. Collin's face was radiant. Leah hadn't realized how much he had missed male companionship.

They both scrambled to their feet.

"I'll say. I'm starving." Collin headed for the dining room, then stopped. "Oops, guess I'd better go wash up."

"Me, too." Max grinned and followed.

Leah shook her head and laughed softly.

The conversation at dinner was light and fun. Leah loved watching the camaraderie between Mr. Reilly and Collin. The boy glowed. It was obvious he had found a new hero.

"Collin, I'd say you are about the luckiest young man in Chicago," quipped Max.

"Why's that, Mr. Reilly?"

"Because, you're mother is the best cook in Chicago, that's why."

Leah blushed and started to speak, but Collin interrupted.

"Yeah, but if you think this stuff's good, wait until you taste the dessert."

Leah shook her head as she watched the two of them clean up a plate of molasses cookies.

Finally, Max gave an exaggerated groan and pushed back from the table.

"You were right, Collin. I've never tasted cookies that good before. Okay, point me to the kitchen sink."

"That's not necessary, Mr. Reilly," Leah said quickly. "I'll just clean up in here while you and Collin finish the model."

"No way, lady. You worked hard preparing this delicious meal, and this fellow pays for his supper. Tell you what—I'll wash, you dry." His eyes danced as he tossed her a smile that just about took her breath away.

"Well, all right, if you insist." Leah stood up and started to clear the dishes from the table. She stopped suddenly and stared as Max removed his coat. Muscles rippled beneath the white dress shirt as he reached forward to hang the jacket on his chair. Leah felt heat rising to her face as he turned and saw her watching him.

His eyes deepened to near blue-black as he stared at her. She stood mesmerized as his hand reached out toward her hair. Leah jerked around quickly and picked up another plate, almost dropping it. She cleared her throat, hoping she could speak normally. "Kitchen sink is right this way, sir."

After Leah filled the dishpan with hot, sudsy water, she handed Max an apron, which he donned with a flourish.

He turned around, flashing a grin at her over his shoulder.

"Afraid you're going to have to tie this. I'm not used to wearing aprons."

Shaking her head firmly, she said, "No way, Mr. Reilly. Your arms can reach behind to those ties quite nicely."

He laughed heartily and tied the apron, then plunged his hands into the suds.

After the dishes were done, they joined Collin, who had disappeared to the living room when he heard the word *dishes.*

Leah watched wistfully as Max helped Collin with the model. It would be wonderful for Collin to have a father. And a husband for Leah wouldn't be bad, either. Especially if that husband was someone like Max Reilly.

He left late in the afternoon, and as Leah followed him onto the wide front porch, he apologized for staying so long.

"Oh no, don't apologize, please. It was so lovely to have you here. I mean for Collin's sake. And, Mr. Reilly, if your kind offer still stands, I see no reason to object to your spending time with my son. He obviously likes you, and you seem to be very comfortable with him."

Max's eyes lit up, and he smiled broadly. "I'm so happy to hear that. Collin is a great kid. I'm going to enjoy this as much as he does."

They stood looking at each other silently for a moment, then Max smiled again.

"By the way, now that I'm going to be a friend, and not just the headmaster, don't you think you could drop the 'mister' and call me Max?"

"Well, I suppose that would be all right. Then I guess you should call me Leah."

He took her hand. "Thank you for a delicious dinner, Leah, and a wonderful afternoon. I can't remember when I've had such a good time."

Leah watched as Max's car pulled away from the curb. There was no denying the attraction there. Her heart raced every time they were in the same room together.

Leah sighed. She had to think about acquiring a job and taking care of Collin. She didn't have time for distractions. Even if this particular distraction did have the most appealing smile she had ever seen.

She went inside and sat on the worn, overstuffed sofa. Her Bible lay on the side table, where she'd set it after this morning's service. The sermon today had touched her in a way she hadn't felt in years. The words of hope and love that had come forth from the gentle lips of the pastor had pierced her heart as words of condemnation never would have.

Leah reached for the small, black book and opened it. Now where was the passage Reverend Hollingsworth had read that morning? *Romans,* she thought.

"Hi, Mom. Hey, are you reading your Bible? I've been reading mine, too. I looked up the part that the preacher was reading today. I wrote it down."

"Oh, Collin. I'm so glad. It was in Romans, wasn't it? Can you tell me the chapter number?

"Sure. Romans, chapter 8. Starting with verse 38."

"Thanks, honey."

Leah leafed through the pages until she found the appropriate verses.

As she read the words of Paul the apostle, hope began to take birth in her heart for the first time since she had received the news about Bob's death: "For I am persuaded, that neither death, nor life, nor angels, nor principalities, nor powers, nor things present, nor things to come, nor height nor depth, nor any other creature, shall be able to separate us from the love of God which is in Christ Jesus our Lord."

Max whistled a popular tune as he drove away from the Halliday home. He had been telling the truth when he'd told Leah he couldn't remember when he'd had such a good time. Collin was a joy to be with. He wondered what it would be like to have a son like him. And a wife like Leah to come home to every day. His eyes gleamed as he recalled the little dimple that appeared next to her mouth when she smiled. And how he would love to run his fingers through the smooth, silky waves that hugged her shoulders.

Suddenly Max sat up straighter and gripped the steering wheel. What was he thinking? He needed to be careful not to get too close to her. She was bound to start asking questions. He couldn't afford for the scandal to rear its ugly head again.

He pulled into his driveway and sat without making a move to open the door.

Would the shadow of that incident with Claudia haunt him for the rest of his life? Would he have to live with this fear hanging over him forever? Why should he have to continue to suffer for something he hadn't done?

Not only could he not pursue a relationship with Leah, but if the scandal resurfaced, she wouldn't let him near Collin. He had to do something. He hit his head against the steering wheel in frustrated agony. But what?

Making a sudden decision, he fired up the engine. He had tried, unsuccessfully, to talk to Jake about this before, but Jake wouldn't even speak to him, much less listen to reason. Of course, he was going to believe his wife over his brother. Max couldn't help but wonder, though, how Jake could be so blind to Claudia's lack of morals.

He drove through the gate and parked in front of the huge brick mansion. His father would object to his not pulling into the garage, but he didn't plan to be here that long anyway.

He found his father in the library polishing a rifle from his collection of antiques.

Max stood just inside the door, inhaling the familiar smell of leather and old books.

"Well, Max, to what do I owe the honor of this rare appearance?"

"Sorry, Dad. I've been busy lately. Is that a new one?" He walked over and put his hand on his dad's shoulder.

James Reilly held up the rifle by the stock, looking at it proudly.

"I have a certificate of authenticity stating that it belonged to Annie Oakley. It's a rifle she used in Buffalo Bill's Wild West Show."

"Hmm, interesting. Where's Mother?"

"She should be here. So busy running around to her charity functions, she forgets charity begins at home. I could use a little of her tender loving care myself." He ran his hands through his thinning hair in obvious frustration.

Max laughed. Everyone knew that Celia Rosemont Reilly doted on her husband and spoiled him rotten.

"Now, Dad, you just can't stand it if she's away from you for an hour. Admit it."

He laughed as his father threw him an indignant glance and placed the rifle back in the oak cabinet.

"Ring for Helen, son. I could use some strong coffee. How about you?"

Only after they had settled into chairs by the fireplace with hot drinks in their hands did his father turn to him with expectation written across his lined face. "All right, Max. Out with it."

Max buried his head in his hands and moaned.

Taking a deep breath, he looked up.

"It's the thing with Claudia. I have to get out from under this, Dad."

A shadow of pain crossed the older man's face, and he surveyed his son. "I don't think anyone believes that old story anymore."

"Some do. You know they do. And most important, Jake believes it. As long as he believes it of me, believes that I could do such as thing. . .well, his attitude gives credence to it. Not just to those who want to believe the worst. It puts a niggling of doubt even in the minds of people who don't want to think it of me."

A log fell in the fireplace, and Max stared at the sparks as they danced and popped around the blazing wood.

"Dad, I was thinking. Do you suppose it would do any good for me to try to talk to Jake again? Surely after all this time, he has gained some insight into Claudia's character."

"They've gone on vacation. I thought you knew. They left on a riverboat last month for New Orleans and places unknown. Claudia's idea, I'd say. Jake never did like to travel. He wanted to take an airplane, but Claudia is afraid to fly. And besides, riverboats are more interesting." He snorted and curled his lips in derision.

"Well, that's that then."

"What brought this on all of a sudden? I thought you had put it behind you. The board knows all about the situation. You don't need to worry about your job, if that's what's bothering you."

"They know?" A sense of shame invaded Max at the very thought of the board members of the school knowing about the tawdry accusations against him.

"Of course they know. Did you think they had their heads in the sand? They, however, also know me and know that I wouldn't try to cover up for you if it had been true. So stop worrying."

"Well, there are a few other reasons. . . . Oh, never mind. I just want my name cleared."

His father gave him a hard look. "It's a woman, isn't it? Who is she? Why haven't you brought her home to meet us?"

"It's not like that, Dad. She's just a friend." He squirmed

in his chair. "The mother of one of the boys at the academy. His father was killed in the war." He smiled as he thought of Collin. "You should see that little fellow. He's great." He ran his hand through his hair. "And she's raised him by herself since he was six."

James Reilly took a sip from his cup, peering at Max over the brim. "I see."

And Max knew that his father did see, way too much.

Chapter 5

I'll miss you, Janie. Are you sure there's not something else you can do?"

"I wish there was. But I'm scared, Leah." Janie's forehead wrinkled, and she bit her lip. "My rent is due in two days, and it would take nearly everything I have left to pay it." Her pink-tipped fingers raked through her hair, and she shrugged her shoulders and smiled sadly. "The last job possibility I had in sight just flew the coop. And believe me, I've pounded the pavement every day."

Leah took a sip of her tea and nodded thoughtfully.

"Yes. Me, too." Leah gave her friend a commiserating smile. "But, Janie, you could live here until something opens up. I have an extra bedroom, you know." Actually, she had been tossing around the idea of renting it out, but Janie didn't have to know that. "So, how about it?"

Janie shook her head. "Thanks, honey. That's sweet of you. But I need to go home while I have money for train fare." She smiled brightly. "Anyway, Dad can always use help in the store."

Leah sighed. "Don't you hate change? Just think how it was a few short months ago. You and Susie and me. The Three Musketeers together forever." She laughed sadly. "Now, Susie is going back to Dallas, and you to Missouri. I'm going to be so lonely."

Janie cut her gaze to Leah, and her lips curved in a teasing smile. "Oh, I don't think you're going to be all that lonely. How are things going with the handsome headmaster? Susie told me you've been spending a lot of time with him."

Leah felt warmth rise to her cheeks. She was going to clobber Susie.

"Really, Janie. Susie is jumping to conclusions. Of course, Max is here quite often because he's spending time with Collin. It's part of the Rosemont program, you know, the one I told you about."

"Um-hmm. And the roses over there? Did *Max* send those to Collin? Are they part of the program also?" She lifted her eyebrows and grinned.

Leah burst out laughing. "Oh, you. All right. I suppose we have been seeing each other some. Actually, he took me to dinner a few nights ago."

"Without Collin?"

"Yes, without Collin. But only because Collin was spending the night with a friend from his Sunday school class."

Suddenly Leah frowned. "Janie, I'm a little bit bothered about something."

Janie, ever the best friend, grew suddenly serious, her eyes alert. "What?"

"It's probably nothing. After all, he has a right to his privacy." Leah paused as anxiety arose as a knot in her stomach. "It's just that every time I ask anything about his family or prior jobs or anything like that, he manages to change the subject." She picked up her spoon and began to tap it against the rim of the saucer. "I'm sure it's okay. After all, a prestigious school like Rosemont surely wouldn't have hired him without a thorough investigation into his personal life. But. . ."

"Hmm. Maybe he's just a private person. Or maybe he's ashamed of his family." Janie slammed her teacup down and snapped her fingers. "Oh, wait, I've got it. His father drinks, and his mother beats him."

Leah exploded into laughter. She was going to miss Janie so much.

After they said tearful good-byes, Leah sat down in her rocker to mend some of Collin's shirts. He'd become so happy and vibrant since Max had taken an interest in him. It was like he had suddenly come to life. There hadn't been a lot of outdoor things they could do because of the cold March winds, but Max had promised fishing trips and baseball games in the spring and summer. In the meantime, he was teaching Collin to play tennis. It never would have occurred to Leah that Collin would be interested in tennis, but under Max's tutelage, the boy was getting quite good at the game.

Still Leah felt she had to be careful where her son was concerned. If only she could be absolutely certain that Max was as upright and responsible as he seemed. It would break Collin's heart if it proved otherwise. And Leah had to be honest with herself. It would just about break hers, too.

Max didn't know what he was going to do about Leah. He was falling in love with her. He couldn't get away from that fact. And she seemed to care for him, too. He hadn't been able to resist pursuing a relationship with her that was fast becoming more than friendship. Yet he knew it was hopeless unless he got the situation concerning Claudia settled. Once and for all.

Leah was already asking questions that he couldn't answer without revealing too much. He hadn't even told her yet that his mother was heiress to the entire Rosemont holdings. He knew he had to at least come clean about that. He wished now he had told her from the beginning. It had been foolish to keep it from her.

He had hoped to speak to his brother by now, but Jake and Claudia were back in New Orleans again after traipsing all over the southern states. Apparently Claudia had been enjoying the antebellum mansions of Georgia, Mississippi, Louisiana, and Alabama and had managed to somehow charm her way into southern society. Now, it seemed she was determined to take part in her first Mardi Gras experience.

Max's lips twisted in a wry grin. Poor Jake. That sort of thing was so contrary to his nature. A picture of the young Jake appeared in Max's mind. A picture of Jake shut up in the library with a stack of books on the floor beside him. Max could hardly ever get him outside long enough to go fishing or play a game of catch. His beloved books were always calling him. It was during a rare period of restlessness on Jake's part that he had met Claudia and fallen hard.

Max had no doubt that his brother was smitten soundly. He couldn't help feeling sorry for him. The brothers had been close once. But when Claudia entered the picture, Jake seemed blind to everything but her dubious charms. His eyes were almost certain to be opened one day, and Collin didn't relish the thought of his younger brother getting hurt.

One Sunday in mid-April when he was driving over to pick up Leah and Collin for church, Max made a sudden decision to come clean about his family connections. He hoped Leah wouldn't be too upset. After all, he hadn't actually lied to her; he had just failed to mention a few things. *Yeah, sure, Max,* he thought. *That's going to impress her.*

Leah came to the door looking like she had just stepped off the silver screen. She flashed him a million-dollar smile that nearly made him trip over his feet.

He smiled warmly back and reached for her hand.

"Hi, Max!" Collin scooted past his mother and grabbed the outstretched hand, giving it a hearty shake.

"Hey, sport. Good to see you." Max sent a sideways smile toward Leah, who attempted to hide an amused grin as she headed toward the car.

The service was inspiring, and Max was pleased to notice that Leah seemed every bit as involved in it as he was. In the beginning, he had wondered at the way she seemed to hold herself back from entering in, but lately she seemed to enjoy the services more. They had even spent a few Sunday afternoons discussing the sermon they had just heard.

As Max and Leah stood in the vestibule visiting with a few people after church, Collin and his friend Tommy came hurrying up.

"Mom, is it okay if I go home with Tommy? His mom and dad say it's okay with them."

"And my dad even said he'll take Collin home later if it's okay with you, Mrs. Halliday," Tommy chimed in.

"Well, I think so, but let me go talk to them first." Leah smiled at the boys, and turning to Max, she excused herself, then headed over to where Tommy's parents stood. After a short, reassuring conversation, she headed back to Max.

As Max watched her walking toward him, he decided to take advantage of the opportunity to have his talk with Leah. A few minutes later, as he opened the car door and waited for her to slide into the seat, he said, "If you don't have plans for the afternoon, I'd like to take you out to dinner."

"That would be lovely."

"Oh!" He snapped his fingers. "Would you mind if I ran back inside for a moment? I need to make a fast telephone call."

Leah looked at him in surprise but shook her head.

After making the phone call, he returned to the car and smiled as he slid in behind the steering wheel. "Sorry about that."

As he passed by their usual restaurant without stopping, Leah threw him a surprised look.

He smiled. "I thought we'd go somewhere different today."

When Max pulled the car into the drive of a very expensive restaurant, she looked at him in concern but didn't say anything.

He gave his keys to the attendant and offered his arm to Leah.

An elderly doorman opened the door for them, and Max motioned for her to step inside.

She did so, but then turned to him with a decidedly worried look on her face. "Max!" she whispered. "You can't—"

"Good evening, Mr. Reilly. It's nice to see you again. It's been too long." The man who spoke was beaming from ear to ear. "Your table is ready. Please come this way."

Leah sat in silence while Max placed their order. The cloth on the table was gleaming white linen, and the settings were silver, crystal, and fine china. Even though it was only noon, a small orchestra played behind palm trees at the end of the room. What was he thinking? She was sure dinner for two here would cost a small fortune. She didn't want to embarrass him by saying anything about it, but. . .

"Max," she said softly, "I wouldn't have minded eating at our usual place. They have excellent food."

"Yes, they do. But I have something to tell you, and I thought this would be the perfect setting. And, Leah, I promise I'm not going to be destitute for the next six months, so enjoy yourself and don't worry about it." He reached over and took her hand for a moment, his eyes warm and affectionate and alive with something else. Uncertainty perhaps?

The food was delicious, and Leah tried to enjoy it, but she was too nervous wondering what he wanted to talk to her about. They both declined dessert, and as they sat with coffee,

Leah looked at Max questioningly.

He took a deep breath.

"Leah, I'm not sure how to begin, but I need to tell you who I am."

She sat up stiffly. Uh-oh, here it came. She knew he was too good to be true.

"Do you mean you're not Max Reilly?" she demanded.

A startled look crossed his face.

"Oh no! I am indeed Max Reilly. I suppose I should have said I need to tell you who my family is." He took a nervous breath, then said quickly, "Leah, I'm a Rosemont on my mother's side of the family."

Leah sat waiting for him to go on. When he didn't speak, she realized he was waiting for a response from her. "Do you mean as in Rosemont Industries, Rosemont Academy, Rosemont Gas and Oil?"

He nodded.

"So your mother is. . .what? A cousin or something?"

"Well, no, not exactly. As a matter of fact, my mother is Templeton Rosemont's daughter."

Leah opened her mouth and tried to speak, finally managing to choke the words out. "What? You're Templeton Rosemont's grandson, and you're just now getting around to telling me?"

"Leah, I didn't tell you in the beginning because there wasn't really any reason to at the time, and I don't like to spread it around. Then later. . .well, I wasn't sure how to tell you, especially since my grandfather's factory had let you go."

Suddenly Leah felt a giggle rising up from her chest to her

throat, and she coughed to try to cover it up, but to no avail. She chortled with glee while he sat and stared at her as though she had lost her mind.

Finally, she managed to get control of herself.

"Oh, Max, I'm sorry. It's just such a relief. I knew you were holding something back, and I was afraid you had some deep, dark secret. And all the time, you were just afraid I'd be mad at you because your grandfather had fired me."

"Well. . ."

"Don't worry about it, Max. I don't hold you responsible at all."

They left the restaurant shortly afterward, and Max took her hand at the door and said good-bye, promising to see her on Tuesday after school when he and Collin had a tennis date.

Leah felt as though she were walking on clouds the rest of the day, and after Collin had gone to sleep that night, she sat in her grandmother's old overstuffed chair and thought over the day.

Suddenly she closed her eyes.

"Father, I'm so sorry for all my doubts. Please forgive me and help me not to ever fall into unbelief again. And, Lord, thank You so much for clearing this thing up about Max. Because I guess You know what I've not been admitting even to myself. I've fallen in love with him."

Chapter 6

Mr. Reilly, do you wish to dictate those letters about the graduation exercises now?"

Max looked up from the stack of applications on his desk. His secretary stood in the doorway with her steno pad and pencil in hand.

He smiled. "Sorry, Edna. I was supposed to do that this morning, wasn't I?"

She gave him an uncertain smile. "Shall I come back later?"

"No, no, they need to be mailed out right away." He waved her to a chair. "Please sit down, and we'll do that now."

He shoved the applications aside and took his notes for the letters out of the top drawer.

Get ahold of yourself, Maxwell. You're slipping. The thought caused him to exhale loudly, and Edna frowned at him. Max couldn't blame her. She wasn't used to him being absent-minded or stressed. He needed to pull himself together.

With an apologetic smile tugging at his lips, he shrugged. "You still have last year's letter on file, don't you?"

"Of course. But—"

"Good! Just use that one, and incorporate these additional notes, please, if you don't mind." He held out his pages of notes to her.

"No, I don't mind, Mr. Reilly." She stood and took the notes, then left the room. But Max couldn't fail to see the confusion in her eyes.

He walked over to the window and looked out. Some of the trees were beginning to bud. A sign of the approaching spring. But he knew that winter could just as easily come rushing back.

His dinner with Leah on Sunday had started out like spring, too. Fresh and joyful. But her words, laughingly spoken, kept ringing through his ears. *I thought you had some deep, dark secret or something.* He hadn't missed the relief in her tone of voice. Apparently she had perceived that everything wasn't as it should be with him. Now he feared he was deeper in the quagmire of deception than before. And he knew Leah didn't deserve to be a part of it.

He had to get this mess straightened out before Leah and Collin got hurt. He supposed he should just back out of their lives. It would probably be the kindest thing to do. But he couldn't. His feelings for both of them were too strong for that now. More than anything, he wanted them for his own. He wanted to be a husband to Leah and a father to Collin. But could that ever happen? Could he ask them to share his life when a shadow hung over his good name? Would God in His mercy show him a way out of this pit?

Max had always believed that God loved him and would take care of the things concerning him. Even when the incident had first happened and the unjust accusations had caused turmoil in his life, he had never doubted God. But now. . . *Why, God? Why?* For the first time in his life, God seemed far away, and no comforting words came to his mind. In sudden grief and frustration, Max doubled up his fist and hit the wall hard, not even feeling the pain.

Leah's high heels clicked against the sidewalk as she almost danced up to her front door. Finally, after all these months of worry, she had a job. Even better, her dream job. The salary was a little lower than she had hoped for, but the owner of the bakery had promised a raise after her initial training. Mrs. Crumply was a widow in her early sixties, and she needed someone who could take over the major part of the pastry making as well as learn the business end. This was just the sort of opportunity Leah had been dreaming of.

God was so good to her. First to clear up her concern about Max and now to provide a real job again. She couldn't wait to tell Collin.

She spent the rest of the day doing laundry and baking cookies. She might as well get all the practice she could. She grinned as she sat at the table sampling one that was warm from the oven.

The door slammed, nearly sending her through the roof.

"Oops! Sorry, Mom!"

Leah grinned at the sound of Collin's voice. Hurrying into

the living room, she grabbed him in a tight hug and whirled him around in circles.

"Mom! What are you doing?" Collin stumbled out of her grasp and stared at her with a frown that tried to hide the smile lurking behind it.

Leah laughed and tousled his hair.

"I have a job, Collin. A really good job. Isn't it wonderful?"

"Wow, Mom. That's terrific. Where you going to be working?"

"Crumply's Bakery. Can you believe it?"

Collin leaned his head back and let out a whistle through his teeth.

"Swell, Mom. Peachy keen. When do you start? Do you get to bring home free stuff?"

"I start tomorrow morning. And we didn't talk about free stuff. But there are cookies on the counter. Get changed while I pour you some milk. Then you'd better get your homework done before Mr. Reilly gets here."

She knew Max planned to take Collin out for hamburgers after their tennis practice. This had become a Tuesday ritual. She smiled softly as she poured the milk and put two cookies on a plate.

The doorbell rang just as Collin was closing his notebook, and he jumped up and ran to the door, throwing it open.

"Hi, come on in," Leah called out from the chair where she sat darning socks.

Max walked in with his hand on Collin's shoulder. His eyes twinkled when he saw what she was doing.

"Boys are hard on socks, aren't they?" he queried.

"Well, this one is." They shared a knowing look, and both laughed.

"Guess what, Mr. Reilly? Mom's got a new job. She starts tomorrow. And it's in a bakery." Collin licked his lips and rubbed his stomach, grinning widely.

Leah and Max burst out laughing.

"I can see this is a job after your own heart, Collin. Congratulations, Leah."

"Thank you, sir. I've been walking on cloud nine all day."

"How about joining Collin and me for hamburgers later to celebrate?"

"That sounds very tempting, but I have ironing to do. I need to get it all done up since I'm starting back to work tomorrow."

"Okay, Mom. We'll see you later. We need to go now." Collin's not-so-subtle hint got through to Max, and he laughed.

"You're absolutely right, sport. Let's go. See you later, Leah. We should be back by six. Is that all right with you?"

She nodded, and he flashed her a smile and headed out the door with Collin.

Leah leaned back in the porch swing and covered a wide yawn with the back of her hand.

Max sent her a crooked smile. "Am I boring you?"

"Oh, sorry. It's not the company. I've just had quite a day."

"I'd probably better be going so you can get some rest."

"Not yet. Let's sit here awhile longer. It's such a beautiful night. I don't know when I've seen the stars so bright."

"Um, you're right." Max leaned back, too, and stretched his

arm out behind her. Collin had gone to bed nearly an hour ago, and they had sat here since, talking softly about the tennis game and how well Collin was doing in school.

"Leah. . ."

"Yes?" she answered softly.

A lock of her hair had fallen loose from the velvet ribbon holding it back. Mesmerized, he took it and wrapped it around his finger. She turned toward him, and they gazed into each other's eyes for a moment. He caught his breath as she smiled lazily at him.

"You are so beautiful," he whispered. "Leah, do you realize how much I care for you?"

"I care about you, too, Max. You are so wonderful with Collin, and. . .well, it's not only because of Collin." She took a deep breath and whispered softly, "I care about you for you."

He swallowed and cleared his throat. "There is so much I want to say to you, but. . ."

She reached over and placed her hand on his arm. "It's all right, Max. Let's just get to know each other a little better. I don't want to rush into anything, either."

She smiled warmly, and he thought his heart would melt.

Maybe, just maybe they could make this work. Maybe, when the time was right, he would tell her everything, and she would understand and believe him. But not now. He couldn't, wouldn't spoil this moment.

Leah swallowed the last bite of her toast, then gulped down her orange juice.

"Collin, you need to hurry, sweetheart. We have to leave in five minutes. I don't want to be late my first day."

Collin stood up silently and took his dishes to the sink. She followed as he turned without looking at her and went into the living room where he donned his coat, still without speaking.

"Is something bothering you? You haven't said a word since you woke up."

He lifted his eyes and shot her an accusing look.

"I saw you and Mr. Reilly on the porch swing last night!"

Leah felt her face flame.

"Oh. Well, Collin, I. . . What do you mean? We were just talking."

"He's my friend, not yours! Anyway, you're my mom. You're not supposed to have boyfriends!"

Stunned, Leah stared at her son as she felt the blood leaving her face. Her hands trembled as she grasped desperately for the right words to say.

"Collin." She reached for him, but he eluded her grasp and stomped out the door. By the time she followed him out, he was halfway down the sidewalk to the bus stop.

Leah rushed to catch up and reached him just as their bus pulled up. Collin flopped onto a seat and moved over so she could sit next to him.

She turned to him only to see him trying unsuccessfully to hide a tear that had slipped from his eye.

"Collin, I'm sorry you're upset. We'll talk about it this afternoon."

He scowled and turned toward the window.

Leah's heart felt like it would break. It never would have occurred to her that Collin would object to her friendship with Max. What would he do if that friendship did grow into something more as it appeared to be doing? How in the world would she handle this new development?

Chapter 7

Max whistled as he placed his freshly laundered shirts in the drawer. He had been so busy this week, he had been down to one clean shirt when he finally got time this afternoon to pick up his laundry. He chuckled softly to himself as he started straightening up his bedroom. He hadn't had time to do much cleaning lately, either. Well, to be honest with himself, he probably could have found time before now, but more important things filled his life these days.

Sometimes he felt like pinching himself to see if he was in the middle of a wonderful dream. Leah was the most adorable woman to grace the earth, and he couldn't believe his extraordinary good fortune that she actually loved him, Max Reilly.

Leah had told him about Collin's angry explosion, and Max had been concerned. The boy was refusing to have anything to do with him, but Max had caught him looking at him several times when he thought no one was watching. The expression on his face was proof to Max that the boy missed their times together. It wouldn't be long now. He was coming around. God was answering prayer.

The aroma of lasagna reminded Max it was probably time to take his dinner out of the oven. Ten o'clock was a little late to be eating, and he was starving. He had just settled himself at the kitchen table when the doorbell rang. Max groaned and considered ignoring it, but it continued to ring, getting more insistent with each peal. With another groan, Max pushed his chair back and headed for the living room.

"Okay, okay, keep your shirt on. I'm coming!" He yanked open the door and stared at the disheveled woman who still leaned against the doorbell, causing the repeated ringing.

"Hi, Maxie. Glad to see me?" Claudia's lopsided smile, obviously meant to be seductive, sent a wave of revulsion through Max.

"What are you doing here, Claudia? I thought you were still in Louisiana, ruining lives there."

"Oh, Maxie. You hurt my feelings. Aren't you going to ask me in?" She giggled, then before he realized her intent, she had brushed by him and made her way across the room, falling onto the sofa.

Pursing her lips into a grotesque pout, Claudia beckoned to him with crimson-tipped fingers.

"Come on, Maxie. Sit here and talk to me." She patted the seat next to her.

"You can't stay here, Claudia. You'll have to leave now."

"But, Maxie. I don't want to go anywhere. I want to stay here with you. You know, Max, you're much more handsome than Jake. I've always liked you, and if you'd just get to know me a little, I think you'd like me a lot." She squinted up at him and gave a tipsy smile.

"Claudia, you're drunk. I'm calling a cab to take you home."

Max headed for the phone, and Claudia jumped up and staggered toward him, screaming in protest.

"Don't you dare pick up that phone, Max. I told you I don't want to go anywhere. I'm staying right here with you. I got you in trouble once, Max. And I can do it again!" A calculating look crossed her face. "I hear you have a girlfriend. Does she know about the time you tried to force yourself upon me?"

"Don't start it, Claudia. No one believes your lies anymore."

"Jake does." She threw her head back and laughed, then suddenly bent over as a fit of coughing overtook her.

Max stood looking at the woman his brother had chosen for a bride. Her hair was coming loose, and the bright red lipstick on her mouth was smeared all over her chin. Maybe a cab wasn't such a good idea. Claudia suddenly put both hands to her head and swayed. Grabbing her arm, Max helped her back to the sofa, where she stretched out with a moan.

"Maybe I'll just take a little nappy, okay, Maxie?" And with that, she was out like a light.

Max stood looking down at her in helpless fury. Would he never be rid of her? Making a sudden decision, he strode firmly to the phone and dialed.

His brother's panicky hello wrenched Max's heart. Apparently Jake had been waiting for the phone to ring. Max hated to cause him pain, but what could he do?

"Jake, you need to come over here and get your wife. She just showed up at my door, and she's not in very good condition."

There was a pause on the other end of the phone, then Jake answered shakily, "I'll be right there."

Max waited anxiously for his brother, hoping Claudia wouldn't wake up before he got there.

When Jake finally did arrive, he hurried over to his wife, barely looking at Max. He lifted her gently in his arms and carried her out to his waiting car. Max noticed he hadn't availed himself of his chauffeur's services. After he had deposited his wife into the backseat, Jake returned to the front door and confronted his brother. His lips were tight, and Max flinched at the pain and humiliation on his brother's face.

"You won't mention this to Mother and Father, will you?"

"No, of course not." Max reached out to put his hand on Jake's shoulder, but Jake drew back.

"I don't need your pity!"

Max watched sadly as the car squealed away from the curb.

Leah's days were passing in unbelievable happiness. She loved her job. The baking itself would have been joy enough, but to make things even better, Mrs. Crumply was giving her increasing responsibility for running the business. And as icing on the cake, her relationship with Max was flowering into something precious and wonderful.

His mother had sent an invitation to dinner, and Leah got butterflies in her stomach just thinking about meeting Max's mother. But she also admitted to herself she felt intimidated at the thought of going to one of the largest and grandest mansions in the city.

The only thing that had marred her life these past few weeks was Collin's attitude. After his initial outburst, he had drawn away from Max completely, hardly being civil to him and outright refusing to go anywhere with him. Leah had tried everything she could think of, from reasoning with him to firmly insisting that he straighten up his attitude, but to no avail.

Finally, after she had burst into tears on Max's shoulder one evening, he had cupped her chin in his fingers, turned her face to him, and spoken gently.

"Darling, please don't be so upset. Collin doesn't know how to handle the change in our relationship. Up to now, you have belonged to him alone, and I was his exclusive pal. Give him time to adjust. I really think if we don't make a big issue of it, he'll come around."

They had prayed together that night, and Leah had felt peace wash over her that she hadn't experienced since she and Bob had used to pray together. Later, when she was alone, she had cried out her gratitude to God.

Max had continued to come over on every scheduled day to see if Collin wanted to play tennis. In spite of the continuous negative answer, lately she had noticed Collin looking wistfully at Max when Leah and Max were talking or laughing about something. And a couple of times she caught him trying to hide a smile. So maybe things were progressing after all, just as Max had said they would.

Leah hummed softly as she took the mail from her mailbox

and went into the house. Another good thing about the bakery was that her day ended at three, and she usually made it home a few minutes before Collin did. Leah had made arrangements with the mother of one of the students to pick him up at their neighbor's house in the morning and bring him home after school. So far it had been working out fine.

She threw her purse on the coffee table, kicked her shoes off, and sat on the sofa. Glancing through the mail, she noticed an envelope addressed in flowing handwriting with no return address and no postage stamp. Puzzled, Leah tore it open. A yellowed clipping fell out, and Leah picked it up and held it while she perused the accompanying note. There was only one line: *I thought you should know the sort of man you are keeping company with.*

Leah's heart pounded as she read the clipping. It was from an old society column, and as Leah read, she felt all her hopes and dreams begin to fade. Her mind grew numb, and her breath came in short, fast gasps.

She started as she heard a car pull up out front, and her heart pounded madly. She had to pull herself together. Collin was home. *Oh no. Collin. What have I done to you? What sort of man have I allowed into our lives?*

How could she have been so wrong? Even in the beginning, when she had doubts, she never would have considered that Max would do the sort of thing this article was accusing him of. Surely this must be a different Max Reilly. But no, it mentioned his father and grandfather by name. How could he have been accepted to his present position if these accusations were true? Leah's mouth twisted, and she gave a short laugh. Of course. The Rosemont name and money could probably buy anything.

She stood up as Collin came bounding into the room.

"Hi, Mom. How was work today?" he asked as he gave her a hug.

She returned his hug, then cleared her throat before speaking. It wouldn't do for Collin to see she was upset. She had no idea what she would say to him if he asked what was wrong.

"Work was fine, Collin. And how was school?" There, that wasn't so hard. It sounded cheerful enough, even to her ears.

"Oh, okay, I guess. Just two more weeks 'til school's out."

"Um-hmm. Looking forward to that, I'll bet."

"Yeah, I guess." He ducked his head and rubbed the toe of his shoe on the worn carpet.

"Is something wrong at school, Collin?"

"No, ma'am."

Suddenly he lifted his face to her, and she could see the pain behind his eyes.

"I'm going to do my homework, Mom. I'll see you later."

"Well, all right, son. Collin, listen. I need to speak to Mr. Reilly privately when he gets here, so would you stay in your room until I call you down, please?"

He tossed her a worried look. "Is something wrong?"

"Nothing for you to concern yourself with, honey."

She watched him tread slowly up the stairs, and anger flared inside her. She could handle the pain of losing her dream, but how dare that cad mess up her son's life? She went outside and sat on the porch swing, clutching the envelope and its contents. The longer she sat there, the angrier she became and the harder she pushed herself back and forth in the swing.

Max drove slowly to Leah's house. After the episode with Claudia and Jake last night, he knew he couldn't put things off any longer. He was going to tell her everything and just trust in God's mercy and Leah's love for him. Surely she would understand and believe him.

As he pulled up in front of the house, he noticed she was waiting for him on the porch swing. He didn't see Collin anywhere. Good. That would make it easier. And he wouldn't have an excuse to put it off.

"Leah, just the girl I wanted to see." Max smiled as he stepped up onto the porch.

Leah stood up and faced him, and he stopped in shocked surprise at the dark fury in her eyes.

"Leah?"

Her lips were pressed together tightly. She stared at him silently for a moment before she spoke. "Mr. Reilly, please take this little token and leave. I never want to see you again."

Thrusting an envelope into his hands, she turned and walked woodenly into the house, closing the door firmly behind her.

Max stood staring at the closed door for a long moment. When he finally glanced down at the envelope in his hands, he knew he had waited too long.

He didn't have to open it to know that Claudia had kept her word. She had ruined his life once more.

Chapter 8

The days dragged by for Leah. Even her job at the bakery, which should have given her joy, was just busy activity to help her get through another day. Only when confronted with Max's true character had Leah realized how much she truly loved him. The knowledge that he wasn't the man she had thought pierced her heart until she could hardly stand it.

The only ray of light in her life was Collin. Dear sweet Collin. He was going through his own private torment. That was plain from the confusion on his face. He didn't understand why Max wasn't coming around anymore. And he hadn't seen fit to ask her. She knew it must be hard on him seeing Max every day at school and wondering why he had stopped coming over.

One night when Collin was taking his bath, Leah sat in the rocking chair, attempting to concentrate on a new book.

"Mom."

Leah looked up. Collin stood there in his pajamas and slippers, and his wet hair was tousled from a not-so-successful attempt to towel it dry.

"Yes, sweetheart?" Leah reached over and brushed a straying lock of the damp hair out of his eyes.

"I'm sorry."

Puzzled, Leah frowned. "Sorry about what, honey?"

"I'm sorry I was so bad and rude and all about Mr. Reilly." His face seemed to crumple. "It's my fault he stopped coming over, and now you're sad."

"Oh, Collin, no." Leah stood up and pulled her son into her arms. "It's not your fault at all. This is something between Mr. Reilly and me. It has nothing to do with you."

"You sure?" The expression on Collin's face as he looked up indicated he wasn't completely accepting her statement.

"Sure as can be. Now, Collin. . ." She bit her lip and studied her son. "I know it must be difficult for you to be around Mr. Reilly every day under the circumstances, so I'm thinking about letting you switch back to your old school after all. What do you think?"

A totally horrified look crossed Collin's face.

"No, Mom! I mean, do I have to?"

Surprised, Leah stared at her son. "I thought that was what you wanted."

"That was a long time ago. I like Rosemont now, and I've got lots of friends there. Besides, I don't even see Mr. Reilly very much anymore."

Leah peered at her son anxiously, trying to ascertain if he was being truthful or if he was just saying what he thought she wanted to hear.

The tears, threatening to spill over, convinced her he really meant it.

Suddenly his eyes grew wide, and he clapped his hand against his leg. "Oh no!"

He bounded up the stairs and into the bathroom. In just a minute he was back, breathing heavily and holding out a piece of folded paper.

"Wow! I'm glad I remembered this before my trousers went into the laundry. Mr. Reilly asked me to give it to you."

She took the note from him with trembling hands and clutched it tightly.

"Well, all right, Collin. We'll leave the matter of changing schools for now since the term is almost over. Maybe we'll talk about it again before next year."

"Okay, Mom." He reached over and kissed her good night, then went upstairs.

Leah closed her eyes, almost afraid to look inside the folded piece of paper. Finally, with trembling hands, she opened it.

Genesis 39.

Leah stood staring at the words for a moment in stunned surprise.

Genesis 39? What in the world?

Leah picked up her Bible from the side table and leafed through it until she found the passage. She had only read for a few minutes when she inhaled deeply, then continued to read. As she came to the end of the chapter about Joseph and Potiphar's seductive, vindictive wife, her knees grew suddenly weak, and she sat down quickly.

Had she been too hasty in accepting the accusations in the clipping as truth? Could it be that Max was innocent of the charges?

In spite of herself, hope began to rise in her heart and mind. Hope that was quickly replaced with shame. She hadn't given Max a chance to defend himself. On the other hand, this wasn't proof positive that he was innocent. Of course, he would claim innocence if he was guilty. But based on what she'd seen of his character, did she truly believe he was capable of the vile actions the article had accused him of?

When Leah finally went to bed, she tossed and turned in an agony of indecision. Should she give him a chance to explain—and risk her heart again? She was already in so much pain she could hardly function. If she gave him a chance, only to discover that the accusations were true, it would be unbearable. And what would it do to Collin?

Finally, she fell into a restless sleep filled with disturbing dreams. One moment, she would see Max with hurt and pain on his innocent face. In the next, the expression would turn into a gloating sneer. When her alarm clock went off, she felt as though she hadn't slept at all.

Somehow she managed to get through the day at work. They were extra busy due to the Easter weekend coming up, so at least Leah's mind was occupied and unable to wander to the subject that was causing her so much anxiety.

That night when Collin was in his room reading, she went to her room and knelt.

"Lord, I need your wisdom."

1 Corinthians 13.

What? Leah inhaled sharply. Where did that thought come from? She knew that was the chapter on love. Could God be speaking to her? Suddenly a peace washed over her, and she knew it had indeed been God who put the thought in her mind.

She quickly got her Bible and fanned the leaves until she came to the passage. She carefully read each line, each word, not wanting to miss something that God might desire to bring to her attention. As she read all the attributes of love, suddenly she stopped at verse seven and reread the last part. She felt as though a sword had pierced her heart.

"Believeth all things, hopeth all things."

Max had been the epitome of moral excellence from the moment they had met. He had been kind, generous, and godly. Yet when she heard a bad report concerning him, she had immediately believed the worst instead of believing in the qualities she had observed, the qualities that had caused her to fall in love with him.

Lord, tell me what I should do. She was met with silence. Making a sudden decision, she rushed from her room.

"Collin, I'll be right back. I'm going to see if Mrs. Wright can stay with you for a little while. I have something I need to do."

"Okay, Mom."

She quickly changed her dress and smoothed down her hair. As she hurried down the stairs, a knock sounded on the door.

Max was having a hard time hiding his misery. He had been so down in the dumps the past weekend when he had gone to his parents' for dinner that his mother had first cried, then grown angry.

"Max, would you like for me to go have a talk with that young lady?" she had asked, her eyes flashing as she patted him on the shoulder.

He had given a little laugh that came out more like a sob.

"Thanks, Mother, but I don't think she would be too convinced by my mother defending me. Mothers tend to do that."

"Well, all I can say is if that woman really loves you, she shouldn't believe a note written by someone she doesn't even know."

"You're right, Mother. But I have to admit, I should have been more forthcoming with her before it was too late."

"Well, be that as it may, we must clear up this misunderstanding." She patted him as only a mother can do, then frowned deeply. "It had to be Claudia who sent the clipping."

"If I thought it would do any good, I would try to reason with Claudia, but she really has it in for me."

Max's father had entered the room about that time, and he emitted what could only be described as a growl. "Good luck if you want to try to talk with Claudia. No one knows where she is. Jake doesn't even know. She's been gone for the past four days."

"Poor Jake." Max couldn't help feeling sorry for his little brother, in spite of his treatment of Max.

"Well, if you ask me, he'll be better off if that woman never comes back," his mother had seethed.

"We may feel that way, Mother, but apparently Jake doesn't."

That had been nearly a week ago. Max wondered if Claudia was still missing. He ate an early supper at the kitchen table and went into the living room. He turned on the radio and searched for something to take his mind off Leah. As if that were possible.

Settling on a music station, he sat on the sofa, leaning his head back against the cushions.

Lord, was I wrong? I was so sure Leah was the woman You intended me to spend my life with.

The doorbell brought him sharply out of his musing. He got up wearily and went to open the door.

"Jake!"

If there had ever been an object of total dejection, it was his brother as he stood in the doorway, hatless, shirt hanging out at the waist. His eyes had the look of a hunted animal, and he ran his hands nervously through his hair.

"Is it all right if I come in and talk to you, Max?" His voice was hoarse as though he had been yelling, or worse, crying.

"Of course." Max stepped back, allowing Jake to come in. "Coffee?"

"Yeah, that'd be good."

"Okay, why don't you just sit down here in the easy chair while I go get it."

Max had never seen his brother so shaken. His face was pale as death, and his hands were trembling when he took the cup from Max. He took a long drink of the hot liquid, then set the cup down on the side table and dropped his head in his hands.

Max sat in silence to give Jake time to pull himself together.

Finally, Jake looked up at Max and took a tortured breath.

The words he spoke were the last thing Max had expected to hear.

"Max, can you ever forgive me?"

Max felt a wave a love for the brother who sat with tears streaming down his face. He knew his own eyes were damp, too. "I forgave you a long time ago, Jake. You're my brother. I love you."

Jake closed his eyes and sighed. "Claudia told me the truth, Max. That she made the whole thing up. She thought it was funny. She played her little games and lied about everything."

Max closed his eyes and breathed a silent prayer of thanksgiving. Finally, after all this time. "Where is she? Did she come back home?"

"Yeah, she came back to try to get some money. A lot of money. Said she needed it to pay off her sister's hospital bill." He emitted a short laugh. "I wasn't buying it. I told her she wanted it to pay off gambling debts and buy booze. That's when she got mad and started screaming and yelling."

Jake's face held an expression of unbelief. "Terrible things. Her language was foul. I couldn't believe some of the things she admitted to. Bragged about, even. Then she laughed and told me she had lied about you."

He dropped his head into his hands for a moment, then looked up at Max.

"I'm so sorry. How could I have believed you would do anything so vile?"

"It's okay, Jake. It's over. She's your wife. She had you fooled. I may have done the same thing in your shoes."

"There's more. She said she had some article from an old newspaper about the supposed attack. Sent it to your friend Leah."

Max was on his feet like lightning and pulling his brother up from the chair.

Jake jerked backward as if he thought Max was about to attack him. "What? What are you doing?"

Max stepped back and looked at his brother.

"Jake, I know you are miserable. I'm going to do everything I can to help you through this. But will you please follow me over to Leah's and tell her about this? She won't talk to me."

"Of course. That's the least I can do for you."

Max drove to Leah's as quickly as he could while making sure Jake was able to follow. When they reached her house, Max knocked on the door with fear and doubt in his heart. Would she believe his brother or just think he was making it up for Max's sake?

The door flew open, and Leah stood there with shock on her face.

"Max!" She was in his arms before he realized what was happening.

"Oh, Max, forgive me for doubting you." She sobbed. "I know you could never do the horrible thing that note accused you of. Will you forgive me?"

"Sweetheart, it's okay. It's my fault." Max cupped her chin and lifted it so that she was looking into his eyes. The love she saw there left no doubt of its sincerity. "If I had had the courage to tell you about it in the first place, you never would have believed the accusation."

At the sound of a cough, Leah saw for the first time that they weren't alone. She felt her face flame and stepped back out of Max's embrace.

"Leah, this is my brother, Jake. He has something he wants to tell you."

As Leah listened to Jake's story, she felt a conflict of emotions. Anger toward the woman who had caused Max so much pain. Anger toward Jake for believing it, and at the same time pity for his obvious pain and heartbreak. Most of all, she felt shame that she had doubted Max for even a moment.

After Jake left, Max took Leah into his arms once more, and she snuggled closely and wrapped her arms around his waist.

"Leah," he whispered shakily.

She looked up at the expression of love on his face, and as his lips came closer to hers, she closed her eyes and waited in anticipation for this moment she had longed for. She sighed against his mouth as it pressed against hers, finally. All the dreams she'd had of his kisses were nothing compared to the reality. He tightened his hold, and their passion rose, leaving her breathless. "I love you, my girl," he whispered, his forehead resting against hers.

"Oh, Max, I love you, too."

"I'm thinking. . .June."

"June? What are you talking about?" She laughed.

"For the wedding."

Swallowing hard, Leah couldn't resist a grin. "What kind of a proposal is that?"

"The prelude to the real one, which I promise will be everything you've ever dreamed of." He kissed her forehead, her cheeks, her nose, her chin, and finally captured her lips once more. "Or maybe June is too long," he said with a husky growl.

Leah's heart nearly stopped. "I think June will be just fine. We have a lifetime after that."

"So is that a yes?"

Caught by her own words, Leah rose on her tiptoes and initiated a kiss. "Did you have any doubt?"

"Mom! Are you still going somewhere?"

Leah and Max both jumped back as Collin came running down the stairs.

"Mr. Reilly! Hi!"

Max took a deep breath, and smiling at Leah, he went to meet Collin at the bottom of the stairs.

Leah felt a fleeting moment of disappointment, but at the joy on Collin's face, she caught her breath. There was plenty of time for their love. Plenty of time. Her eyes brimmed with happy tears as she watched Max catch Collin into a tight embrace.

Deep contentment swelled Leah's chest, and her heart soared with the truth that God was good indeed.

TRACEY V. BATEMAN

Tracey V. Bateman lives with her husband and four children in southwest Missouri. She believes in a strong church family relationship and sings on the worship team. Serving as vice president of American Christian Romance Writers gives Tracey the opportunity to help new writers work toward their writing goals. She says she is living proof that all things are possible for anyone who believes, and she happily encourages those who will listen to dream big and see where God will take them. To learn more about Tracey, visit her Web site, http://www.traceybateman.com. Her e-mail address is tvbateman@aol.com.

FRANCES DEVINE

Frances Devine was born and raised in the great state of Texas but has been a resident of the beautiful Missouri Ozarks for the past twenty years. She is a substitute teacher and part-time school library aide. She is the mother of seven adult children and grandmother to fourteen perfect grandchildren for whom she gives God her eternal gratitude.

Love of a Lifetime

by Rhonda Gibson

Dedication

A special thanks goes to my own true-life hero, James Gibson.
Thank you for believing in the work God has given me.
Also, thanks go to my mother, Louise McConnell,
for believing in her little girl.
Above all, I want to thank the Lord for all things.

Chapter 1

Silver Mine, Colorado—Present Day

"Oh no! Not again!"

Smoke billowed in the small kitchen. The fire alarm blared. Colleen Halliday grabbed an oven mitt and pulled the burned cinnamon buns from the oven.

She tossed the pan on the stove. Holding her breath, she snatched the step stool. The offensive alarm continued to blare as she climbed onto the stool and jerked out the alarm's battery.

"Now, Colleen, don't take out your frustrations on the poor alarm." Mr. Wilson chuckled from his seat at the round table by the window.

She wanted to tell the old man to mind his own business but resisted the unchristian temptation. Hanging on to her temper, she hopped off the stool. She set the battery on the counter, then made her way to the back door.

"Lord, this bakery is going to be the death of me. I'm not so sure I should keep it open anymore." Colleen grumbled the prayer as she opened the door to escape the smoke and odor of burnt sugar. It wasn't a matter of money. Granddaddy Max's side of the family made sure Grammy's Bakery would never lack for funds, but if she continued to burn everything, she was sure to lose her customers.

"Hey, Colleen. Was that your smoke detector going off again?" Jenny Walker grinned, revealing red, white, and blue braces.

"I'm afraid so. I burned the cinnamon buns." She waved the screen door back and forth. Fresh fall air filled the small kitchen.

Colleen knew the teenager didn't mean anything by her words, unlike Mr. Wilson, who enjoyed making fun of her lack of cooking skills.

Jenny pulled her backpack up higher on her slim shoulder. "I've got a few minutes before I have to get to school. Want me to help you with those buns?" At Colleen's nod, she dropped her backpack and jacket just inside the door.

Colleen hated to admit it, but the sixteen-year-old could cook circles around her. "Are you sure you have time? I don't want you to be late for school again."

The young girl brushed past her. "I'm sure. I'm keeping an eye on the clock. Adam wasn't happy the last time I was late." Jenny went to the stove and grabbed an apron. She tied it around her small waist. "I want to go into Durango tomorrow with my friends, so I'm toeing the line. Adam says if I step over it, I can just forget the trip."

Thoughts of Jenny's older brother, Adam Walker, took Colleen's mind off the burnt food. She hated to admit, even to herself, that she looked forward to his daily visits. As a postman, Adam used Grammy's Bakery as the spot where he took his morning break. The memory of his light blue eyes, dark brown hair, and easy smile softened the frown on her brow.

Colleen shook her head to clear it. Enough daydreaming about a man who would never take her seriously. He hadn't had time for her in high school. What made her think he'd notice her now? Besides, everyone in town expected him to marry Cassie Masters, the kindergarten teacher at the elementary school. They had been dating for more than a year.

The sound of the small bell ringing over the door indicated that Mr. Wilson was leaving. She couldn't suppress the sigh of relief. Since she'd moved back to the small community of Silver Mine, Colorado, Mr. Wilson had made a real effort to come to the bakery every morning. She suspected her dad had something to do with Mr. Wilson hanging around so much.

The two men were friends from days gone by, and Colleen knew her dad felt guilty for leaving on another mission trip to Africa. His solution was to have his friend keep an eye on her. Most days, Mr. Wilson just ordered coffee and read his paper. But there were days, like this one, when he really got on her nerves.

Colleen pushed all thoughts of Mr. Wilson from her tired mind and focused once more on what Jenny said.

"You would think after two weeks you'd get the hang of making simple cinnamon rolls and pastries." The young girl's voice trailed off as though she realized how insulting her words sounded, and an expression of horror covered her features.

"It's okay, Jenny."

Jenny wiped her hands over the front of her apron. "No, it's not. I'm so sorry, Colleen."

"Really, it's okay. You didn't mean anything by it." Colleen mixed together fresh dough for hot rolls.

"No, I didn't mean it that way, but I still shouldn't have said anything. Your grammy has only been gone a month. Adam would say, 'There I go again; speaking before I think.' "

Pain, sharp and real, sliced through her. Oh, how she missed her grandmother. Guilt still ate at Colleen for not being there during her grandmother's last moments. Tears pricked the back of her eyes. She wouldn't think about it now. She smiled at the teenager. "Jenny, are you going to be late?"

"No."

Colleen sensed Jenny's dark blue eyes studying her. She dreaded the words she knew were forthcoming. She narrowed her eyes and stared back at Jenny. "What? Do I have flour on my nose?"

"I still can't believe Grammy left you this shop and apartment. Why didn't she teach you how to cook?"

They stared at each other for a moment. The comical way Jenny talked at motorboat speed took the sting out of her words.

"Well, she tried, but I wasn't as good a student as you." A smile tugged at the corners of Colleen's mouth. "It's not as though I can't cook at all; I just have a little trouble with pastries."

Jenny returned the smile. "I'll teach you if you want."

"I'm not proud. Teach away," Colleen joked, bending to watch how Jenny worked her magic with sugar and flour.

After Jenny left for school, Colleen slid a pan of cookies into the oven. She wiped off the counters and smiled. Chocolate chip cookies were her specialty.

She hummed as she washed up the last of the morning dishes and thought about Jenny. The girl knew her way around the kitchen. Colleen could imagine Grammy teaching the young lady in this very room.

She rubbed the back of her hand across her stinging, watering eyes, thankful for the empty bakery. She looked to the table where Mr. Wilson had sat earlier. Why did he choose Grammy's favorite spot to sit every morning? Memories washed over her as tears trickled down her cheeks.

She remembered the day she'd told Grammy she was going away to college. Oklahoma State University had offered her a full scholarship. At the time, it felt like the chance of a lifetime, and she'd moved to Oklahoma against her grandmother's wishes.

Grammy had held her hands, listened, and then said, "Colleen, you can't run from God and family forever. When you're ready to come home, I'll be here."

Had that really been only five years ago? Why hadn't she done as her grandmother wanted and stayed in Silver Mine? Even now, Colleen didn't want to admit she'd been bitter toward God over the death of her mom.

"Grammy, I'm not running from anything. I'm going to college to get a business degree. I'll be able to run a business and help supplement your income."

"I love ya, angel. I'm going to pray God sends you home

soon." The tenderness in Grammy's eyes had almost changed Colleen's plans to leave.

At Grammy's funeral, Colleen remembered something else her grandmother had said daily. "Child, why don't you give your broken heart to the Lord? He'll heal it, and the pain will go away."

Those words came back to haunt her as she'd stood and looked down at Grammy's casket. Her heart too pain-filled to endure, she'd made her way to a private corner and sought comfort only her heavenly Father could give. If only Grammy had been there to rejoice with her.

Colleen picked up the dishcloth and moved to the tables. As she wiped them clean, she prayed. "Lord, I need help if I'm to keep Grammy's bakery open. Jenny has agreed to teach me how to bake something other than hot rolls, but I'm thinking I need more than a teenager teaching me how to cook. I don't know for sure what I'm asking for, but I know You can supply my every need." Just whispering the words lightened her heart.

The bell over the door jingled. She looked up and smiled when Adam Walker pushed through the door. He carried a large package in his arms.

Her heart surged like a cake rising in the oven's heat at the sight of Adam. She forced herself to focus on the box as she walked toward him. "Is that for me?"

"It's got your name on it." He set it down and sighed. "Boy, am I bushed. Between taking care of a teenager at night and delivering heavy packages during the day, this postman is worn out."

Colleen caught the hint of teasing in his voice. She shifted her gaze from the box to him. He smiled. A dimple in his right cheek winked at her. His light blue eyes sparkled with merriment.

"Would some caffeine perk you up? I've got fresh coffee. Want some?" She found it impossible not to answer his smile.

Adam pulled out a chair and sat down. "I'd love some, thank you."

She hurried to the coffeepot. Her heart flip-flopped from the effect of his grin and the warmth of his voice. What was it about Adam that set her heart to fluttering? "Everything," she whispered for her ears alone.

Colleen poured two cups of coffee. She handed one to Adam and cradled the other in her hands. The heat distracted her from the warmth in her cheeks.

Dark brown hair brushed his forehead when he bent his head to the cup. The mug looked fragile in his large hands. His blue eyes met her gaze. Intensely aware of his scrutiny, she watched as his gaze swept over her face, then settled on her mouth.

Heat rushed to Colleen's face. She looked away from him. "What do you suppose is in that?" She went into the kitchen for a knife to cut through the tape on the box.

The timer on the stove went off, reminding Colleen of her cookies. She pulled them out, set them on a cooling rack, then grabbed a knife and headed back into the dining room.

Adam offered her a clipboard and pen to sign with. "It sure is big, isn't it?"

This time Colleen smiled. Colleen knew Adam had seen

larger packages. "Yes, it is." She handed him back the pen and clipboard.

Colleen turned her full attention to the box. The mailing label read: From Ethel Collins. Colleen's brow puckered. She had just spoken with her great-aunt over the weekend, and the elderly lady had never mentioned a package.

"Aren't you going to open it?" Curiosity filled his voice. He had moved and now stood behind her. A shiver ran down her spine as his warm breath whispered across her ear.

The tape pulled off with ease. Colleen opened the flaps and peeked inside. Several shoe boxes filled the container. A slip of notebook paper lay on the top.

Colleen squinted at the small, scribbled handwriting. Aware of Adam and his interest, she read aloud.

Dear Colleen,

Leah told me to send this to you at the store if anything happened to her. She left it here when she moved down there to be closer to you and Collin. She said you should have it all. Since I'm in my eighties and have no other relatives, I'm of a mind to agree with her. Please keep our family's memories alive. In the boxes are pictures, letters, scraps of our heritage, and something that every woman in our family has discovered. I hope you can come visit me in the spring. I'm looking forward to seeing what this treasure box brings you.

Love,
Ethel

Colleen sat back. It was almost like a message from Grammy. She smiled at Adam and lifted the first of the shoe boxes.

Chapter 2

Colleen was still looking through the many boxes when Jenny arrived a little after three that afternoon. "You aren't going to believe what our teacher wants us to do." She tossed her backpack beside the table and yanked off her coat.

"It can't be that bad," Colleen replied distractedly. She asked herself for the hundredth time what to do with all these old photos, letters, postcards, and scraps of material. Colleen hadn't even gotten to the bottom of the box before she began repacking it.

Jenny dropped into the chair across from her. "It is," she declared.

Colleen finished packing the box. "Okay, tell me. What does your teacher expect you to do that's so horrible?" She closed the flaps over the contents.

"She wants us to create a scrapbook of our family and anything we know about our ancestors. It's fifty percent of our grade." Her voice went up like only a frustrated teenager's can.

"Why do we have to do that for a history class?" Jenny picked up the two coffee cups and followed Colleen into the kitchen.

"How long do you have to complete this assignment?" Colleen asked, sliding warm cookies onto platters. Kids of all ages would be storming the bakery in a few moments. A smile crossed her face. Maybe her cookies would save the store from going under.

Jenny set the cups in the sink and started running hot water. "Oh, we have the whole school year. But I really don't know if I can do it, Colleen."

"Why not? That should be plenty of time." Colleen set the platters of cookies on the counter, then turned to pull a new bag of flour from the pantry.

"It's not the time," Jenny grumbled. "I don't know how to do a big project like this."

Colleen filled the flour canister, then studied the young girl. She knew Jenny's mother and father had died five years earlier in an automobile accident. If it hadn't been for Adam taking his half sister in, Jenny would have been alone in the world.

"I do." Colleen moved to the sink and stood beside Jenny. "I'll make you a deal." She waited to see if she had Jenny's full attention.

Jenny grabbed several cups and saucers and dunked them into the hot, soapy water. She refused to meet Colleen's gaze. "I'm listening."

Colleen placed an arm around her shoulders and gave her a gentle hug. "If you will teach me to bake pastries after school, say from four to five, then from five to six I'll help you put together your scrapbook." She released the teenager and picked up a cup to rinse.

"Really?" Jenny continued to wash the dishes as if she were afraid Colleen would take back the offer.

"Sure." Colleen began drying and putting away the clean cups and saucers. She set a cup inside the cupboard and paused. "Did you see the big box over there?"

"Yeah." Jenny's teenaged voice took on a note of caution.

"Well, it's from my aunt Ethel, Grammy's sister. She sent a letter saying she would like for me to preserve the memories of all my ancestors. I thought I might put together a scrapbook, too." She chewed the side of her lip.

Jenny squealed with delight. "That would be great! We really would be doing it together."

Colleen smiled at the sudden joy she'd just brought her young friend. Silently she thanked the Lord that she was able to give Jenny a reason to enjoy the school project.

"What do I have to do?" Jenny asked, wiping the counter.

"First, gather up all your pictures, old letters, and stuff that you think will help you remember your family. Then you put them together in a photo album." Colleen dried the remaining dishes and set them in the cabinet.

Jenny pulled the stopper out of the sink and dried her hands on a nearby towel. "Mrs. Sword says we can use stickers, die cuts, special letters, all kinds of stuff on our pages."

Colleen smiled. "We can."

"When can we start?" Jenny asked eagerly.

"How about we meet at the scrapbook store in Durango tomorrow? I'll close the bakery at ten, and then I can meet you and your friends after lunch." Colleen's gaze moved to the box. Her mind swirled with ideas for the scrapbook. "I'd like to get started as soon as possible on mine."

Adam told himself he was just being polite as his feet carried him back to Grammy's Bakery. That box had been very heavy. He didn't want Colleen hurting her back trying to carry it the short distance to her living quarters even if the apartment was attached to the bakery. He didn't dare question himself as to why he cared.

The smell of hot apple pie caused his mouth to water. Adam pushed the door the rest of the way open and hurried into the shop. His stomach growled.

"Adam, come see what Colleen baked all by herself," Jenny called.

He walked into the kitchen. Colleen pulled a pie from the oven while Jenny looked on with excitement. Adam smiled at Colleen. Flour dusted her pert little nose. Green eyes met his gaze and sparkled with pride. Her curly black hair was pulled back in a ponytail. Ringlets had escaped the hair tie and softened her heart-shaped face.

Adam didn't understand his sudden attraction to Colleen. He admired the way she'd taken over the bakery and tried to make a go of the business. And the way she'd befriended Jenny was wonderful. But there was more, something he couldn't quite put his finger on.

"Isn't it beautiful? I can't believe she did it all by herself." Jenny pointed at the golden crust of the pie Colleen held in her hands.

Adam's gaze ran over Colleen's face once more. He cleared his throat. "Very beautiful."

Colleen's flushed cheeks deepened to crimson.

A woman who still blushes at a compliment—now that is rare, thought Adam.

She ducked her head and turned to place the pie on the counter behind her. "Thank you, Adam."

"Is that your first apple pie?" He leaned against the wall and watched her wipe her hands.

"It's not an apple pie. I made the apple pie. Colleen made a chicken pot pie." Jenny turned off the oven. "She said we could stay for dinner if you want to."

Colleen finished wiping down the counters and drained the sink. Adam noticed she still hadn't met his gaze since he'd complimented her.

He moved away from the wall. "I don't know, Jenny. We wouldn't want to put Colleen out." The last thing he wanted to do, however, was leave.

"Please stay. I never could have made this beautiful pie if it hadn't been for Jenny. Seems only right she should share it." Colleen's soft voice halted his footsteps.

He turned and found her looking at him. For a moment, Adam thought he would drown in the beautiful sea of green. Her eyes compelled him to stay.

"Great! It's settled then." Jenny whipped off her apron and

grabbed three plates and silverware.

Once more, Colleen caught his attention with her warm voice. "I'm glad. I'll make a salad. Adam, would you shut the windows and turn the OPEN sign to CLOSED?"

How could he refuse to stay? Why would he want to?

Chapter 3

What is that pounding noise?

Colleen didn't want to know. She pulled the pillow over her head and groaned. The pounding didn't stop. If anything, it grew louder. Just when she'd been in a wonderful dream of listening to Adam tell her she was the girl he'd been looking for all his life.

"It's Saturday. Go away." She groaned into the mattress. Her head felt thick.

"Colleen, wake up! It's me, Jenny!"

Jenny? What in the world was she doing up early on a Saturday morning? "Aren't teenagers supposed to sleep in on the weekend?" Colleen grumbled and pulled her head from under the pillow. She squinted at the clock beside her bed.

Twelve o'clock glared red at her.

Midnight? The question rattled through her groggy mind.

"Colleen, please wake up!" Jenny's voice pleaded loudly.

She pushed back the covers and swung her feet to the floor. "I'm coming."

"Hurry."

Cold air entered the house when she opened the back door. "What's wrong? Do you know what time it is?" Colleen demanded in a harsher voice than she meant to.

Jenny burst into tears. "I had to come."

Colleen stepped back to let the teen into the house. Only then did she notice that Jenny carried her suitcase.

"Calm down, sweetie. What are you doing here?" Unease stirred at the sight of the overnight case.

The young girl dropped her luggage and covered her face. Loud sobs filled the room. Jenny's shoulders shook. Her tears broke Colleen's heart.

Colleen took Jenny in her arms and let her cry. When the sobs trailed off, she patted Jenny's shoulders and released her. "Let's go into the kitchen. I'll make some hot chocolate; then maybe you can tell me what's going on."

She led the way. A hiccupping Jenny followed close.

Colleen set a kettle of water on to boil and turned her attention to Jenny. Thankfully the young girl had gotten her emotions under control and no longer sobbed. Colleen offered her a stool to sit on at the small island in the center of the kitchen and gave her a box of tissues.

Colleen prepared two cups of hot chocolate and handed one to Jenny, then sat on the stool beside her. "Now tell me why you've run away."

"Adam said I couldn't go to Durango." Jenny blew her nose. "So I snuck out of the house. I sorta hoped I could stay with you."

"Did he say why?" Colleen's question was tentative. She wasn't sure she should get involved in a dispute between the two of them.

Jenny shrugged her shoulders. "Not really."

"He just decided for no reason that you couldn't go?" Colleen's voice held skepticism.

The young girl nodded and took a sip from the hot beverage. Colleen noted Jenny wouldn't meet her gaze.

"Well, I guess I'd better call him and tell him where you are."

"No." The single word burst from Jenny's lips.

"Why not? I'll tell him you're here, and then he won't worry about you." Colleen could only imagine Adam's distress.

"No, please don't tell him I'm here. He'll be angry." Jenny set down her cup. Her eyes pleaded with Colleen.

Questions raced through Colleen's sleepy mind. Could Jenny be telling the truth? She thought so, but there was more here than what Jenny conveyed. Her gut feeling said that the teenager overreacted to something Adam had said.

Lord, please let me be right.

"Jenny, I can't let you stay here and not tell Adam where you are. It wouldn't be right." She reached for the phone.

"Why do you and Adam always go on about what's right?" Jenny demanded. She continued on in anger. "You both have that holier-than-thou attitude. Why can't you just leave me alone and let me do things my way?" She glared at Colleen, waiting for an answer.

Colleen searched her face. "Our ways aren't always God's ways, Jenny. I'm not always right, and I don't always do what I should, but I do pray and ask for guidance. Would you like to pray with me?"

"No, I don't want to pray about it. I guess since you won't let me stay here, I'll go to my friend Sarah's house. She'll let me sleep on her couch." Jenny flounced to her feet.

Lord, I'm no good with teenagers. Please help me use the right words now. Colleen watched Jenny grab her suitcase off the floor.

"Jenny, why did you really leave home tonight?"

Jenny's eyes filled with more tears. "Adam and I fight all the time. He said I'm pushy and willful." A tear slid down her face.

This time Colleen knew the tears were real. The hurt ran deep, and the misery in Jenny's eyes tore at her soul. She opened her arms, and the young girl eagerly came into them.

An hour later, Colleen hung up the phone. The fact that Adam wanted to work the problem out immediately gave Colleen an even higher opinion of the man. He finally agreed with her that Jenny needed time to settle down and decided that she could stay the night.

She returned to the kitchen. "Adam said you could spend the night."

Jenny smiled and sighed in relief.

"Come on. Let's get to bed." Colleen led Jenny into her small apartment. They went through the living room and down the hall to the last bedroom on the right.

"You should be comfortable in here." Colleen went to the bed and pulled back the light blue quilt that matched the curtains hanging over the window. It was a small room with a twin bed and a matching oak nightstand. A writing desk sat against the opposite wall.

Jenny put her suitcase down just inside the doorway. "Thank you, Colleen."

"You're welcome. Running away won't fix your problems. Tomorrow you have to face your brother." She knew all about running away.

A dejected look crossed Jenny's young face. "I know." She moved into the room and dropped down on the bed.

"Were you being pushy and willful?"

Jenny looked up at her. "A little."

Colleen walked back to the door. "You know how to fix this, right?" She put her hand on the light switch.

"Yes, but it's going to be hard." Jenny laid her head on her crossed arms.

Colleen gave her what she hoped was an understanding smile. "Asking forgiveness isn't always easy, especially when you are sincere, but once you take that step, the relief and cleansing is well worth the agony."

Moments later, Colleen crawled back into her own bed. She wondered if Adam would forgive Jenny and allow her to go to Durango with her friends. She thought of her own trip into town and wished she had the nerve to ask Adam if he'd like to go with her.

She recalled the way they had laughed and talked during the simple meal. He seemed happy to be there. When Jenny moaned about the school history project, they shared a knowing smile. Colleen wondered now if she'd misread Adam

Walker's interest in her.

Who said he was interested in her? She scolded herself mentally. The image of Cassie Masters filled her tired vision.

Cassie portrayed everything Colleen wasn't. She had big Bambi eyes surrounded by long lashes that fluttered with every blink. Her silky blond hair was cut into a short style that curled around her ears. Creamy white skin and perfect teeth completed the package.

Colleen flipped over onto her stomach and groaned into the pillow. What if Adam had already scheduled a date with Cassie? Colleen decided it would be better not to ask him to make the trip with her.

Tears of exhaustion seeped into the pillow.

Adam poured himself another cup of coffee. He stared at the empty pot in his hand. How many did that make, two or three pots? And he was no closer to the answer. The question pressed upon him again. What was he going to do with Jenny?

He raked a trembling hand through his disheveled hair. She'd never run away before. Adam drained the last drop of coffee from the cup and wished his father were still around to talk with about Jenny.

He set the empty cup and coffeepot in the sink. "Lord, I should have come to You first. Father, what am I going to do about Jenny? She is stubborn, willful, and my baby sister. I just don't know what to do."

Peace settled over him as he released his concerns to his heavenly Father. The thought that he should just love her first and foremost and the rest would be taken care of came to mind. "If only it were that easy, Lord."

Adam looked up at the clock. Time to go pick up Jenny. He changed into jeans and a warm sweater before stepping into the chilly autumn morning.

He decided to stop by the post office before confronting Jenny at Colleen's. Saturdays off were rare for a postman his age, even in a small town like Silver Mine where everything was within walking distance.

Adam felt a pang of guilt. He knew Sly Mason was working for him today. No one knew Sly's real age, but he was old. Sly had been the one to make the arrangements for him to be off on Saturdays after Adam and Jenny's parents had been killed. The old man had reasoned that Adam would need the time off to keep an eye on his young sister. For that, Adam was grateful.

"Morning, Sly," he called as he pushed the door open.

Sly Mason looked over the rim of his glasses. "What are you doing here this morning, Adam?" The older man's gaze moved to the calendar. "Son, this is your day off."

Leave it to Sly to point out the obvious. Adam shut the door against the brisk morning air. "I just thought I'd come by and see if there was anything pressing you need delivered." The words sounded phony in his ears.

The old man studied him for several long moments, causing Adam to squirm. Sly laughed.

Adam realized he must look as guilty as he felt. Why had he come here? Did he really dread the conflict with Jenny so much, or could it be that he dreaded seeing Colleen even more? After all, she probably thought they were the most dysfunctional family she'd ever had the misfortune of befriending.

"Well, since you're here, would you mind throwing this big trunk in the back of your Blazer and delivering it to Grammy's Bakery this morning?" Sly grunted as he pushed a large box in Adam's direction.

Adam looked at the item in question. The chest was huge and black. "Hold on, Sly. I'll need to go get the SUV."

The old man stood and placed both hands on his hips. "It's a mite heavy. Think you can lift it by yourself?" he asked. His bones popped as he pushed on the small of his back.

Adam laughed. "I'll see what I can do. Give me a few minutes to get the Blazer."

After he collected the trunk from the post office, it didn't take Adam long to drive over to Grammy's Bakery. He drove slowly, telling himself it was in the interest of the old chest not to drive too fast.

The closer he got to the bakery the more his stomach knotted. What must Colleen think of them? Last night she had sounded concerned. He wondered how much Jenny had told her.

He pulled up in front of the bakery and hopped out of the Blazer. He moved to the back of it and pulled the heavy trunk toward him. Its weight tugged on his shoulders and back.

Adam carried it to the porch and set it down. The scent of fresh bread filled the frosty air. His stomach growled. He took a deep breath and knocked.

Colleen opened the door. The dark circles under her puffy, red eyes told him what kind of night she'd had. Something deep down told him it was his fault.

Chapter 4

"Come on in, Adam. I hope you don't mind, but Jenny is still asleep." Colleen stepped back so he could pull the trunk into the entryway. Then she closed the door.

She bent down and looked at the old trunk. The address label said it came from Aunt Ethel. What could this be? She pulled on the lid. It didn't budge.

Out of the corner of her eye, she could see Adam looking around the small living quarters. "I don't mind, but I think we've imposed on you enough."

"Not at all. Help me open this, and we'll call it even." She searched his face. A soft smile lifted the corners of his mouth.

"Deal." Adam knelt beside the old trunk.

"Would you like some coffee?" Colleen asked, standing up to get out of his way.

Adam looked up at her. "I'd love some, thank you."

Colleen went into the kitchen and made a fresh pot of coffee. Her hands shook and her heart pounded. How could one man shake her up like this?

To keep busy, Colleen fixed bacon and eggs. It gave her hands something to do and calmed her nerves. She filled two plates, making sure to leave plenty of bacon for Jenny.

Just as she set the plates on the small table, Adam walked in. "It's open."

"Great! Why don't you sit down and start eating. I'll go see what my aunt sent." She moved past him and returned to the entryway.

She knelt beside the chest and carefully lifted the old lid. A child's coat lay on the top. The fabric looked old and fragile. Being careful not to damage it, Colleen set it on the floor beside her.

She sifted through the remaining clothes. At the bottom of the box were several books and a sewing box. She gently lifted an old Bible from the bottom. The black leather was worn and ragged around the edges.

"Wow, that is really old." Adam's voice drifted over her shoulder, startling her.

Colleen jumped. The Bible slipped from her hand, and they both caught it. Their fingers brushed. Her heart rebounded against her ribs.

Adam released his hold on the book.

How long had he been kneeling beside her? She felt heat crawl up her neck and into her face. She quickly returned all the items to the chest except the Bible.

"I'm sorry, I didn't mean to startle you." Adam straightened and took a step back.

Colleen closed the lid. "It's okay. I just thought you were

eating breakfast." She picked up the Bible, stood, and smiled.

He returned her grin. "I hate to eat alone."

The low reverberation of his voice turned her knees to mush. He probably had no idea how appealing he sounded when he spoke in low tones like that.

"Me, too." Colleen led the way back to the kitchen. Adam wanted to eat with her. Did that mean anything? She was afraid to hope. She poured them both coffee.

When she turned back to the table, Adam stood waiting behind her chair. Colleen didn't know what to do. She felt just as funny as she had the night before at dinner. If sharing meals was going to be a regular occurrence, maybe she'd better put a stop to this now. "I'm not real formal, Adam. You don't have to do that." She thought the protest sounded a little weak.

"I know." He continued to wait with a soft smile on his face that showed off the dimple in his right cheek.

Colleen realized he had no intention of sitting down until she did. She carried the coffee to the table and allowed him to seat her.

As soon as he sat down, Adam asked, "Shall I say the blessing?" He extended his hand palm up on the table.

She placed her hand in his. "That would be nice, thank you."

His smile warmed her heart, and she bowed her head. The prayer was simple and straight to the point. Just the way it should be.

"Amen."

She echoed him, pulled her tingling palm from his, and looked up. "I hope you like your eggs sunny-side up." Unable to keep from staring at him, Colleen tried to focus on spreading strawberry jam on her toast.

Adam sampled the eggs and grinned. "Love them. Thanks."

They ate in silence for several moments. Adam laid his fork down. "Great breakfast." He watched Colleen sip at her coffee.

"I hope you don't mind that Jenny came here last night. I'm really not sure why she came to me. I would have thought she would have gone to one of her friends' homes." She stared into her cup.

Adam picked up his own coffee. "She thinks of you as her friend, Colleen."

Her eyes met his. "I know, but most kids run to other kids."

She watched him set his cup back down. He reached across the table and took her hand in his. Warmth surrounded her fingers.

"I'm glad she chose to come here, but I'm really sorry we placed you in the middle of our family problems."

The roughness of his fingers on the back of her hand sent goose bumps up her arm. Colleen pulled her hand away. "I'm glad I could be here for her."

Adam lifted his coffee cup again and held it with both hands.

Jenny stumbled into the room, rubbing sleep from her eyes and focusing on her brother. She said, "I'm sorry, Adam," as she sank into a chair.

Colleen didn't know if she felt happy or sad about the interruption. She stood up. "Would you like some eggs and bacon, Jenny?" She gathered up her plate and coffee cup.

"If you don't mind," Jenny answered. She pulled her legs up into the chair.

Adam's gaze on Colleen made her self-conscious. She turned and smiled at Jenny. "I've got some bacon ready for you. How do you like your eggs cooked?"

"Scrambled, please." Jenny laid her head on her knees and faced Adam.

"I shouldn't have left home like that last night, Adam. I'm really sorry, and as soon as I get done with breakfast, I'll call Sarah and tell her I'm not going to Durango today." She rubbed her cheek against the sleeve of her yellow terrycloth robe.

Blue eyes shimmered with tears. Truth shined in their depths. Adam wondered what had caused the change in her attitude. "Why didn't you just tell me you were meeting David and the other boy and going up there together, instead of trying to sneak around and do it?"

Jenny glanced in Colleen's direction. Colleen gave a slight nod of encouragement.

"I was afraid you wouldn't let me go." Jenny turned to face him once more. "Honest, that's the truth."

Adam stared at his sister, then glanced at Colleen. She smiled and nodded to show him she believed Jenny.

Adam scowled. "You were right. I wouldn't have let you go."

Jenny sighed heavily.

"I expect you to tell me the truth, Jenny."

"I'm sorry," she whispered.

Adam reached over and patted her leg. "Me, too."

They sat in silence for several long minutes. Colleen felt a little left out. She wished she had a brother who cared as much about her as Adam did about Jenny. She set a steaming plate of food in front of Jenny. "More coffee, Adam?"

"Please." Adam held his cup out to her.

"How about you, Jenny? Coffee or hot chocolate?" Colleen took Adam's cup and smiled at her young friend.

"Chocolate." Jenny picked up her fork and moved the eggs around.

"Jenny?"

She looked over at Adam.

"I'll make you a deal. Agree to always tell me the truth and to never run away again, and I'll agree to drive you and Sarah to Durango." Adam accepted the coffee from Colleen. He took a sip, his eyes on Jenny.

Jenny searched his face. "Aren't you letting me off easy?"

The guarded look in her eyes spoke volumes. "Maybe. But I'm praying I can trust you and your word."

Jenny lowered her eyes and chewed her bottom lip.

Adam's gaze flickered to Colleen. Colleen couldn't help herself and directed a beaming smile of approval at him. He was handling this just right.

"I promise to never run away again, and I'll try not to lie anymore." Jenny's statement drew his attention once more.

Adam laughed.

"What's so funny?" Jenny snapped.

"I appreciate your honesty, Jen. You thought about it and decided you might need to lie to me again, so you said you'd try not to lie. That's not quite what I meant."

Jenny gave him a sheepish look. "I didn't want to lie."

He hugged her to him. "I appreciate that." He tightened his arms around her, then let her go. "So how soon can you ladies be ready to drive into Durango?"

Adam meant her, too? Colleen almost dropped the coffeepot. Maybe the day wouldn't turn out to be so bad after all.

Chapter 5

Colleen enjoyed Jenny and Sarah's chatter on the way to Durango. They talked about everything from boys to magazines and back to boys. She hoped Adam wasn't too bored with their girl talk.

Adam drove with expertise. He took the curves up and down the mountain with skill and alertness. His eyes remained trained on the road, but every time Jenny mentioned David, a frown marred his features, a sure giveaway that he was paying attention to the girls.

As they passed one of the many small waterfalls, Colleen smiled.

"I notice you've smiled every time we pass one of those." He grinned at her, then returned his gaze to the winding road.

"I love waterfalls. I'm not sure what it is about them that I enjoy. Grammy always said it was because they are so peaceful and soothing." Colleen eased back into her seat and allowed the scenery to comfort her. When would the pain of losing her grandmother diminish? she wondered as she surveyed the passing scenery.

Cottonwoods and pine trees lined the highway. In some spots, large walls of rock hugged one side of the road, and on the other side a steep drop-off took her breath away.

The girls squealed in the backseat as a truck passed a little too close to them. So much for relaxing. Colleen sat up straighter in her seat. The road curved and twisted all the way into Durango.

"Adam, don't forget we're meeting David and Matt at Denny's." Jenny leaned against the seat. She flashed a red, white, and blue grin at Colleen, then scooted back into her seatbelt.

"Do you want to eat at Denny's or someplace else?" Adam turned his head and asked Colleen.

His boyish grin turned her stomach into a cage of hovering hummingbirds. She wiped her clammy palms on her jeans.

"Denny's is fine."

Did her voice quiver? Colleen sneaked a peek over her shoulder. Both Jenny and Sarah were deep in conversation. If her voice had trembled, they would have looked up. She relaxed to see them still attentive to one another.

Once Adam parked, the girls wasted no time getting into Denny's and finding the boys. The four of them were seated at a small table with their heads together behind menus when Adam and Colleen caught up.

A waitress led them to a nearby booth. She waited until they were seated and asked, "What would you like to drink?"

Colleen answered first. "I'd like an iced tea, please." She

took the offered menu.

Adam watched Jenny smile at David. "I'll have the same." He made eye contact with his sister. She nodded slightly as if to reassure him. Adam relaxed and turned around to face Colleen. He immediately didn't like having his back to his sister and her friends.

"Looks like we've been abandoned for the boys." Colleen drew his attention. She studied her choices from the menu with a slight frown.

"Something wrong?" he asked, picking up his own glossy menu.

A soft laugh answered him. "Not really. I'm looking for chicken-fried steak and don't see it here." She continued to study the lists.

Adam's gaze moved over the menu with speed. "Here it is." He pointed it out to her.

"Where? I still don't see it." Her gaze darted from his menu to hers. The frown deepened on her forehead.

Adam moved from his side of the booth and scooted in next to her. He noticed she didn't shift away from him but leaned forward to see where he pointed.

"Oh, my menu is missing that page. See?" Colleen held hers up for his inspection.

He smiled, glad it was missing a page. It gave him the perfect excuse to move into her side of the booth.

She returned his smile and quickly looked back at his menu as she pushed a black curl behind her ear.

Adam watched a pink flush travel up her neck and into her

cheeks. He wasn't sure what caused her blush but had to admit he enjoyed the freshness of her shyness. The feeling of being watched drew his head up.

He looked toward Jenny's table. She wasn't looking at him at the moment, but he felt pretty sure she had been watching them. He wondered what she would think if he asked Colleen out on a date.

The waitress came by and took their orders. Colleen surprised him by ordering a ham and cheese sandwich with chips.

"I thought you were going to order the chicken-fried steak," he commented when the waitress left their table and moved to Jenny's.

She scooted away a little and turned in her seat to face him. "I was, but it's pretty heavy, and I plan on walking up and down historic Main Street." She took a sip from her tea.

He faked a sour face. "I wish you'd told me that before I ordered the steak and baked potato."

Colleen laughed. "You still have time to change your order."

Two hours later, Adam wished he had changed his order. His meal rested in the pit of his stomach like heavy metal.

Jenny and David stood on the opposite side of the street. Jenny called, "Hey, Colleen, I found the scrapbook store." She motioned for them to cross the road.

Colleen grabbed Adam's upper arm and attempted to pull him across the busy street. "Come on, slowpoke. You're going to get us run over."

Adam reached for her hand and slipped it into his as they ran across the street. The warmth from her soft palm lightened his heart. He continued to hold it even after they were safely across. They fell into step behind the two teenagers.

"It's called Scrapaholics. It's right up here," Jenny called over her shoulder as she and David continued to lead the way.

Adam noticed that David held Jenny's hand. His gaze moved to his and Colleen's interlaced fingers. Was he acting like a lovesick teenager?

As they traveled up the small hill, Colleen tightened her grip on his hand. He moved his gaze to her face. She rewarded him with a smile.

"Here it is," Jenny announced needlessly.

Disappointment spread over him when Colleen released his hand and followed Jenny and David inside. Through the glass window of the scrapbook store, he could see Jenny and Colleen already engrossed in a wall of stickers.

Adam decided to stand outside for a few moments and enjoy the fall air. He leaned against the red brick building and looked up and down the side street. He could see Main Street from where he stood.

Adam glanced around Durango's downtown. Many of the original buildings were constructed by Durango's pioneers. He wondered if Colleen would like to visit the Rio Grande Land that contained the restored depot built in 1881. It had been years since he'd been inside it.

Colleen had already mentioned she'd like to have dinner at the Strater Hotel. Adam admitted he enjoyed the quaintness of the building that was built in 1887. A reflection of the town's prosperity, it remained a central attraction in downtown

Durango for locals and visitors.

He prayed she wouldn't want that dinner anytime soon. His stomach still felt full from lunch. Adam smiled. He'd enjoyed the teasing and lightness during the meal. Colleen, quiet and shy one moment, proved quick-witted and playful the next.

"What are you all smiles about, Adam Walker?"

Adam turned to see Cassie Masters walking down the hill toward him. "Cassie, how good to see you. What did the doctor say?"

Cassie laughed. Her cheeks filled with color, and she nodded.

"You are? Really?" Adam hugged her to him. He released her quickly and held her out to look at her.

"Yes. Really." She laughed again. "Oh, Adam, I am so very happy."

Chapter 6

Colleen and Jenny stopped inside the doorway. They couldn't believe all the things one could use for scrapbooking. There were stickers, eyelets, die cuts, scissors, punches, accessories, and many different types of papers.

"Where do we start?" Jenny asked, her voice filled with awe.

"I'm going to start by sitting right here at this table and not moving." David pulled a hot-rod magazine out of a deep pocket in his cargo jeans and sat down.

"Well, why don't we start by choosing a couple of photo albums?" Colleen stepped down the steps and moved toward the walls of paper.

Colleen moved around the papers and came into an aisle with photo albums of different sizes and shapes. "Wow, I had no idea there were so many decisions to make when starting a scrapbook," she muttered to herself.

"I know exactly what you mean. Are you just getting started?"

She looked over at a dark-haired woman who held several

pages of papers and a fistful of stickers. "I'm afraid so. Do you work here?" Colleen asked, praying she wasn't about to get suckered into buying the whole store.

"Oh no. I have enough stuff that I could open my own store, but I'm not brave enough to take that step just yet. I'm Shelly Young. I'm just hooked. Do you want me to get Debbie? She owns the store."

Colleen shook her head. "No, thanks. Jenny and I need albums, but I'm not sure what size. I guess I'll just have to study them for a moment."

Jenny chose that split second to come around the corner. She held several stickers in her hand. "Colleen, did you know you have to use special pens to write in the albums if you want to keep your pictures in it forever?" She stopped and looked from one woman to the other. "Oh, I'm sorry. I didn't mean to interrupt."

"You have a very nice daughter." Shelly smiled at the two of them.

Jenny spoke first. "She's not my mom."

Shelly laughed. "I'm sorry. She doesn't look old enough to be your mother.

Colleen smiled. She didn't know what it was about this woman, but she found herself liking the total stranger. "It's okay. I hope to have a daughter just like Jenny someday." She placed an arm around the teenager's shoulders and gave her a gentle squeeze.

"Oh, you found the photo albums." Jenny stepped away from Colleen and knelt down in front of the many books.

She chose a blue one, turned it over, and asked, "What size do we need?"

Colleen noticed Shelly standing a few feet away looking at the many different precut paper picture frames. She hesitated for a moment, then asked the other woman, "Shelly, can you recommend a good size to buy?"

The small woman looked to be in her mid-fifties. She hurried to assist them. "Well, it depends. What are you going to do with it? Is it going to be a heritage album? A school album? A gift album for a relative? A sports album? It really depends on what you are going to use it for."

Colleen thought of the many shoe boxes at home. She knew she'd need a big one. "I've just inherited the family memorabilia. So I guess mine should be a big one."

Shelly turned to Jenny. "What about you?"

"Mine is for a school project. I don't think I need a real big one." Jenny ran her hand over the front of a five-by-seven album. "Do you think this will be big enough?"

"If all you plan to put on a page is one to two pictures, a few stickers and a place to journal, that should be okay for you, Jenny. Plus, with that one, you can add extra pages. See?" Shelly found an open album and showed Jenny where she could add the extra pages if she wanted to.

Colleen picked up a twelve-by-twelve book. She made sure she could add pages, too, if need be. "Thanks, Shelly."

"No problem. Like I said earlier, this hobby can be overwhelming." She paused as if thinking about her next question. "Do you know what to do now?"

Jenny looked up. Colleen saw the familiar flash of red, white, and blue braces. "I thought we'd go look at those magazines over there. They will probably help us."

"Good idea, Jenny. Well, if you ladies don't need me right now, I'll get out of your hair. But please feel free to ask me any questions if you need help."

"Thanks, Shelly."

As the woman walked away, Colleen silently thanked the Lord for sending Shelly to help them get started.

After looking at the suggestions in the magazines and choosing two of their favorites to buy, Colleen and Jenny moved about the store selecting paper, stickers, different-shaped scissors, glue pens, and a few die cuts to get started.

Colleen walked to the front of the store. She looked out the big glass window. The scene occurring outside caused her heart to feel as if someone had just stepped on it.

Adam stood hugging Cassie. A smile as big as the San Juan River graced his handsome face. She saw his breath move the other woman's hair as he said something to her.

She moved back into the aisle and away from the window. Colleen fought the tears that threatened to spring forth. How could she have been so stupid to forget that Adam was dating Cassie? Had they planned on meeting in Durango? What must he have thought when she'd held his hand?

Twenty minutes later, Colleen was still wandering around the store. She'd picked up various papers, die cuts, and stickers. The sound of Adam's voice carried back to her.

"Are they buying up the store, David?"

"Did you find everything you needed?" Shelly asked, coming up behind her.

Colleen exhaled and turned with a pasted smile on her face. "I think so."

If Shelly noticed anything out of the ordinary, she didn't act like it. "Don't forget to get an acid-free pen to journal with. Some people get all the colors of the rainbow, but all you need is one to start with."

This time when Colleen smiled, it was genuine. "I'd forgotten about the pens. Jenny said we need a special kind." At Shelly's nod, Colleen pressed on. "I don't know how I could have done this without your help, Shelly. Thanks again."

Shelly patted her hand. "Come on. I'll show you where the pencils and pens are."

Jenny sat between Adam and David at the round table, showing them all the items she'd chosen.

Colleen continued to follow Shelly past the table and to the front wall. When she walked by Adam, he gave her a warm smile. She prayed the smile she returned was as warm as his.

"Jenny, did you choose a pen?" Colleen asked. She studied the wall. This, too, was a little overwhelming. Pens of all shapes and sizes were displayed. Some in packs and others as stand-alones.

Jenny joined them. "I looked at them. Do you want to buy a pack and share them? Or do you want to just get one color each?"

"If you're going to share them, it would be cheaper to buy a small pack. Just make sure you have one black and one blue pen," Shelly advised, then moved to the register.

"Let's get a set," Colleen decided.

Jenny hugged her. "I hoped you'd say that."

They picked out a collection they both liked and turned toward the register. Shelly had just finished paying for her purchases.

"I want you two to have these." She held out double-sided tape dispensers, one for each of them.

Colleen gasped. "Oh, you shouldn't have done this."

Shelly laughed. "I wanted to. Just don't blame me when your projects become your hobbies." She used her fingers to put quotes around the words *projects* and *hobbies* as she said them.

"Thank you," Colleen and Jenny echoed each other. Colleen couldn't imagine this becoming a hobby.

"You're both very welcome. I hope to see you in here again. Next time bring your albums. If I'm here, I'd like to see what you do with them." Shelly turned to leave.

"Wait a minute." Colleen quickly grabbed one of her business cards and handed it to Shelly. "If you're ever in Silver Mine, stop by; coffee and cinnamon rolls are on me."

Adam paid for the items Colleen and Jenny had selected while Colleen said farewell to Shelly. He noted Colleen's eyes no longer possessed their sparkle. He wondered if she was saddened by the thoughts of preserving her grandmother's memories.

Jenny gathered up the bags. Adam watched her turn and frown at David. If he knew his sister, David was about to be dumped.

Colleen turned back to the register. "Hey, why did you do that?"

Adam was shocked by the demanding tone and the new flames in her eyes. "You were busy. I just took care of it."

"Since when did you start paying my bills, Adam?"

Adam looked over his shoulder at the gawking cashier. "Colleen, you are making too much of this. It's the least I could do. After all, if you weren't helping Jenny with her homework, you probably wouldn't even be here." His own anger began to grow. One thing he didn't enjoy was being the center of attention.

"I see. Thanks."

Adam watched her eyes tear up. Now what had he said? Women were so hard to understand.

Sarah and her boyfriend chose that moment to enter the store. "Hey, I didn't know this store had stickers." She made her way to the first wall with a vast array of brightly colored decals, unaware of the tension in the store. Her boyfriend followed.

Jenny looked at David, who had his nose buried in a magazine, shook her head, and followed the other two teenagers.

Adam watched Colleen walk to the big window and stare out. The urge to take away David's magazine and hide behind it tempted him. Hurting Colleen's feelings had been the last thing Adam wanted to do, and if he could figure out what he'd done wrong, he would change it.

Fact was, though, he was clueless.

And from the squaring of her shoulders, she wasn't going to tell him, either.

Chapter 7

Colleen pulled another faded, black-and-white snapshot from the shoe box. A man and woman faced the camera. His arm was draped over her shoulders. She could tell by the expressions on their faces that they were in love. She turned the photo over and read the names, Leah and Max Reilly.

Her grammy?

She flipped the picture back over and studied her grandmother's young face. Grammy couldn't have been much older than Colleen herself. And she looked so happy. Colleen wondered if she would ever find the man of her dreams and look that content.

Thoughts of Adam invaded her mind. Could she be happy with him? She sighed. Even if that were possible, Cassie Masters already held his heart.

Colleen separated her family photos into two piles. The Hallidays and the Reillys. She laid the picture on top of the Reilly pile of family photos. The clock chimed.

Jenny would arrive shortly, ready to scrap. The teenager had taken to scrapbooking like a bear to honey. She loved everything about it.

Colleen started her pages with the old notes and letters from the past. She'd found several scripture quotations jotted on the sides of notes as if they were someone's favorite verses. Grammy had said that Peter Collins, one of her grandfathers, had been a minister. So Colleen assumed they were his.

A soft knock sounded on the side door to the apartment. Assuming it was Jenny, Colleen called out, "Come in."

She picked up another photo and examined the strangers staring back at her. Their faces were blurred, so she pulled it closer to get a better look.

"I hope I'm not disturbing you."

Colleen jumped. She dropped the snapshot.

"I'm sorry. I thought you knew I was here." Adam bent and picked up the picture.

She held her hand to her pounding chest. "I thought you were Jenny."

He held the photo out to her. "I don't normally get that," Adam teased.

Colleen couldn't help but smile, too. "No, I don't guess you would." She took the picture. "Thank you."

For several long seconds, they stared at each other. Colleen hadn't seen Adam since Saturday when they'd gone to Durango and she'd overreacted to him paying for her scrapping supplies. Jealousy and the knowledge that he was simply grateful to her for helping Jenny had made her act hastily.

He broke eye contact first. "I came by to tell you Jenny wouldn't be coming today." Adam stuck his hands into his pockets. "And to give you this." He held out an envelope.

"I hope everything is okay." Colleen took the letter. A quick glance told her it was from her father. She raised her gaze from the envelope. Adam cleared his throat. "She got sick. Something she ate for lunch didn't agree with her."

"I'm sorry to hear that. Is there anything I can do?" Colleen laid the picture on the table.

He pulled his hands out of his pockets and shifted his feet. "Thank you, but I think she just needs some rest. She'll probably feel fine in the morning."

"Well, if she needs anything, let me know, and I'll try to help." Colleen knew she should say something about Saturday, but her brain refused to give her mouth the command.

His eyes softened. The light pools of blue turned into dusky pools of liquid. "I better go. Thanks again." He spun on his heels and hurried to the door. He paused at the door and turned.

"One question, Colleen."

She studied his intent face and nodded. "Okay."

"Why are you mad at me? I thought we were getting along great at Durango, but then you clammed up. What gives?"

Her stomach clenched. No way would she admit to jealousy. "Nothing."

"Is that why you didn't say a word on the way home from Durango? You wouldn't even look at me."

She couldn't look at him now. Was that how she'd seemed

on Saturday—angry? She'd been hurt, not mad.

The telephone rang. Reprieved. She smiled in relief. "Excuse me." Colleen walked to the living room to answer the phone.

⁂

Adam moved to the table and looked down at her pictures. She had divided them into small piles. He saw faces of young and old staring up at him. A picture of a little girl and a woman smiled serenely. He wondered if the child was a young Colleen.

He picked up the photograph and turned it over. "Me and Colleen" was inscribed on the back of it. Adam flipped the picture over again and smiled at Colleen's young image. She must have been six or seven when the picture was taken. Her two front teeth were missing, and her hair had been pulled up into pigtails.

"Sorry about that." Colleen stopped a few feet from him. Her gaze moved to the photo in his hand.

Adam grinned. "You sure were a cute little thing. Is this your mom?" he asked, handing the picture to her.

Colleen looked down and nodded. "I was six. I remember the day it was taken. We were getting ready to go to church. Dad took the picture and said we were the two most beautiful women in the world."

He watched a soft smile touch her lips at the memory. *You are beautiful,* he thought. Adam wished he had the courage to tell her so. For the first time, Adam saw Colleen as someone with whom he could spend the rest of his life.

If only he hadn't agreed to keep Cassie and Richard's marriage a secret, he could ask Colleen out. It had been okay to take Cassie to all the church functions when he hadn't been interested in Colleen, but now that he was, the arrangement no longer worked for him. Adam knew even as he entertained the thoughts, he'd continue the charade as long as his friends needed him to.

"I'd better get back to Jenny."

She raised her head. "Call if you two need anything."

There seemed a new softness in her eyes. Maybe she was over whatever had been bugging her.

He drove through town and pulled into the drive of his home, then went inside to check on Jenny.

"Adam? Is that you?" Jenny called from her bedroom.

He hurried to the door. "I'm here. How are you feeling?"

She pushed herself up. "I'm doing okay. Cassie called. She wants you to call her back." Jenny extended her hand with a piece of paper in it.

He entered her room of stuffed animals and lace and took the number. "Did she say what she needed?"

"No, but she sounded kind of upset." Jenny scooted back down under the sheets.

Adam sat down on the edge of Jenny's bed. He touched her forehead. It felt a little warm, but he didn't think she had a fever.

She gave him a weak smile.

"Do you need anything?" Adam brushed the hair from her forehead.

Jenny yawned. "No, I just want to sleep."

"Okay, I'm going to go call Cassie back. Yell if you need me." He stood slowly to his feet. By the time he'd gotten to the door, Jenny had already fallen back to sleep.

Adam made his way into the living room and sat down. The phone sat on an end table beside him. He looked at the number again and reached for the receiver.

Cassie's voice sounded weak when she answered.

"Cassie, this is Adam. Jenny said you called."

"Adam, I'm scared. I think I'm miscarrying. Can you come over?" She sobbed into his ear.

"I'll be there in a few moments. Be ready to go to the doctor," he ordered, then hung up. He felt torn. Jenny lay sick in her bedroom, and Cassie needed him to take care of her and the baby. Cassie needed him more than Jenny right now, he decided. Adam picked up the phone again and dialed Colleen's number.

Chapter 8

Colleen answered the phone.

"Can I bother you for a favor?"

If Adam's voice hadn't been so full of concern, she would have laughed. Only a man would begin a telephone conversation like that. "Sure, is something wrong with Jenny?"

"No, I just need to run to Durango, and I hate to leave her alone when she's sick. Would you mind coming over and sitting with her?"

She wondered why he'd leave his sick sister to go to Durango, but since he hadn't volunteered that information, Colleen decided it would be better not to ask. "I'll be over there in a few minutes."

"Thanks. Just let yourself in. She's asleep right now. I'll be back as soon as I can." Adam hung up the phone.

Colleen hurried to gather a few things. She grabbed *Without a Trace,* a mystery by Colleen Coble she'd been reading, and a cross-stitch project she'd been working on. A small bag of pinion nuts and a couple of diet colas completed her quick selections as she hurried out the door.

Adam's vehicle was gone from the driveway when Colleen got to the house. Disappointment gripped her heart. She'd really hoped she could catch Adam before he left. The thought of seeing him had sent shivers of anticipation down her arms.

She let herself in the front door. Colleen's mind did a mental inventory of the room. A lamp in the corner illuminated the cozy room. A large, plush, dark brown couch filled most of the space. An oversized matching chair sat off to one side, and a mahogany bookshelf stood beside it. End tables with lamps sitting on them completed the furniture in the room. Family pictures decorated the walls. She would have enjoyed looking at each one but decided her first priority was to check in on Jenny.

Colleen made her way down the short hallway. She opened the first door on the left. A very masculine bedroom greeted her. Adam's scent assaulted her. She inhaled deeply, enjoying the earthy fragrance. She could tell that Adam used half the room for sleeping, the other half as a small office.

She moved on to the next room. The door stood partway open, so she gave it a gentle push. Plush animals, posters of young men, and lacy curtains greeted her. Definitely Jenny's room. Colleen tiptoed inside.

Jenny lay on her side with her arm under her pillow and head. She seemed to be sleeping peacefully. Colleen turned around and slipped out of the room. She pulled the door halfway closed.

A bathroom across from Jenny's room completed the

hallway. Colleen turned around to go back into the living room. She passed Adam's room and shut the door.

She picked up her bag and decided to put the colas in the refrigerator. The kitchen had been decorated in rich hunter greens and deep blues. There were no frilly curtains, no cute magnets on the refrigerator, and no country cup towels hanging about. Definitely a man's kitchen.

"What are you doing here, Colleen?"

Colleen jumped. She spun around and saw the yawning Jenny standing in the doorway. What was it with the Walkers? Did they always sneak up on people? Jenny's pale face stopped Colleen from scolding her.

"Adam asked me to come over." Colleen opened the fridge and set the colas inside. "How are you feeling?" She turned back around to face the young girl.

Jenny sat down at the little table to the side. "My stomach is still a little queasy. Would it be too much trouble to make some tea?"

"Of course not. Where do you keep it?" Colleen leaned against the counter and smiled.

"Right behind you in the green canister."

Colleen turned to the cabinet and opened the doors. Several canisters greeted her. "They're all green."

"The middle one," Jenny's muffled voice answered.

She pulled the canister down and opened it. Inside she found a varying collection of tea packets. Colleen looked over her shoulder at Jenny. The girl sat with her head resting on the table.

Colleen looked through the tea bags. "Chamomile's supposed to calm the digestive system and soothe stomach cramps. We'll try that one."

"Okay," Jenny mumbled from the table.

A navy blue teakettle sat on the back of the stove. She filled it with water. After placing it on the burner, she turned her attention back to Jenny.

"The tea should be ready in a few minutes." Colleen sat down in the chair next to Jenny.

Jenny lifted her head. "Thanks. Mom used to make me tea when I was sick."

Colleen smiled as she remembered. "Mine made me potato soup."

"Colleen?"

She looked up and met Jenny's serious gaze. "What?"

"How old were you when your mom died?" She fingered the blue and green tablecloth as she waited for an answer.

"I had just turned sixteen. My father was away on a trip to Africa." Her thoughts went to the night the policemen had showed up at their house. That had been the worst night of her life. She'd given up on life and God that night. Thankfully, her grammy had been there, or Colleen felt sure she would have done something foolish and ended her own life.

"Is that when you moved in with your grammy?" Jenny picked at a small thread.

The teakettle whistled. Colleen stood up and poured them both a cup of hot water. She handed Jenny a cup and a tea bag then answered, "No, when my granddaddy Max died, Grammy moved here to be closer to us and to open her bakery. But after Mom's death, nothing was the same."

"Really?" Jenny dipped her bag in the hot water and scooted up in her chair.

Colleen knew Jenny was fishing for something. But what? She decided to be honest with the girl. "Sure, nothing was the same. The house didn't feel like home, and I felt as if my whole world had come tumbling down around me. My grammy and dad were grieving, too, so to me it seemed as though no one cared about me." She allowed her thoughts to drift for a moment and then continued explaining her old feelings to Jenny. "Mom and I were very close. You see, my parents had me late in life. Mom always told me I was a gift from God because He allowed her to carry me full term. My parents had lost two babies before me and were afraid they would lose me, too. So when Mom died, I felt as if I'd lost my best friend, and I didn't react well to her loss."

Jenny stood up and pulled a small canister of sugar out of one of the many hunter green cabinets. "What did you do?" She returned to the table and plopped back into her chair.

"I pouted, blamed God, and cried a lot." She bent her head to her drink and peeked at Jenny over the rim of the cup.

The teenager's voice came out a whisper. "You really did that?"

Colleen looked up at her. "I'm not proud of it, but yes. Because I was bitter, I pushed God, Daddy, and Grammy away from me."

"How did you fix it?" Jenny gulped her hot tea, then winced in pain.

"At Grammy's funeral, I took the advice she had given me years before and turned it all over to God. I asked Him to forgive me. And He did." Colleen smiled at the memory of God's forgiveness. She glanced over at Jenny. The girl fanned her tongue and frowned.

"And dat fixed it?" Jenny asked, sticking her tongue out and waving her hand over the hot spot.

Colleen laughed. She went to the fridge, pulled open the door, and got Jenny a piece of ice. "Yes, but I still grieve for my mom and my grandparents. It's only natural, Jenny."

"You really think so?" A tear slid down Jenny's cheek. "Sometimes it feels like my heart is being ripped from my chest. I miss my mom and dad so much. Adam doesn't understand me, and now David and I have broken up. Oh, Colleen, it's just awful." She buried her head in her arms.

Colleen walked around the table and pulled a chair up beside Jenny's. She put her arm around the girl's shoulders and hugged her close. "I know it is."

She found herself repeating the advice of her grandmother. "Jenny, if you will turn all the hurt over to God, He will heal the wounds of your soul."

⁂

Adam glanced down at his watch. He groaned. Three o'clock. The emergency room had taken forever to finish treating Cassie. What must Colleen think? He hurried into the house and found her asleep on the couch.

He stood for several long moments just staring down at her sleeping face. Should he let her sleep? Wake her up? Or just continue to stare at her? If he let her sleep, would her reputation be ruined by those who might see her leave in the morning? The questions buzzed around in his tired mind.

He moved to the closet at the end of the hall and pulled out a soft quilt. Made with flannel on one side and a cotton print on the other, comfortable was the only way to describe it. He smiled as he carried the colorful wedding ring quilt back to the living room.

Jenny stuck her head out of her door. She whispered, "Is Colleen spending the night?"

Adam walked back to her. "How are you feeling?"

"Much better."

"Good. I'm sorry I took so long. Cassie needed me to do something for her tonight, and it took longer than we'd planned." He glanced over his shoulder and down the hall. "Do you think I should wake Colleen or let her stay the rest of the night?"

He felt his little sister studying his profile. Adam turned his attention back to Jenny. The tilt of her head and the glow in her eyes made him realize he'd never asked her advice before. Why hadn't he? She was old enough to make some decisions. He decided he must be more tired than he'd first thought.

"Let her stay." Jenny smiled and turned back into her bedroom. "I'll see you tomorrow."

Adam stuck his head in the door. "Jenny, I have to go to work early tomorrow. I'll probably be gone before you or Colleen wake up."

She yawned. "I'll set my alarm for six. That should give us both time to get up and get going, don't ya think?" Jenny reached for the clock beside her bed.

"That should be plenty of time. Night."

He went back to Colleen. She lay in the same position she'd been in earlier. Adam spread the quilt over her and returned to his bedroom.

Adam set his alarm clock for four-thirty. He'd only get an hour of sleep, but by leaving early, he'd avoid being seen at the house in the early morning hours with Colleen. He lay down across his bed, and right before he went to sleep, he heard the front door open and close.

Adam pulled himself up and went to the living room. Colleen was gone. The quilt lay neatly folded on the couch. The sound of her car starting up filled the night air. Adam looked out the window and watched her drive away.

He returned to his bedroom. Just as sleep overtook him, Adam decided he could see himself married to Colleen. She would be a good wife, and he knew she loved God.

When had thoughts of marriage entered his mind? Was this something God was bringing to his attention?

Chapter 9

Two weeks later, Colleen marveled at the difference in her baking skills. Thanks to Jenny's lessons, Colleen could now make several different types of pastries.

She and Jenny had fallen into the habit of making dinner for all three of them. While the meal cooked, they worked on their scrapbooks, adding this item and taking away that one. Adam usually arrived in time to eat with them.

Colleen suspected he had decided to spend this time restoring the bond between himself and Jenny. She could see the two of them growing closer every day. After dinner, Adam and Jenny looked over photos and reminisced about their childhoods.

Inevitably, Colleen sank deeper into loneliness. Her own pictures brought back memories as well. She missed her mother and Grammy Leah. At times, she longed to see them, talk to them, pour out her heart, then cry on their shoulders offered with sympathy and caring.

Another problem that snipped away at her conscience was

the fact that Adam was still seeing Cassie. Colleen had seen them several times from a distance. She thought about that for a moment. They really hadn't acted like a couple, but then maybe she was just fooling herself.

Colleen pulled her coat on and prepared to go to the grocery store. Her thoughts returned immediately to Adam and the last few days together. He had a sweet tooth, and his favorite way of appeasing it was to go out for ice cream. He'd invited her out twice, and even though the evenings were getting much cooler and ice cream wouldn't have been her first choice for a dessert, Colleen hadn't turned him down.

She closed the door and headed down the quaint dirt street toward the only grocery store in town. Colleen ducked her head against the sharp wind and made a mental note to get more hot chocolate. Once more Adam invaded her thoughts. He'd invited her to dinner the night before. She wished she'd taken him up on the date.

"It wasn't a real date," Colleen whispered to herself. It was an invitation, not a date. Adam only appreciated the change in Jenny. His request was because of gratitude, not romantic interest, Colleen told herself as she pushed the door open and entered the citrus-scented store. She picked up a small red basket and made her way to the produce section.

Just when she had convinced herself Adam wasn't really interested, a small voice nagged at her. *If he's not interested in you, then why did he start attending your church and sitting by you during the service?*

She felt the gentle pull of a smile as it touched her lips. He had started attending First Community Church. And he did sit by her.

"Hello, Colleen. Isn't this weather turning nasty?"

Colleen looked into the soft brown eyes of Cassie Masters. She held the smile in place. "Hi, Cassie. It is getting cold out there."

"Daddy says it's going to be a harsh winter. I hope he's wrong." She rested a protective hand over her stomach. "It wouldn't do for me to catch a cold in my condition." Cassie's voice held a far-off dreamy texture to it.

She knew she was being nosy, but Colleen couldn't stop the words from popping from her lips. "Are you ill?"

Cassie looked up at her as if she'd forgotten she'd been talking to her. Colleen watched a soft smile touch the other woman's lips.

"Oh, I just have to tell someone besides Adam." Cassie looked around and leaned toward Colleen. "Please don't tell anyone, but. . ." She paused, looked around again, and whispered, "I'm pregnant."

The way her brown eyes sparkled told Colleen that Cassie was a little more than thrilled about the prospect. "Please don't tell anyone. Daddy would have a fit. So far the only one who knows is Adam. He took the news in stride and has been helping me keep it a secret."

Colleen didn't know what to say. She wondered if her face showed the amount of shock she felt at the news. They weren't even married, and Cassie acted as if having a baby out of wedlock was the best thing in the world. "I won't say anything to anyone. Adam knows?" She asked the last to make sure she'd heard Cassie right.

Cassie picked up a tomato and gave it a little squeeze. "Oh, yes. He's been real good about helping me with. . . " She looked around again then continued. "The doctor's appointments and stuff."

Colleen chose two tomatoes and put them into a plastic bag. She felt as if someone had kicked her in the stomach.

She silently prayed in anguish. *Why, God? Why can't I find someone to love me?*

⁂

"No, I don't want to go out with you, Adam Walker."

Adam stared into Colleen's flashing green eyes. Her face radiated pure anger. Now what had he done? He did a mental inventory. Nothing came to mind except asking her to dinner at the Handlebar Restaurant. What was wrong with her?

"I can't believe you would even ask." She marched back into the bakery kitchen.

He followed. The smell of warm cinnamon rolls welcomed him. "Why wouldn't I ask you out?" Adam watched her grab an apron and tie it around her slender waist.

Colleen pulled the buns from the oven and slammed the pan on top of the stove. She turned and glared at him. "For starters, there's Cassie Masters."

She was jealous! So Colleen did have feelings for him.

He smiled. Now that Richard was coming home to collect his wife, Adam could tell Colleen the truth about his and Cassie's relationship.

But first he'd tease her a little. "What does she have to do with me taking you out?" He wiggled his eyebrows and leaned over the bar that separated them.

She met him at the counter. Her words came out slow and chopped. "Let's see. . ." She drummed her fingernails, then continued. "She might not want the father of her baby out dating other women." Colleen pushed herself away from him.

Adam tried to absorb her words. They echoed in his ears. Why would Colleen think such a thing? He and Cassie had never even held hands.

Colleen continued. "How could you do such a thing? I thought you were a man of God. I thought you were better than everyone else. I thought. . ." The rest of her sentence hung in the air.

Adam watched the anger seep from her eyes. Tears filled them—and loathing. He had questions of his own. How could she think such a thing of him? Why hadn't she asked him about it instead of questioning him like a common criminal?

"I know what you thought and what you are thinking now." He swallowed as sorrow threatened to choke him.

The phone rang. He watched as Colleen turned to answer it. He thought he was in love with her before, but now he knew it. This kind of pain could only be inflicted by those you love.

But how could he love a woman who didn't believe in him? A woman who judged him before hearing all the details?

He couldn't.

His gaze moved to the table where he'd spent many evenings falling in love. The scrapbook projects were almost complete.

After tonight, he wouldn't be coming back to the warmth of Colleen's home. He had to put some distance between them. *She's not the woman I thought she was,* he decided.

Colleen covered the mouthpiece to the phone and whispered, "Adam, this call is going to take awhile. It's my dad from Africa. Can we talk about this some other time?"

He studied her face. She was serious. "Sure, but I'd appreciate it if you wouldn't say anything to Jenny about this."

"I won't," she mouthed, then returned to her phone call. "I'm sorry. . ."

Just like that, Colleen dismissed me, Adam thought bitterly as he let himself out. His feet carried him to the little cemetery on the hill. It was the only place in town where he felt it would be safe to voice his hurts. He stopped beside the graves of his parents, Mary and Robert Walker.

Chapter 10

Fluffy white snowflakes drifted to the cold ground. How fitting that the first snow came on such a sad day in her life, Colleen observed. All her dreams and hopes of finding love lay buried like the ground beneath the glistening white covering. She shivered. Adam hadn't even bothered to deny his actions.

"Colleen, what do you think of this?" Jenny asked.

She turned back to the teenager and looked at the page Jenny had been working on for the past hour. Adam's smiling face stared up at them from the page. It was his senior picture with both his parents. "It looks good."

"I'm going to put the words 'We're very proud of you' at the top. Do you think he'll like that?" Jenny didn't look up as she wrote the date on the bottom of the paper.

"I'm sure he'll love it." Colleen wondered how Jenny would take the news that she would soon be an aunt.

Adam and Jenny's relationship had blossomed. Colleen hoped Jenny wouldn't be too disappointed in her older brother.

Then the question hit her. What would Jenny think of a Christian man behaving as Adam had?

A knock sounded at the front door.

"That's Adam. Don't let him in until I can hide this page. I want it to be special when he sees it." Jenny hid the paper in the back of her scrapbook. She opened the book to a new page and pulled out fresh paper. "Okay, I'm ready now."

With a heavy heart, Colleen went to answer the "shave and a haircut, two bits" musical being tapped out on her door. She opened the door and hurried away without making eye contact with Adam.

He shut out the chill that whipped in about her ankles. The sound reminded Colleen of her heart's door now closed tight against any emotion that threatened to escape or enter. The sting of tears pricked her eyes.

She wandered back to the window but listened to the conversation taking place behind her.

"Hi, Jen. How was your day at school?"

The sound of a chair scraping across the hardwood floors and the creak of the table as he sat down familiarized Colleen with his location. She assumed he'd taken his regular seat and knew his back would be to her if she chose to turn back around and face the room. Why was she having so much trouble facing him? He was the one with the explaining to do, not her.

Still, something nagged at her. Colleen pushed all thoughts of his innocence to the back of her mind. She turned and found herself staring into stormy blue eyes.

"What's up between you two?" Jenny asked. She looked at

Adam, then Colleen, and back to Adam for an answer.

"You didn't say anything?" Adam asked. His voice sounded scratchy.

Colleen folded her arms over her chest. "Of course not. I said I wouldn't." She didn't like him questioning her word. Unlike him, she knew right from wrong.

Jenny laid down the pen she'd been journaling with. "Adam? What's wrong?"

Adam turned his attention to Jenny. "Nothing's wrong, but I do need to tell you something. Cassie Masters is pregnant."

Colleen felt sick to her stomach as she watched Jenny's eyes get wide.

"No way!"

Adam smiled. "The doctor says she's about three months along."

"Who's the dad?" Jenny asked as she picked her journaling pen back up.

"Richard." His gaze met Colleen's again.

Jenny looked down at her paper. "I bet her dad is furious."

Shock and confusion rushed through Colleen's system. Her knees went weak.

"He will be for a while, but Cassie has decided to tell him the whole story tonight." Adam focused back on Jenny.

Jenny's blue gaze met his. "Adam, I didn't think Cassie was that kind of girl." The words came out a whisper.

"She isn't, Jenny. Cassie and Richard were secretly married last summer right before he went to boot camp. They were husband and wife when the baby was conceived." Adam smiled at his sister.

Jenny returned the smile. "I'm glad, but why did they sneak off? Why not just tell her dad they were married? She's old enough to get married." The last sentence came out sounding as though she were thoroughly disgusted at the adult population.

Adam laughed. "Yes, she's old enough, but her dad didn't want her to marry a military man like himself. He wanted his little girl to have a stable home and not have to move around."

"So when is she going to tell him?"

"Tonight. Are you about ready to go?" Adam stood.

"I'm glad she's going to tell him. I don't think she should have lied in the first place. Do you?" Jenny closed her scrapbook and began gathering her things.

"No. I think she should have told her parents, but we don't always do what we should." Adam's gaze met Colleen's.

Colleen turned back to the window.

She'd been wrong.

The realization that she'd judged and convicted Adam without knowing all the facts took her by surprise. What could she say?

Jesus' words from Matthew 7 floated through her mind. "Judge not, that ye be not judged."

"Bye, Colleen," Jenny called.

Colleen turned to call out to Adam that she was sorry. The door closed before she could get the words out. She ran to the door, then stopped.

Tears slid down her face as she realized no matter what she said, the damage had already been done.

"Why don't we ask Colleen if she'd like to ride up to Grand Junction with us?" Jenny folded another pair of jeans and put them into the suitcase.

Adam leaned against the doorframe of his sister's bedroom. He'd had the same thought but knew that if they did, Colleen would just bury herself deeper into his heart. He couldn't allow that to happen. She hadn't believed in him. "I don't think so, Jenny."

"Why not? She'd enjoy the trip, and Sarah said Grand Junction has a great big scrapbook store. Plus, she could do her Christmas shopping." Jenny sat on the lid of her suitcase.

Adam smiled as Jenny struggled to fasten the latches. As usual, his little sister had packed too much. He moved to her side to help her. Placing his hands on the suitcase top to add his weight for closing it, he voiced his thoughts. "I don't plan on seeing Colleen anymore, Jenny."

The catch snapped into place. Adam smiled and turned to Jenny. The look on her face erased his grin.

"Why? What has Colleen done?" Jenny dropped down on the side of her bed.

Adam scooted the suitcase back and joined her. "Colleen thought Cassie's baby was mine. She believed I would have a baby out of wedlock, Jenny."

"Why would she think that? She knows you and I go to church. Are you sure?"

"I'm sure." Adam studied his hands. He didn't know why she would believe him capable of such a sin, but she did.

"So just like that, you aren't even going to talk to her about it. You're just dropping her like yesterday's old mail," Jenny accused and stood up. "Aren't you the one who says that if we have a problem with someone, we should talk to them about it?" She picked up her compact CD player and stuffed it into a book bag.

Adam stood up, too. "This is different, Jenny. Colleen and I aren't like you and your friends." He turned to walk out the door.

"No, you love each other."

Adam chose to ignore her. What did a kid like Jen know about love? "Let's go, Jen. Cassie's waiting."

They drove the short distance to Cassie's house. She stood on the front porch with her parents when they pulled into the driveway. Adam hopped out of the Blazer and picked up her suitcases while she hugged her parents good-bye. "You call as soon as you get there," her father ordered from the porch.

Adam helped Cassie in. As soon as he closed her door, she rolled down the window and answered, "I will, Daddy. I love you both."

Adam clicked shut the clasp of his seat belt and turned to the tearful Cassie. "Ready?"

She nodded and waved good-bye to her parents.

They drove in silence.

Cassie wiped at her eyes. Jenny put on her headphones and turned on the CD player. Adam didn't know what to say to either one of them.

He really didn't think there was much he could say to

Cassie. From the phone call the night before, he knew her talk with her parents had been rough, but in the long run, they had forgiven her and were looking forward to having a new grand-baby to cuddle. Her tears were tears of sorrow at having to leave them.

As for Jenny, she sat sulking in the backseat. He'd dealt with her anger before, and it always passed. But this was the first time in two months that she'd been this angry with him. Since the night she'd stayed with Colleen until the night he'd gone to the hospital with Cassie, they'd gotten along fine. Now this had to happen. He told himself she didn't understand grown-up things, but he knew deep down he was wrong. Jenny had matured a lot in the last few months, thanks to Colleen.

"You two are quiet today." Cassie blew her nose and glanced toward the backseat where Jenny sat with her photo album.

Adam tried to smile. "We had an argument this morning, and she's pouting."

"I'm not pouting, and I can hear you." Jenny flipped the page of her scrapbook with anger.

Cassie turned sideways in the seat and faced Adam. "Want to tell me about it? Maybe I can help you work through it."

Silence.

"You know, like an unbiased third party?" she hinted.

Jenny sat up straighter. "Yeah, Adam. Why don't you tell her what we are arguing about? After all, it's partly her fault." She met Adam's eyes in the rearview mirror.

"That will be enough, Jenny." Adam didn't want to have this discussion with Cassie or Jenny. This was his business and no one else's.

"Why is it my fault?" Cassie turned farther in the seat to face Jenny.

Jenny ignored the threatening look from her brother and pressed on. "Well, it seems someone told Colleen you were pregnant. Since you and Adam have been going out a lot, she assumed he was the father and refused to go out on a date with him."

Cassie's sharp intake of breath didn't stop Jenny.

"So my brother thinks he's too good to forgive and forget, and now he doesn't want to see Colleen at all, even though everyone in town knows they are both crazy about each other."

"Jenny, that's enough," Adam warned.

Cassie's voice came out weak. "I'm sorry."

"It's not your fault, Cassie." Adam reached over and patted her hand.

She nodded her head. "Yes, it is."

Adam watched fresh tears fill her eyes. "It really isn't, Cassie. Colleen jumped to the conclusion that the baby is mine. She didn't ask me; she just assumed." He moved both hands to the steering wheel and looked straight ahead.

Cassie touched his arm. "Adam, I didn't mean to, but I sort of told her the baby is yours."

"You what?" His voice, edged with disbelief, echoed within the cab.

Cassie jerked her hand back. "I didn't mean for it to sound

as though you were the father, but I guess it did. I told her you were fine with me being pregnant and that you were helping me get to my doctor's appointments and everything. Now that I think back on the conversation, I never said Richard and I had gotten married or that he is the baby's father. I'm so sorry, Adam." Tears spilled down her cheeks once more.

Chapter 11

Colleen finished straightening up the bakery. She turned off the lights, locked the door, and made her way back to the apartment. The scrapbook lay on the kitchen table. It beckoned her to come and finish it. She ignored the summons and made her way to the teapot instead.

She'd worked on the photo album off and on during the last week, but it just didn't spark her interest now that Adam and Jenny were out of town and out of her life.

Once more she asked the Lord why she had been allowed to fall in love with Adam just to have him snatched away from her. Tears welled up in her eyes, threatening to spill over. She bit down hard on her lip and blinked, determined to maintain the mood she'd left the bakery with.

While the teakettle heated, she sat down at the table and looked at the scrapbook. Each page captured her family's history. Colleen had made special notes throughout the pages. She wanted to remember the love and laughter of her ancestors. A smile touched her lips.

For now, the scrapbook and journaling were finished. She'd used the pictures, scraps of notes and letters, and even a few lacy handkerchiefs to fill the pages. She felt each item represented her relatives' lives.

Upon reflection, Colleen realized that Jenny's school project had brought back the Hallidays and Reillys from days gone by. She felt a smile tug at her lips. Warmth enveloped her as she thought about her family. She turned to the last page and looked at the picture of her parents. They smiled up at her. Love filled their eyes.

"Lord, please let Adam forgive me. I love him so much, but I'm afraid he won't forgive me and I will never find true love again." Colleen whispered the prayer and closed the scrapbook.

Her hands moved over the front cover. *What if Adam doesn't forgive me?* She would be alone forever.

Colleen walked to the stove where the water in the teakettle boiled. She poured the steaming liquid into a cup.

Her thoughts returned to her morning devotions. She'd skimmed the scripture and the notes in the devotional. As clear as a summer's day, Psalm 136:26 echoed through her mind: *"Give thanks to the God of heaven. His love endures forever."* Colleen decided she should reread the devotional.

Colleen collected her Bible and devotion book. She spread them out on the table and began to read aloud. "God's love endures forever. People come and people go, but the Lord God Almighty will always be here for you and will always love you."

My love endures forever. The words echoed through her mind. Colleen bowed her head and prayed. For the first time since Adam left, Colleen felt at peace. Adam might not forgive her, but she knew with confidence that the Lord would be there for her.

❖

Sunday morning arrived with fresh snow. Colleen hurried home from the morning services. She looked forward to having a light lunch and then getting to work. Last night she'd decided that the photo album needed a cover.

She pushed the door open with the help of the winter wind. Snow blew in with her, and she laughed as she shoved the door closed.

Now that she knew the Lord would never desert her, she looked forward to Adam's return. It would hurt if he didn't forgive her, but thanks to her newfound knowledge, she knew that, in time, she'd be fine.

Colleen put a pot of water on the stove and pulled down the chocolate mix. While the water heated, she made a grilled cheese sandwich and warmed up some tomato soup.

After hurriedly eating lunch, Colleen opened the trunk. She searched the many articles of clothing for the child's coat. It would be small enough that she wouldn't have to waste much of the material.

What better way to preserve her family's memories than to use its lining as the cover for her scrapbook?

"Here you are." Colleen pulled the item of clothing out. The black coat's lining held many faded colored patches. Light green dominated the garment, but faded blues and yellows could still be distinguished.

She looked back into the chest. The coat had been covering a small sewing basket. Colleen pulled it out. "I wonder if there's anything in here that I can use."

Colleen lifted the wicker lid. Inside were antique spools of thread and a few rusted needles. The lining of the little basket was torn in several places. She ran her hand over it and, to her surprise, felt something inside.

Her heart leaped as she pulled out an envelope. She set the basket off to the side and stood up and carried the faded envelope to the table. Then she sat down and opened it.

Inside she found a piece of paper. Colleen unfolded the treasure.

Tears filled her eyes as she read the letter from the past:

My dearest son,

This quilt is the story of your family and the love that binds us together as truly as the threads that hold together these pieces of cloth.

I began this quilt as a new bride. I didn't know any more about sewing than I did about being a wife, but I knew about love. The pieces of my wedding dress are in here and form the center block. They are the delicate spring green swatches. It's the same green, by the way, you'll see when the first wildflowers poke their brave stems through the winter-worn earth.

There are a few patches of white in this quilt. They are cut from the shirt your father wore when we got married. Ah, John, what a fine figure he presented that day!

I can still see him in my mind, so elegant, so handsome, so sure. . .and so very much in possession of my heart.

The little patches were once your blanket. This was the first earthly fabric that touched your newborn skin. Yellow-spotted flannel looked so warm against your infant skin, like God had poured sun around your tiny body. It was cold the night you were born—so cold the doctor's breath froze midair—but you quickly warmed our hearts.

As our family grew, so did our love—and the quilt. Notice how the stitches get more even and practiced on the outer patches. I was just learning in the center section, but the patches, straggly though they may be, are still holding together after many years of hard use.

Love is like that, John. At first, it's all very new and awkward, but if you're willing to put your heart into it, it'll hold steadfast. There aren't any silk or satin or velvet pieces in this quilt, but to me, its beauty far exceeds the grandest coverlet. Even the littlest, most mundane pieces of life make an extraordinary tapestry when united by love. . .these scraps of love.

Your loving mother,
Brigit Streeter Collins

No longer able to control her tears, Colleen wiped the streams from her face. Had Grammy known Adam would enter her life again when he delivered the coat?

Colleen picked up the coat and sewing basket, then stood

to her feet. She walked back to the kitchen table and set all the items down. The scraps brought Adam into her life, but indirectly they had brought her closer to God.

Colleen reached for her cup of chocolate. Fear of rejection shot through her as she whispered to the quiet room, "I have to tell him I love him and ask his forgiveness."

Chapter 12

Adam paced his living-room floor. He and Jenny had gotten home the night before. He'd asked Jenny not to go to Colleen's before he had a chance to talk to her. He knew he owed Colleen an apology. Would she forgive him? He'd walked out on her and hadn't looked back.

He opened the small jewelry box and stared down at the wedding set that sat on a cushion of red velvet. Adam couldn't believe he'd bought the ring. But he knew in his heart that Colleen was the woman for him, and he thought she knew it, too.

He pulled his coat on and stepped into the cold afternoon air. The desire to talk to Colleen filled him with longing. Adam walked in the direction of her house.

All the way, he tried to come up with ways to say he was sorry. Adam finally gave up. He stopped two blocks from her house. A small park on the side of the road beckoned him to enter its sanctuary. He took the path that led to a beautiful river.

Adam sat down on a huge rock beside the water, which

trickled through the ice. He looked up into the heavens. "Lord, I can't find the words to tell her how sorry I am, to tell her how much I love her. Father, what am I to say?"

He stuck his hands in his coat pockets and waited for the Lord to answer. Too late, he realized he should have come to the Lord earlier last week when he'd thought the worst of Colleen.

The longer Adam sat in the cold, the more he realized he ought to be up-front with her. Tell her the truth, tell her he loved her, and ask her to marry him.

Adam left the park with a new bounce in his step. He felt confident Colleen was the woman God had chosen for him.

"Thanks for the coffee, Colleen. I'm sure looking forward to Adam resuming his route." Sly groaned as he picked up his mailbag.

Colleen took a deep breath. "Jenny and I are working on a school project. Did Adam say when they would get back into town?" She felt a prickle of guilt for using Jenny as an excuse to learn more about Adam.

The postman took a last long drink from his cup. "Got home last night." He set the cup back on the table.

He was home.

Colleen felt her heart speed up and her palms turn to a hot swampland. She wiped the moisture on her apron.

Sly headed for the door. "Thanks again for the coffee," he called on his way out.

"Any time." Colleen tugged on the apron strings. They

refused to budge. Hot and anxious, she fretted about what to say to Adam. How would she voice her sorrow for her quick judgment?

The knot wound tighter and tighter. She turned completely around, facing the kitchen. Her fingers couldn't loosen the tie.

The bell over the door tinkled, alerting her that someone had just entered the store. She looked up at the clock on the wall. A few minutes after two, too early for Jenny. A wave of disappointment enveloped her.

"I'll be right with you," Colleen called over her shoulder, still fighting the knot.

Warm hands enveloped hers. "Here, let me get that."

Adam.

Colleen couldn't hold still. She turned swiftly and looked into his clear blue eyes. An endearing smile touched his lips and caused the dimple in his cheek to wink at her.

"Adam, you're home." Her voice sounded breathless to her own ears.

"We got in last night."

Words exploded from her lips. "I'm so sorry, Adam. I never should have judged you. Can you ever forgive me?" Her throat closed up, tears filled her eyes, and Colleen silently prayed for the strength to continue.

He guided her to the nearest chair and indicated that she should sit down. Colleen chewed on her bottom lip. There was so much she wanted to say, but her tongue stuck to the roof of her mouth.

"I'm sorry, too, Colleen. I was wrong. My pride got in the way of my thinking. Please forgive me for being so rude to you." Adam continued holding her hands.

His eyes pleaded with her to forgive him. Colleen wanted to sink to the floor and sit with him, but her body refused to do as her mind screamed. All she could do was nod. He must think she was an idiot.

Tears streamed down her cheeks when he released her hands. She wanted to scream that she did forgive him and that she had been wrong, too. Silently, she prayed, *Lord, what's wrong with me? Why can't I speak or move?*

Adam took a small box from his pocket. "I love you, and I'm praying you love me, too." He opened the box and held it out to her.

He loved her. The words screamed through her mind.

"Colleen, will you marry me?" Adam held the box out to her with one hand and took her cold fingers in the other.

Colleen smiled through her tears. She opened her mouth, and the words she'd silently been thinking burst forth. "Yes! Yes! Yes!"

His rich laughter filled her heart and home. Colleen gasped as he stood up, pulled her from the chair and into his arms, and swung her around."I was so afraid you would say no." He laughed and held her close for several moments.

Colleen hung on to him. He'd forgiven her and asked for her forgiveness as well. He really did love her.

Adam pulled back from her and cupped her face in his hands. "Are you sure?"

Colleen saw the worry in his eyes and wanted to erase all doubt from his mind. "Adam, I have loved you forever." She watched in wonder as he pulled her face to his. Adam's kiss felt gentle and sweet—just what she expected from him.

Epilogue

Three weeks later, Colleen's fingers shook as she fitted the veil on her hair. Today was the day. Her wedding day. She wondered if Adam felt as nervous as she at this moment.

Jenny came into the room wearing a red dress that fit her young figure beautifully. "Adam is pacing the floor," she giggled. "You better hurry." She stopped mid-stride, her mouth forming a perfect O. "Wow, you look fantastic." She circled Colleen, and her hand raised several times as if she wanted to touch the fabric but didn't dare.

"Adam's just gonna die when he sees you," Jenny said, her voice tingled with awe.

Colleen had chosen a simple satin, A-line dress with long sleeves that tapered to a V ending at the base of her middle finger. Tiny pearl beads were sewn along the sleeves and neckline. The pink and white shine of the pearls shimmered as she moved. Colleen's hair hung full and shiny in a natural sweep. She placed trembling fingers lightly across her lips, feelings of confidence warring with major insecurities.

"You really think he'll like it?" she questioned anxiously with a little giggle.

"Oh, yeah. He's gonna love it. You'll blow him away."

"Thanks." Colleen caught Jenny in a quick hug, then turned once more for a final glance in the full-length mirror. She ran her hands down the satin fabric of the dress. "Okay." She breathed deeply. "I'm ready."

The small church would be drafty—something Colleen had anticipated, it being the middle of winter. Over a hundred years old, the building had stopped being used, and it had taken a couple of days to clean, but she loved it. The old wooden pews, the intricate carvings in the woodwork along the walls, and the high ceilings evoked an earlier time that spoke to her heart.

Jenny handed Colleen a bouquet of red roses with baby's breath mixed throughout it. She then picked up her own bunch of artificial white tulips. "You know, Colleen. When you first said you wanted a Christmas wedding with Christmas colors, I thought you were crazy. But I was wrong. The church is beautiful, and the red and white colors are absolutely gorgeous."

They both turned at the knock on the door. Giggles burst from Jenny's lips. "We'd better get going." She hugged Colleen, then opened the door and walked out.

Colleen followed and came face to face with her father. She gasped with happiness. "Daddy, you made it." His black hair had turned silver around the temples since she'd seen him last.

"I couldn't miss my only child's wedding." Collin Halliday hugged her to him for several moments.

Colleen returned his warm hug. "I'm so glad you're here, Daddy."

He pulled away from her and held her at arm's length. "You are so beautiful."

She felt her cheeks grow warm under her father's green-eyed gaze. "Thank you."

He smiled at her, then tucked her right hand into the crook of his left arm. "Are you sure about this, honey?"

Colleen smiled at the protective question. She squeezed the muscles in his arm. "I've been waiting all my life for Adam Walker. I'm ready."

He patted her white-gloved hand. "I wanted to make sure."

She smiled. "I've never been surer of anything in my life."

Her father nodded. "Then let's not keep your young man waiting."

Colleen's heart pounded in her throat as the pianist began playing the wedding march on the upright piano at the front of the sanctuary.

Jenny glanced over her shoulder, raised her eyebrow as if to say, "This is it," then proceeded down the aisle.

"Time to go." Colleen's dad squeezed her arm

He took a step, and they turned the corner.

She'd been down this aisle many times, but it had never seemed to take this long. Adam stood in front of an arch decorated with red poinsettias and white mums. To her, he appeared at least a mile away, and her legs moved in slow motion. Adam wore a black tuxedo. It complemented his dark complexion and soft blue eyes. He would always be the most handsome man she'd ever seen.

A smile tilted his lips, and love lit his eyes with a shining glow. His love drew her down the aisle.

"Who gives this woman?" the minister asked.

"I do," Colleen's father answered.

Colleen gave his arm one last squeeze before he released her and placed her hand in the groom's.

Adam's palm felt warm in hers. Colleen listened to the preacher and followed his lead. When it came time for the rings, she glanced at the ring bearer standing beside Adam. She knew he was a cousin on Adam's mother's side of the family. The little boy looked about three years old. He held in his small hands her scrapbook.

Her scrapbook! She checked the child's hands again. Sure enough, it *was* her scrapbook.

Tears of happiness filled her eyes. Jenny had asked if she could pick the pillow for the ring bearer. Colleen had no idea Jenny would use the scrapbook. The very item that brought her and Adam together today helped bind them for life.

Adam untied the ribbon that held their rings to the coat-of-many-colors that covered the photo album. The memory of her great-great-grandmother's letter floated through her happy thoughts as Adam slipped the ring on her finger and they repeated their vows.

With certainty, Colleen knew theirs was a love to last a lifetime.

RHONDA GIBSON

Rhonda Gibson resides in New Mexico with her husband and two children. She writes inspirational romance because she is eager to share her love of the Lord with readers. Besides writing, her interests are reading and scrapbooking. Visit Rhonda's Web site at http://www.RhondaGibson.com.

A Letter to Our Readers

Dear Readers:

In order that we might better contribute to your reading enjoyment, we would appreciate your taking a few minutes to respond to the following questions. When completed, please return to the following: Fiction Editor, Barbour Publishing, Inc., P.O. Box 719, Uhrichsville, OH 44683.

1. Did you enjoy reading *Scraps of Love*?
   - ❑ Very much—I would like to see more books like this.
   - ❑ Moderately—I would have enjoyed it more if ______________

____

____

2. What influenced your decision to purchase this book? (Check those that apply.)
   - ❑ Cover ❑ Back cover copy ❑ Title ❑ Price
   - ❑ Friends ❑ Publicity ❑ Other

3. Which story was your favorite?
   - ❑ *Marry for Love* ❑ *The Coat*
   - ❑ *Mother's Old Quilt* ❑ *Love of a Lifetime*

4. Please check your age range:
   - ❑ Under 18 ❑ 18–24 ❑ 25–34
   - ❑ 35–45 ❑ 46–55 ❑ Over 55

5. How many hours per week do you read? ______________

Name ______________________________________

Occupation ______________________________________

Address ______________________________________

City ____________________ State ___________ Zip ___________

E-mail ______________________________________